I0642230

Charles G. Leland

The Unpublished Legends of Virgil

Charles G. Leland

The Unpublished Legends of Virgil

ISBN/EAN: 9783337152796

Printed in Europe, USA, Canada, Australia, Japan

Cover: Foto ©Andreas Hilbeck / pixelio.de

More available books at **www.hansebooks.com**

THE
UNPUBLISHED LEGENDS

OF

VIRGIL.

COLLECTED BY

CHARLES GODFREY LELAND.

LONDON:

ELLIOT STOCK, 62, PATERNOSTER ROW, E.C.

1899.

TO THE

SENATOR AND PROFESSOR

DOMENICO COMPARETTI,

AUTHOR OF

"VIRGIL IN THE MIDDLE AGES,"

THIS WORK IS DEDICATED

BY

CHARLES GODFREY LELAND.

FLORENCE, *September*, 1899.

PREFACE.

ALL classic scholars are familiar with the Legends of Virgil in the Middle Ages, in which the poet appears as a magician, the last and best collection of these being that which forms the second volume of "Virgilio nel Medio Aevo," by Senator Professor Domenico Comparetti. But having conjectured that Dante must have made Virgil familiar to the people, and that many legends or traditions still remained to be collected, I applied myself to this task, with the result that in due time I gathered, or had gathered for me, about one hundred tales, of which only three or four had a plot in common with the old Neapolitan Virgilian stories, and even these contained original and very curious additional lore. One half of these traditions will be found in this work.

As these were nearly all taken down by a fortune-teller or witch among her kind—she being singularly well qualified by years of practice in finding and recording such recondite lore—they very naturally contain much more that is occult, strange and heathen, than can be found in the other tales. Thus, wherever there is opportunity, magical ceremonies are described and incantations given; in fact, the story is often only a mere frame, as it were, in which the picture or true subject is a lesson in sorcery.

But what is most remarkable and interesting in these traditions, as I have often had occasion to remark, is the fact that they embody a vast amount of old Etrusco-Roman minor mythology of the kind chronicled by Ovid, and incidentally touched on or quoted here and there by gossiping Latin writers, yet of which no record was ever made. I am sincerely persuaded that there was an immense repertory of this fairy, goblin, or witch religion believed in by the Roman people which was never written down, but of which a great deal was preserved by sorcerers, who are mostly at the same time story-tellers among themselves, and of this much may be found in this work. And I think no critic, however inclined to doubt he may be, will deny that there is in the old mythologists collateral evidence to prove what I have asserted.

It may be observed that in these Northern legends, Virgil is in most cases spoken of as a poet as well as magician, but that he is before all, benevolent and genial, a great sage invariably doing good, while always inspired with humour. Mr. Robinson Ellis has shrewdly observed that, in reading the Neapolitan tales of Virgil, "we are painfully struck with the absence, for the most part, of any imaginative element in them." I would, however, suggest, that in these which I have gathered with no small pains— having devoted a great part of my time for several years to the task—there is no want of imagination, romance or humour.

Such are, in brief, the contents of this book. Sincerely trusting that the press and public may treat it as kindly as they did the "Etrusco-Roman Remains," and "The Legends of Florence," I await the verdict, which will probably determine whether I shall publish other Italian traditions, of which I have still a very large collection.

CHARLES GODFREY LELAND.

FLORENCE,
1899.

CONTENTS.

INTRODUCTION.

"C'est bien raison que je vous compte des histoires de Virgille de Romme lequel en son temps fis moult de merveilles."—*Les Faictz Merveilleux de Virgille. XVIth Century.*

THE reader is probably aware that during the Middle Ages, Virgil, who had always retained great fame as a poet, and who was kindly regarded as almost a Christian from a conjectured pious prophecy in his works, underwent the process of being made romantic and converted into a magician. How it all came to pass is admirably set forth by Professor Domenico Comparetti in his truly great work on "Virgil in the Middle Ages." *

During the twelfth century, and for some time after, many learned pilgrims or tourists from different parts of Europe, while in Italy, hearing from the people these tales, which had a great charm in an age when the marvellous formed the basis of nearly all literature, gave them to the world in different forms. And as the fame of Virgil as a poet was almost the first fact learned by those who studied Latin, legends relating to him spread far and wide. The Mantuan bard had been well-nigh deified by the Romans. "Silius Italicus used to celebrate his birthday every year, visiting his tomb as if it were a temple, and as a temple the Neapolitan Statius used to regard it." † And this reverence was preserved by the Christians, who even added to it a peculiar lore.

"These tales," says Comparetti, "originated in Naples, and thence spread into European literature, in the first

* Of which there is an English translation by E. F. M. Benecke, entitled 'Virgil in the Middle Ages." London, Swan Sonnenschein and Co.
† Comparetti.

instance, however, outside Italy. Their origin in Italy was entirely the work of the lower classes, and had nothing to do with poetry or literature; it was a popular superstition founded on local records connected with Virgil's long residence in Naples, and the celebrity of his tomb in that city."

This latter is a shrewd observation, for as the tomb is close by the mysterious grotto of Posilippo, which was always supposed to have been made by magic, it was natural that Virgil, who was famed for wisdom, should have been supposed to have wrought the miracle, and it may well be that this was really the very first, or the beginning of all the legends in question. These were "connected with certain localities, statues and monuments in the neighbourhood of Naples itself, to which Virgil was supposed to have given a magic power." . . . Foreigners who visited Naples thus learned these legends, and they passed "even into Latin works of a learned nature." So it resulted that from the twelfth century onward the fame of Virgil as a magician spread all over Europe. Among those who thus made of him a wonder-worker were Conrad von Querfurt, Gervase of Tilbury, Alexander Neckham, and John of Salisbury.

That these marvellous tales were localized in Naples, and there first applied to Virgil, may be freely admitted, but that they really originated or were first invented there will be claimed by no one familiar with older or Oriental legends. This has not escaped Senator Comparetti, who observes that wonders attributed long before to Apollonius of Tyana and others "are practically identical with those attributed in Naples to Virgil." The idea of setting up the image of a fly to drive away flies, as Virgil did in one legend, is Babylonian, for in Lenormand's Chaldæan Magic we are told that demons are driven away by their own images, and Baalzebub, as chief of flies, was probably the first honoured in this respect.

That is to say, that little by little and year by year the tales which had been told of other men in earlier times—magicians, sorcerers, and wizards wild—were remade and attributed to Virgil. The very first specimen of an ancient Italian *novella*, given by Roscoe, is a Virgilian legend, though the translator makes no mention of it. So in the "Pentamerone" of Giambattista Basile of Naples we find that most of the tales come from the East, and had been of old attributed to Buddha, or some other great man.

The Neapolitan stories of Virgil were spread far and wide, into almost every language in Europe; but they had their day, and now rank with black-letter literature, being republished still, but for scholars only. I had read most of them in my youth, and when the work of Senator Comparetti appeared, I was struck by the singular fact that there is next to nothing in all the vast amount of Virgilianæ which he quotes, which appears to have been gathered of late among the people at large. A great number of classic and mediæval names and characters are very familiar to the most ignorant Italians. How came it to pass that nothing is known of Virgil, who appears in the " Divina Commedia " as the guide, philosopher, and friend of Dante, whose works are read by all.

Inspired with this idea, I went to work and soon found that, as I had conjectured, there were still extant among the people a really great number of what may be called post-Virgilian legends, which possibly owe their existence, or popularity, to the Virgil of Dante. A very few of them are like certain of the old Neapolitan tales, but even these have been greatly changed in details. As might have been expected of Northern Italian narratives, they partake more of the nature of the *novella* or short romance, than of the nursery-tale or the mere anecdote, as given by the earlier writers. That is to say, there was, after Dante, among the people a kind of renaissance in the fame of Virgil as a magician. It is by a curious coincidence that, as Senator Comparetti admits, all the earlier legends of the bard were gathered and published by foreigners; so have these of later time been collected by one not to the country born.

One good reason why I obtained so many of these tales so readily is that they were gathered, like my " Florentine Legends " and " Etrusco-Roman Remains," chiefly among witches or fortune-tellers, who, above all other people, preserve with very natural interest all that smacks of sorcery. It is the case in every country—among Red Indians, Hindus or Italians—that wherever there are families in which witchcraft is handed down from generation to generation there will be traditional tales in abundance, and those not of the common fairy-tale kind, but of a mysterious, marvellous nature. Now, that the narratives in this book contain—

quite apart from any connection with Virgil—in almost
every instance some curious traces of very ancient tradition,
is perhaps to be admitted by all. Such is the description
of Agamene, the Spirit of the Diamond, which is one of the
oldest of Græco-Roman myths, and Pæonia, who kills or
revives human beings by means of flowers, wherein she
is the very counterpart of Minerva-Pæonia, who taught
Esculapius, as mythology expressly states, "the power
of flowers and herbs," even as the statue Pæonia teaches
Virgil. These are only two out of scores of instances, and
they are to me, as they will be to every scholar, by far the
most valuable part of my book.

These incidents, which I in many cases did not know,
until after subsequent search in mythologies, were ancient,
certainly could not have been invented by the very ignorant
old women from whom they were gathered. And this
brings me to the important consideration as to whether
these stories are really *authentic*. A learned Italian professor very lately asked me how I could be sure that the
common people did not palm off on me their own inventions
as legends of Virgil. To which I replied that I would not
be responsible for the antiquity or origin of a single tale.
For, in the first place, any story of any sorcerer is often
attributed to Virgil, so that in two or three instances which
I have specially noted "a Virgil" means any magician.
And very often I have myself told some story as a hint or
suggestion, in order to give some idea as to what I wanted,
or to revive the memory. But in all cases they have come
back to me so changed, and with such strange fragments of
classic lore of the most recondite kind added, that I had no
scruple in giving them just for what they were worth,
leaving it for critics to sift out the ancient from the modern,
even as the eagles described by Sinbad the Sailor, brought
back the legs of mutton with diamonds sticking to them.
"You would not," I said to the professor of classical lore,
"reject newly-mined gold because it is encumbered with
dross; and that there may be much dross in all which I
have gathered I am sure; but there is gold in it all."

The nursery peasant tales collected by Grimm and Crane,
and many more, represent surface-diggings. Those who
were first in the field had an easy time in gathering what
thousands knew. But these finds are becoming exhausted,
and the collector of the future must mine out of the rock,

and seek for deeper traditions which have been sedulously concealed or kept secret. There are still many peasants who know this lore, though their number is very rapidly diminishing, and they are, as a rule, without exception, extremely averse to communicating it to anyone whom they know or think is not what I may call a fellow-heathen, or in true sympathy with them. I may give in illustration of this an incident which occurred recently as I write: Miss Roma Lister, who had an old Italian witch-nurse, still living in Rome (and who has contributed several of these tales of Virgil), who taught her something of the art "which none may name," while walking with a priest near Calmaldoli, met with a man whom she knew had the reputation of being a *stregone*, or wizard. She asked him, *sotto voce*, if he knew the name of *Tinia*, one of the Etruscan gods, still remembered by a few, and who is described in the "Etrusco-Roman Remains." He hastily replied in a whisper: "Yes, yes; and I know the incantation to him also—but don't let the priest hear us." At a subsequent meeting they interchanged confidences freely. Maddalena, whom I have chiefly employed to make collections among witches and others, has often told me how unwilling those who knew any witch-lore are to confess it, especially to ladies or gentlemen. One must literally conjure it out of them.

These tales of Virgil were collected in Florence, Volterra, Rocca-Casciano, Arezzo, Siena, and several places near it, and Rome. I have several not to be published, because they are so trifling, or so utterly confused and badly written, or "shocking," that I could make nothing of them. In all, however, which I have collected, with one exception—which is manifestly a mere common fairy-tale arbitrarily attributed to the subject as a *magus*—Virgil appears as a great and very benevolent man. He aids the poor and suffering, has great sympathy for the weak and lowly, and is ever ready to reprove arrogance and defeat the plans of evil sorcerers. But while great and wise and dignified, he is very fond of a joke. Sometimes he boldly punishes and reproves the Emperor of Rome—anon he contrives some merry jest to amuse him. The general agreement of so many stories drawn from different sources as to this character is indeed remarkable.

As regards the general "value" of these Virgilian tales, and a vast number of others which I have collected, all of

them turning on magic or occult motives, it is well worth
mentioning that from one to three centuries ago a great
number of tales very much resembling them were published by Grosius, Prætorius, and others, as at a later date
the " Histoire des Fantômes et des Demons," Paris, 1819,
which work unquestionably supplied Washington Irving
with the story of the Spectre Bridegroom, and another
tale.* In Italy, the writers of *novella*, such as Boccaccio,
Bandello, Cinthio, and in fact nearly all of them, shook off
and ridiculed all that was associated with barbarous superstitions and incantations, and yet in the " Metamorphosi "
of Lorenzo Selva, Florence, 1591, and here and there in
similar obscure works by writers not so painfully afflicted
by " culture " and style as the leaders, there are witch and
fairy-tales which might have come from very old women,
and would be certainly recognised by them as familiar
traditions. That these mysterious stories contained an
immense amount of valuable old Latin classic lore and
minor mythology, or that they were not altogether silly and
useless, does not seem to have entered the head of any one
Italian from Dante downward. Men like Straparola and
Basile made, it is true, collections of merry tales to amuse,
but that there was anything in them of solid traditional
value never occurred to them. I mention the few and far-
between witch-tales which are found in certain writers, because
they are marvellously like those which I have given. Some
of these, especially the later, are so elaborate or dramatic, or
inspired with what seems to be literary culture, that many
who are only familiar with simple fairy-tales might doubt
whether the former are really traditional folklore of the
people, or even of fortune-tellers. There is a curious fact,
unnoted now, which will be deeply dwelt on in a future age
when folklore and phases of culture will be far more broadly
and deeply or genially considered than they are at present.
This is, that among the masses in Italy there exists an
extraordinary amount of a certain kind of culture allied to
gross ignorance, as is amusingly illustrated in the com-

---

* Alexandre Dumas also used this book very freely for his " Mille et
Une Fantômes "—in fact, the latter work may be said to be based on it.
The " Histoire des Fantômes " was the first and principal source from
which French lovers of the supernatural derived the interest in were-
wolves and vampires which manifested itself during the time of Napoleon
and more recently.

monest language, in which, even among the lowest peasants, one hears in every sentence some transformed or melted Latin word of three or four syllables, suggesting excess of culture—like unto which is the universal use of the sonnet and *terzarime* among the most ignorant.

If there are any readers who find it strange that in these legends and traditions there are not only extraordinary but apparently incredible remains of culture, fragments of mythology and incantations, which pierce into the most mysterious depths of archæology, they would do well to remember that the same apparent paradox struck " Vernon Lee," who treated it very fully in her " Euphorion," in the chapters on the Outdoor Poetry of Italy. And among other things she thus remarks :

" Nothing can be too artificial or highflown for the Italian peasantry; its tales are all of kings, princesses, fairies, knights, winged horses, marvellous jewels . . . its songs, almost without exception, about love, constancy, moon, stars, flowers. Such things have not been degraded by familiarity and parody, as in the town ; they retain for the country-folk the vague charm, like that of music, automatic and independent of thorough comprehension, of belonging to a sphere of the marvellous—hence they are repeated with almost religious servility."

But it must be remembered that with elaborate poetic forms and fancies, which would be foreign or unintelligible, and certainly unsympathetic, even to the fairly well-educated citizen of England or America, there has been preserved to the very letter, especially in Tuscany, a mass of literature which, while resembling the romances of chivalry which Chaucer ridiculed, is far ruder ; it even sur-passes the Norse prose sagas in barbarism. The principal work of this kind is the " Reali di Francia," which is reprinted every year, and which is at least a thousand years old. This work, and several like it, are the greatest literary curiosities or anomalies of the age. In them we are hurried from battle to battle, from carnage to carnage, with rude interludes of love and magic, as if even the Middle Age had never existed. The " Nibelungen Lied " and " Heldenbuch " are by comparison to them refined and modern.

Can the reader imagine this as existing in combination with the literary relics of the Renaissance and many strangely-refined forms of speech ? Just so among the youngest children in Florence one sees gestures and glances

and hears phrases which would seem to have been peculiar
to grown-up people in some bygone stage of society. It is
really necessary to bear all this in mind when reading the
legends which I have collected, for they present the con-
tradictions of barbarism and culture, of old Latin traditions
and crass ignorance, as I have never seen them even
imagined by students of culture.

And here I would remark, as allied to this subject, that
folklore is as yet far from being understood in all its fulness.
In France, for example, no scholar seems to have got
beyond the idea that it consists entirely of *traditions popu-
laires*, necessarily ancient. In England we have advanced
further, but we are still far from realizing that with every
day there springs up and grows among the masses that
which in days to come will be deeply interesting, as expressing the spirit of the age. This accretive folklore is just
as valuable as any—or will be so—and it should be gathered
and studied, no matter what its origin may be. So of this
book of mine, I express the conviction that it contains many
tales which have, since the days of Dante, and many perhaps
very recently, been attached to the name of Virgil, yet do
not consider them less interesting than those collected in the
twelfth century by Gervais of Tilbury, Neckham, and
others. In fact, these here given actually contain far more
ancient and curious traditional matter, because they have
not been abridged or filed down by literary mediæval
Latinists into mere plots or anecdotes as contracted as the
"variants" of a modern folklorist. The older writers, and
many of the modern, regarded as ugly excrescence all that
did not belong, firstly, to scholarship or "style"; secondly,
to the fact or subject in hand. Thus, Lorenzo Selva gives
a witch story with six incantations, which are far more
interesting than all the washy poetry in his book, but is so
ashamed of having done so, that he states in a marginal
note that he has only preserved them to give an idea of
"the silliness of all such iniquitous trash"—the "iniquitous
trash" in question being evidently of Etrusco-Roman
origin, to judge from form and similarity to other ancient
spells. In these later Virgilian tales there has been no
scruple, either as regards literary elegance or piety, to
prevent the chronicler from giving them just as they were
told, the "sinful and silly" incantations, when they occurred,
being faithfully retained, with all that can give an idea of

the true spirit of the whole. The mean fear of appearing to
be vulgar, or credulous, or not literally "genteel," has
caused thousands of such writers to suppress traditions
worth far more than all they ever penned.

I write this in the belief that all my critics will admit
that in these, as in my " Florentine Legends " and " Etrusco-
Roman Remains," I have really recovered and recorded a
great deal of valuable ancient tradition. Also that what
was preserved to us of ancient Etruscan or Græco-Latin
lore regarding the minor gods and sylvan deities, goblins,
etc., by classic writers is very trifling indeed compared to
the *immense* quantity which existed, and that a great deal of
it may still be found among the peasantry, especially among
wizards and witches, is unquestionable. That I have
secured some of this in my books is, I trust, true ; future
critics will winnow it all out, and separate the wheat from
the chaff.

I have entitled this work "The Unpublished Legends of
Virgil," which may be called a contradiction in terms, since
it is now given in type. But it is the only succinct title of
which I can think which expresses its real nature, and
separates it from the earlier collections of such tales, the
latest of which was issued by Mr. D. Nutt.

And, finally, I would remark with some hesitation in
advancing so strange an idea, that in all the legends which
I have gathered, I find persistence in a very rude and earlier
faith, which the Græco-Roman religion and Christianity
itself, instead of destroying, seem to have simply strength-
ened. Indeed, there are remote villages in Italy in which
Catholicism in sober truth has come down to sorcery, or
gradually conformed to it, not only in form, but in spirit ;
from which I conclude that, till science *pur et simple* shall be
all-prevalent, the oldest and lowest cults will exist among
those whose minds are adapted to them. And as Edward
Clodd, the President of the Folklore Society, has clearly
shown,* there are thousands, even among the highly-
educated in Europe, who really belong to these old believers.

There will come a day, and that not very far off, when
the last traces of these strange semi-spiritual-romantic or
classic traditions will have vanished from the *people*, and
then what has been recorded will be sought for and studied

---

* " Pioneers of Evolution."

with keenest interest, and conclusions drawn from it of which we have no conception. To some of us they are even now only as

> " Departing sunbeams, loth to stop,
> Still smiling on the mountain-top."

To the vast majority even of the somewhat educated world, collecting such lore is like sending frigates to watch eclipses and North Pole explorations, and the digging up old skulls in Neanderthals—that is, a mere fond waste of money and study to no really useful purpose. There is a law of evolution which is so strictly and persistently carried out, that it would seem as if the mocking devil, who, according to the Buddhists, is the real head of the Universe, had it in his mind to jeer mankind thereby—and it is that the work of man in the past shall perish rapidly, and those who seek *vestigia rerum* shall have as little material as possible, even as dreams flit. So the strife goes ever on, chiefly aided by the ignorant, who " take no interest " in the past ; and so it will be for some time to come. I have often observed that in Italy, as in all countries, children and peasants take pleasure in destroying old vases and the like, even when they could sell them at a profit ; and there is something of the same spirit among all people regarding things which they do not understand. Blessed are they who do something in their generation to teach to the many the true value of all which conduces to culture or science ! Blessed be they who save up anything for the future, " and they shall be blest " by wiser men to come ! The primeval savages who heaped up vast *koken middens*, or thousands of tons of oyster-shells and bones, did not know that they were writing history ; but they did it. Perhaps the wisest of us will be as savages to those who are to come, as they in turn will be to later men.

THE STORY OF ROMOLO AND REMOLO.

' In quei buon tempi, ne i primi principii del Mondo, dicon li Poeti che
gli uomini e le Bestie facevano tutti una medesima vita. . . . E che sia
il vero ch' eglino s' impastassino del feroce, como loro, e s' incorporassino,
leggete di Romolo e Remulo i quali si pascevon di latte di lupa. Ecco
già che divennero in opera lupi ingordissimi, e voraci."—*La Zucca del
Doni Fiorentino*, 1607.

THERE was of old a King who had a beautiful wife, and
also two children, twins, who were exactly alike. This
King was named Romo and his wife Roma, and the children
were called Romolo and Remolo.

Now, it came to pass that the Queen and her twins, both
as yet sucklings (*ancora poppanti*), were besieged in a castle
when the King was far away. The enemy had sworn
to kill the whole royal family and to extirpate the kingly
race.

Now, when the Queen was in sore distress, seeing
death close upon her, there came to her a wizard, who
said :

" There is only one way by which you can save your life
and that of your babes. I can change you all three into *lupi
manari*, or were-wolves, and thus in the form of wolves you
may escape."

Then the Queen had the power to become a she-wolf or
a human being at her will, and it was the same with the
children. So they fled away, and lived in the woods for
seven years ; and the boys grew up like young giants, as
strong as six common children. And the Queen became
more beautiful than ever, for she lived under a spell.

One day the King was hunting in the forest, when he

found himself alone, and surrounded by such a flock of
raging wolves that his life was in great danger, when all at
once there came a very beautiful woman, who seemed to
have great power over the beasts, as if she were their queen,
for they obeyed her and retreated. Then the King recognised in her his lost wife. So, they returned with the twins
to their castle, but the King did not know that his wife and
children were themselves were-wolves.

One day the same enemy who had sought to kill the
Queen seven years before, of which the King knew nothing,
came to the castle pretending to be a friend, and was kindly
treated. But when the Queen and her two sons beheld
him, they flew at him as if they were mad, and tore him to
pieces before all the Court, and began to devour him like
raging wolves. Yet still the King did not know the whole
truth.

Then a brother of the King who was thus slain gathered
an army and besieged Romo, who found himself in great
danger. One evening he said :

> " There is danger within the walls,
> The sound of enemies without,
> The sun set in blood,
> To-morrow it may rise to death.
> Would that I had more warriors to fight !
> Two hundred fierce and bold ;
> Two hundred would save us all,
> Three hundred would give us full victory."

The Queen said nothing, but that night she stole secretly
out of the castle with her sons, and when alone they began
to howl, and soon all the were-wolves in the country
assembled. So the Queen returned with three hundred
men, so fierce and wild that they looked like devils.

They were strange in every way, and talked or howled
among themselves in a horrible language, which, however,
the Queen and her sons seemed to understand. And in the
first battle Romo gained a great victory. And it was
observed that the three hundred men ate the dead. However, the King was well pleased to conquer.

When Romolo and Remolo were grown up to be men
they learned that in a land not far away were two Princesses
named Sabina and Sabinella, who were the two most beautiful, and also the strongest, maidens in the world. And it
was also made known that he who would win either must

come and conquer her in fight and carry her away by main strength.

So Romolo and Remolo went to their city, and on an appointed day the two Princesses appeared in the public place, ready for the combat. But Romolo advanced with his brother riding on his shoulders, pick-back, *sulle spalle*, as boys do, and, catching up Sabina with one hand and Sabinella with the other, he ran away like the wind—so rapidly that he soon distanced all pursuers. And when Romolo was tired, Remolo took his place, carrying the sisters and bearing his brother. And Romolo made a song on it :

> " Up and down the mountain,
> Over the fields and through the rivulets,
> Over gray rocks and green grass,
> I saw a strange beast run ;
> It had three bodies and three heads,
> Six arms and six legs,
> Yet did it never run on more than two.
> Read the riddle rightly, if you can."

The two brothers wished to build a new and great city of their own. They went to a certain goddess, who told them :

> " The city which ye hope to build will be
> The greatest ever seen in Italy ;
> Above all others it will tower sublime,
> And rule the world in a far future time ;
> But know that at the first, ere it can rise,
> It calls for blood and human sacrifice.
> I know not where the choice or fate doth lie,
> But of ye two the one must surely die."

Now, men were greatly wanting for this city, because in those days there were but few in the land. Then the brothers assembled many wolves, bears, foxes, and all wild beasts, and by their power changed them into men. And they did it thus : A sorcerer took an ox and enchanted it, and slew it, and sang over it a magic song, and left it in an enchanted place. Then the wolves and other wild beasts came by night to the great stone of the sacrifice, by a running stream. A god beheld it. They ate the meat— they became men. These were the first Romans.

Last of all came a serpent with a gold crown—the Queen of the Serpents. She ate of the meat and became the most beautiful woman in the world. She was a great magician. Thus she became the goddess of the city, and dwelt in the tower of the temple. And her name was Venus. She was like a star.

Then Romolo and Remolo wished to know which of them was to die to save the city. And both desired it. Then they resolved to take an immense stone and cast it one at the other. So Remolo picked it up and cast it at his brother, and all who beheld it thought he must be slain. But Romolo caught it in his hands and threw it back; yet Remolo caught it easily. But in that instant his foot slipped, and he fell backward over the Tarpeian Rock, and so he perished. This is an old story.

And thus it was that Rome was built.

[Now, it was in this city, or near by, that in after-time Virgil was born, who in his day did such wonders. But the first wonder of all was the manner of his birth. For Virgil was the glory of Rome, and the greatest poet and sorcerer ever known therein.]

It did not occur to me to include this tale among the Virgilian legends, but finding that the compiler of "Virgilius the Sorcerer" (1893) has begun with a legend of Romulus and Remus, I have done the same, having one by me. As the giant said to the story-telling ram, "There is nothing like beginning at the commencement."

HOW VIRGIL WAS BORN.

"And truly this *aurum potabile*, or drinkable gold, is a marvellous thing, for it worketh wonders to sustain human life, removing all disorders, and 'tis said that it will revive the dead."—PHIL. ULSTADT: *Cælum Philosophorum, seu Liber de Secretis.*

"And there be magic mirrors in which we may see the forms of our enemies, and the like, battalions for battle, and sieges, and all such things."—PETER GOLDSCHMID: *The Witch and Wizard's Advocate over-thrown* (1705).

There was once in an old temple in Rome a great man, a very learned Signore. His name was Virgilio, or Virgil.

He was a magician, but very good in all things to all men ;
he had a kind heart, and was ever a friend to the poor.

Virgil was as brave and fearless as he was good. And
he was a famous poet—his songs were sung all over Italy.
Some say that he was the son of a fairy (*fata*), and that his
father was a King of the magicians; others declared that
his mother was the most beautiful woman in the whole
world, and that her name was *Elena* (Helen), and his father
was a spirit. And how it came about was thus :

When all the great lords and princes were in love with
the beautiful Elena, she replied that she would marry
no one, having a great dread of bearing children. She
would not become a mother. And to avoid further wooing
and pursuing she shut herself up in a tower, and believed
herself to be in safety, because it was far without the walls
of Rome. And the door to it was walled up, so that no one
could enter it. But the god Jove (*Giove*) entered ; he did so
by changing himself into many small pieces of gilded paper
(gold-leaf), which came down into the tower like a shower.

The beautiful Helen held in her hand a cup of wine, and
many of the bits of gold-leaf fell into it.

" How pretty it looks !" said Helen. " It would be a
pity to throw it away. The gold does not change the wine.
If I drink the gold I shall enjoy good health and ever
preserve my beauty."

But hardly had Helen drunk the wine, before she felt a
strange thrill in all her body, a marvellous rapture, a change
of her whole being, followed by complete exhaustion. And
in time she found herself with child, and cursed the moment
when she drank the wine. And to her in this way was born
Virgil, who had in his forehead a most beautiful star
of gold. Three fairies aided at his birth ; the Queen of
the Fairies cradled him in a cradle made of roses. She
made a fire of twigs of laurel ; it crackled loudly. To the
crackling of twigs of laurel he was born. His mother felt
no pain. The three each gave him a blessing ; the wind as
it blew into the window wished him good fortune ; the light
of the stars, and the lamp and the fire, who are all spirits,
gave him glory and song. He was born fair and strong
and beautiful ; all who saw him wondered.

Then it happened, when Virgil was fourteen years old, that
one day in summer he went to an old solitary temple, all
ruined and deserted, and therein he laid down to sleep.

But ere he had closed his eyes he heard a sound as of a voice lamenting, and it said:

> "Alas! I am a prisoner!
> Will no one set me free?
> If any man can do it,
> Full happy shall he be."

Then Virgil said:
" Tell me who thou art and where thou art."
And the voice answered:

> " I am a spirit,
> Imprisoned in a vase
> Under the stone
> Which is beneath thy head."

Then Virgil lifted the stone and found a vase, which was closed; and he opened it, and there came forth a beautiful spirit, who told him that there was also in the vase a book of magic and necromancy (*magia e gramanzia*).

> " Therein wilt thou find all secrets
> Which thou desirest to obtain,
> To make what thou wilt into gold,
> To make the dead speak,
> To make them come before thee,
> To go invisibly where thou wilt,
> To become a great poet.
> Thou wilt learn the lost secret
> How to become great and beautiful;
> Thou wilt rediscover the mystery
> Of predicting what is to take place;
> Yea, to win fortune in every game."

By the vase was a magic wand, the most powerful ever known. And from that day Virgil, who had been as small as a dwarf, became a tall, stately, very handsome man.

This was his first great work: he made a mirror wherein one could see all that was going on in any country in the world, in any city, as well into any house as anywhere. Keeping the mirror hidden (beneath his cloak), he went to the Emperor. And because he was a very handsome man, well dressed, and also by the aid of the mirror, he was permitted to go into the hall where the Emperor sat. And, conversing with him, the Emperor was so pleased that he spoke more familiarly and confidentially than he was wont to do with his best friends; at which the courtiers who were present were angry with jealousy.

Turning to Virgil, the Emperor said:

" I would give a thousand gold crowns to know just what the Turks are doing how, and if they mean to make war on me."

Virgil replied :

" If your Highness will go into another room, I can show in secret what the Turks are now doing."

" But how you can make me see what the Turks are doing is more than I can understand," replied the Emperor. " However, let us go, if it be only to see what fancy thou hast in thy head."

Then the Emperor rose, and giving his arm to Virgil, went to a room apart, where the magician showed and explained to him (*per filo e per segna*) all that the Turks were about. And the Emperor was amazed at seeing clearly what Virgil had promised to show. Then he gave to Virgil the thousand crowns with his own hand, and was ever from that day his friend. And so Virgil rose in the world.

In this tale there is as quaint and naïve a mixture of traditions and ideas as one could desire. The fair Helen, in her tower of Troy, becomes Danae visited by Jupiter, and as the narrator had certainly seen Dantzic Golden Water, or some other cordial with gold-leaf in it, the story of the shower is changed into aureated wine. It is evident that the one who recast the legend endeavoured to make this incident intelligible. All the rest is mediæval. " Gold," says Helen, " will preserve my beauty." Thus the *aurum potabile* of the alchemists was supposed to do the same as Paracelsus declared.

We all recognise a great idea when put into elaborate form by a skilled artist, but to perceive it as a diamond in the rough and recognise its value is apparently given to few. It is true that those few may themselves be neither poets nor geniuses—just as the Hottentot who can find or discern diamonds may be no lapidary or jeweller. What I would say is, that such ideas or motives abound in this Italian witch-lore to a strange extent.

Thus, the making Virgil a son of Jupiter by a Helen-Danae is a flight of mythologic invention, far surpassing in boldness anything given in the Neapolitan legends of the poet. Thomas Carlyle and Vernon Lee have expressed with great skill great admiration of the idea that Faust begat with the fair Helen the Renaissance. It was indeed a magnificent conception, but in very truth this fathering of Virgil, the grand type of poetry and magic, and of all earthly wisdom, by Jupiter on Helen-Danae is far superior to it in every way. For Virgil to the legend-maker represented the Gothic or Middle Ages in all their beauty and exuberance, their varied learning and splendid adventure, far more perfectly than did the mere vulgar juggler and thaumaturgist Faust, as the latter appears in every legend until Goethe transfigured him. And, strangely enough, the Virgilian cyclus, as I have given it, is as much of the Renaissance as it is classic or mediæval. The Medicis are in it to the life. In very truth it was Virgil, and not Faust, who was the typical magician *par éminence* after Apollonius, some of whose legends he, in fact, inherited. And Virgil has come to us with a traditional character as marked and peculiar as any in Shakespeare—which Faust did not. He has passed through the ages not only as a magus and poet, but as a personality, and a very remarkable one.

There is another very curious, and, indeed, great idea lurking in these witch-Virgilian legends, especially set forth in this of the birth and continued in all. It is that there is in them a cryptic, latent heathenism, a sincere, lingering love of the old gods, and especially of the *dii minores*, of *fate* or fays, and fauns and fairies, of spirits of the air and of rivers and fountains, an adoration of Diana as the moon-queen of the witches, and a far greater familiarity with incantations than prayers, or more love of sorceries than sacraments. Whenever it can be done, even as a post-scriptum, we have a conjuration or spell, as if the tale had awakened in the mind of the narrator a feeling of piety towards "the old religion." The romances of Mercury, and Janus, and Vesta, and Apollo, and Diana all inspire the narrator to pray to them in all sincerity, just as a Catholic, after telling a legend of a saint, naturally repeats a prayer to him or a novena. It is the last remains of classic faith.

Or we may say, as things fell out, that the Goethean-Helen-Faust-Renaissance poem represents things as they were, or as they came to pass, as if it were the acme, while the Virgilian tradition which I here impart indicates things as they might have happened, had the stream of evolution been allowed to run on in its natural course, just as Julian the apostate (or rather apostle of the gospel of letting things be) held that progress or culture and science might have advanced just as surely and rapidly on the old heathen lines as any other. According to Heine, this would have saved us all an immense amount of trouble in our school-studies, in learning Latin and mythology, had we kept on as we were.

I mean by this that these traditions of Virgil indicate, as no other book does, the condition of a naïvely heathen mind, "suckled in a creed out-worn," believing in the classic mythology half turned to fairies, much more sincerely, I fear, than many of my readers do in the Bible, and from this we may gather very curious reflection as to whether men may not have ideas of culture, honesty, and mercy in common, whatever their religion may be.

The marvels of the birth of Virgil of old, as told by Donatus, probably after the lost work of Suetonius, are that his mother Maia dreamed, *se enixam laureum ramum*, that she gave birth to a branch of laurel ; that he did not cry when born, and that the pine-tree planted according to ancient custom on that occasion attained in a very short time to a great height, which thing often happens when plants grow near hot springs, as is the case on the Margariten Island, by Budapesth, where everything attains to full-size in one-third of the usual time. The custom of planting a pine-tree on the birth of a child, in the belief that its condition will always indicate its subject's health and prosperity, is still common among the Passamaquoddy, and other Red Indians in America, I having had such a tree pointed out to me by an old grandfather.

In the Aryan or Hindu mythology Buddha, who subsequently becomes a great *magus* and healer of all ills, like Christ, "was born of the mother-tree Maya," according to J. F. Hewitt (" L'Histoire et les Migra-tions de la Croix et du Su-astika," Bruxelles, 1898). He was the son of Kapila Vastu, who was born holding in his hands a medicament, whence he became "the Child of Medicine," or of healing. Buddha appears to be confused with his father.

Now Virgil is clearly stated to be born of Maya or Maia, who is a mythical tree ; his life is involved in that of a mysterious tree, and in more than one legend he is unquestionably identical with Esculapius, the god of medicine.

VIRGIL, THE EMPEROR, AND THE TWO DOVES.

" Qualis spelunca subito commota Columba,
Cui domus, et dulces latebroso in pumice nidi,
Fertur in arva volans, plausumque exterrita pennis
Dat tecto ingentem ; mox ære lapsa quieto
Radit iter liquidum, celeres neque commovet alas."

VIRGILIUS : *Aen.*, V. 213.

This is another story, telling how Virgil first met the Emperor.

It happened on a time that the Emperor of Rome invited many of his friends to a hunt, and on the appointed day all assembled with fine horses and hounds, gay attendants, and sounding horns—*tutti allegri e contenti*, " all as gay as larks."

And when they came to the place, they left their horses and went into the forest, where it befell, as usual, that some got game, while others returned lame ; but on the whole they came to camp with full bags and many brags of their adventures and prowess, and supped merrily.

" It is ever so," said the Emperor to a courtier, " one stumbles, and another grumbles ; then the next minute something joyful comes, and he smiles.

" ' Thus it is true in every land
Good luck and bad go hand in hand.' "

" When men speak in that tone," replied the courtier, " they often prophesy. Now, there is near by an ancient grotto, long forgot by men, wherein if you will sleep you may have significant dreams, even as people had in the olden time."

So when night came on some of the courtiers went to a contadino house to lodge, while others camped out *alla stella*, or in the *albergo al fresco*, while the Emperor was guided by the courtier to an old ruin, where in a solid rock there was a door of stone, which Virgil opened by a spell. (*Sic* in MS.)

The Emperor was then led through a long passage into a cave, which was dry and comfortable enough, and where the attendants made a bed, whereon His Highness lay down, and, being very weary, was soon asleep.

But he had not slumbered long ere, as it seemed to him, he was awakened by the loud barking of a dog, and saw before him to his amazement a marvellously beautiful lady clad in white, with a resplendent star (crescent) on her forehead.   In her right hand she bore a white dove, and in her left another, which was black.

When the lady, or goddess, saw that the Emperor was awake, she let both the doves fly.   The white one, after circling several times round his head, alighted on his shoulder.   The black one also flew about him, and then winged its course far away.

Then the lady disappeared, and the white dove followed her, and sat on her shoulder as she fled.

The Emperor was so much amazed, or deeply moved, by this strange sight that he slept no more, but remained all night meditating on it, nor did he on the morrow give any heed to the chase, but ever reflected on the lady and her doves.

The courtier asked him what had occurred.   And the Emperor replied :

" I have had a wonderful vision, and I cannot tell the meaning thereof."

The gentleman replied :

" There is in Rome a young man, a poet and sage, of whom I have heard strange things, and I believe that he excels in unfolding signs and mysteries."

" It is well," replied the Emperor.   So when they returned to Rome he sent for the magician, who came, yet he knew beforehand why he was summoned to Court.   And it is said that this was the first time when the Emperor knew Virgil.*

Now, Virgil was as yet a young man.   And when the Emperor set forth what he had beheld, he replied :

" It is a marvellously favourable sign for you, oh my Emperor, for in that lady you have seen your star.   There is a planet allotted to every man, and thine is of the greatest.   Thou hast one—call to her, invoke her ever when in need of help, and she will never abandon thee. Thou hast seen thy star.   Her greeting to thee (*saluto*) means that a year hence a danger will threaten thee.   The black dove signifies that one year hence thou wilt have an enemy who will make war on thee.   When the dove fled afar, it was not the dove but the enemy, who will be put to

* Possibly meaning that it was the first time when he recognised his power as a sage or sorcerer.

flight.   And the white dove was not a dove, but your victory announced to you in that form, and your star has announced it because in one year you will have, as the proverb says, 'the enemy at your heels.'"

And all this came to pass as he had foretold.

Then the poet and magician became his friend, and from that time the Emperor never moved a leaf (*i.e.* did nothing) without taking the advice of Virgil.

The goddess, or planet, described in this tale is very evidently Diana, appropriately introduced as the deity of the chase, but more significantly as the queen of the witches, and mistress of mysteries and divination.   In both forms the dog has a peculiar adaptation, because a black dog was the common attendant of a sorcerer, as exampled by that of Henry C. Agrippa.

The dove is so widely spread in this world, and is everywhere so naturally recognised as a pretty, innocent creature, that it is no wonder that very different and distant races should have formed much the same ideas and traditions regarding it.   It is a curious anomaly that while doves, especially in Roman Catholic symbolism, are the special symbols of love and peace, there are in reality no animals or birds which fight and peck so assiduously among themselves, as I have verified by much observation.   However, herein the pious mythologists "builded better than they knew," for the *odium theologicum*, either with heretics or among rivals in the Church, has been the cause of more quarrelling than any other in the world —woman perhaps excepted.

In the Egyptian symbolism, a widow who, out of love for her husband, will not wed again was typified by a black dove.*   The dove who brought the olive-

* Horus Apollo, "Hieroglyph.," II. 32.

leaf to Noah was generally recognised as symbolizing the new birth of the world, or its regeneration after a divine bath or lustration, and the same meaning is attached to its appearance at the baptism of Christ. A German writer named Wernsdorf has written two books on the dove as a symbol, viz., "De simulacro columbæ in locis sacris antiquitas recepto," Viterbo, 1773; and "De Columba auriculæ Gregorii adhærente," Witteberg, 1780.

As Diana always bears the crescent, here confounded or identified very naturally with a star—both being heavenly bodies—the representing her as the peculiar planet of the Emperor is very ingenious. In seeing her he beholds his star, and, in the mute language of emblems, hears her voice. Truly there is unto all of us a star, but it is within and not without, and its name is the Will, which, when revealed or understood, can work miracles.

"So mote it be!"

VIRGILIO AND THE ROCK.

One night, when he was young, Virgil was in Naples; he went to visit a very beautiful woman. And when he left her at midnight he found the house surrounded by *bravi* or assassins, who had been placed there to kill him by a signore who was his rival.

Then the magician ran for his life, followed by all the crew, till he came to a steep rock like a high wall. And here he paused, and cried aloud during the minute which he had gained, this incantation :

"Apri spirito della rupe,
Apri il tuo cuore a me.
Spirito gentile, abbi,

Abbi pietà di me,
Se tu vuoi che Iddio
Abbia pietà di te."

" Mighty spirit of the mountain,
Ope thy rocky heart to me.
Gentle sprite, I pray thee
Have mercy upon me,
As thou truly hopest
That God may pity thee."

Then the rock opened, and Virgil fled into it and was saved.

Those who sought his life followed. And Virgil went forth, but while they were in the passage it closed at both ends, and they all perished. So was Virgil saved.

It came to pass in time that Virgil, seeing it would be of great use, opened the grotto, and it is there to this day.

There was no place where Virgil did not leave some great work, whence it came that his name is known to all the world.

There is a curious reflection, and one of great value to folk-lore, to be drawn from this, and in fact from all of these stories. It is believed—actually believed, and not merely assumed to make a tale—that the conjurations given in them have the effect attributed to them when they are uttered by any wizard or witch or person who is prepared by magic or faith. Therefore such tales as told by witches are only a frame, as it were, wherein a lesson-picture is set. This induces a deeper, hence a more advanced, kind of reflection or moral than is conveyed by common, popular fairy-tales. The one condition naturally leads to another. There is very little trace of it in the " Mährchen " of Grimm, Crane, Pitré, or Bernoni. In the *novelle* of Boccacio, Sachetti, Bandello and others, of which literally thousands were produced during and after the Renaissance, there is very often a commonplace kind of moral, such as follows all fables, but it is not of the same kind as that which is involved in witch-stories. Even in this of Virgil the invocation to the Spirit of the Rock, adjuring it to be merciful as it hopes for mercy from God, is beyond what is generally found in common traditions.

All of these conjurations, to have due effect, must be intoned in a certain manner, which is so peculiar that anyone who is familiar with it can recognise at a distance, where the words are not to be distinguished, by the mere sound of the voice, whether an incantation is being sung. Hence the greatest care and secresy is observed when teaching or chanting them.

Among the Red Indians of North America this is carried so far that, as one who took lessons from an Oneida sorcerer informs us, it required study every day for seven years to learn how to correctly intone one spell of twelve lines. The same is told of the old Etruscan-Latin spells in the "*Dizionario Myth. Storico.*"

This legend is specially interesting because the tomb of Virgil is close by the grotto of Posillippo, and it is conjectured that as it was, according to tradition, made by magic, Virgil probably made it. Therefore it may have been the first of these tales. Why the grotto was specially regarded as mysterious is almost apparent to all who have studied cave and stone worship. In early times, in the mysteries, the going through a hole or passage, especially in a rock, signified the new birth, or illumination, or initiation, hence the cult of holy or holed stones, great or small, found all over the world. Such writers as Faber and Bryant have, it is true, somewhat overdone guess-work symbolism, or fanciful interpretation, but that the passing through the dark tunnel and coming to light played a part in old rites is unquestionable, and that this respect for the subject extended to all perforated stones and even beads.

Incantations or spells are of two kinds—the traditional, and those which a powerful or gifted magician or witch improvises. This of Virgil is of the latter kind.

VIRGIL, THE EMPEROR, AND THE TRUFFLES.

"Quo ducit gula?"—*Latin Saying.*
"I am passionately fond of truffles, though I never tasted them."—
XAVIER DE MONTEPIN.

One day Virgil was at table with the Emperor, and the latter complained that his cook was a dolt, because he could never find anything new to tempt his appetite, and that he had to eat the same kind of dishes over and over again.

"What I would like," he said, "would be some kind of new taste or flavour. There must be many a one as yet unknown to the kitchen."

Then Virgil, reflecting, said :

"I will see to-morrow if I cannot find something of the kind which will please your Highness." Whereupon all who were present expressed delight, for no one doubted that he could do whatever he attempted.

So the next day Virgil went into the forests, where there were many pigs, and considered attentively what the roots might be which they dug up with such great care ; for he had remarked that whatever men eat pigs also like, above all other animals. And having obtained some of the roots, which were like dark-brown or black lumps, he took them to the Emperor's cook, and said :

" Wash these well and cut them fine, and I will see to the cooking."

That day the Emperor had invited several friends to see what new dish Virgil would produce ; and when they were assembled at table, Virgilio took the roots, cut fine, put them into a pan with oil and beaten eggs, and served them up with his own hands. And the smell thereof was so appetizing that all cried, " *Evviva Virgilio !*" even before they had tasted the dish. But when they had eaten of it, they were delighted indeed, and one and all wished to know what the roots were which gave such a delicate flavour ; to which Virgil, rising, replied :

" Truffles !"*

And ever since that time, even at the table of the Pope, or any other rich man, no one has ever discovered any better flavour for food than this which was first found out by Virgil.

One day not long after this took place Virgil was in his study, when, looking at the stone in a ring which he wore, he exclaimed : " The Emperor wishes to see me !" And sure enough, a few minutes later a messenger entered, saying that his imperial master desired to speak to the sage. And, having obeyed the call, he found the Emperor ill and suffering from an indigestion.

" *Caro Virgilio*," exclaimed the Emperor, " I have made thee come because I am suffering from disorder ; and as that pig of a cook who caused it can give me nothing to eat to relieve it, I have recourse to science, for I know that thou art a great doctor."

" Truly," replied Virgil. " Very simple doctoring is needed here. Just tell the cook to boil wheat-bran in water, mix it with the yolk of an egg, and drink it in the morning before you rise."

" Bran boiled in water !" repeated the Emperor slowly. " Just what they give to pigs ! Truly, it seems that you have brought me down to a pig's level, since you give me ' hogs' broth,' as they call it."

" I wonder," exclaimed Virgil, ' since your Highness is so humble, that you do not put yourself below the pigs, because you have abused like a pig, and many a time, that

---

* Simply an *omelette aux truffes*, the common fashion of eating truffles among the peasants. It is possibly an old Roman dish, and may be in Apicius.

poor devil of a cook for not pleasing your palate. It is not long since I delighted you, and had applause from all, for serving truffles at your imperial table. Had *he* done so, you would have curiously inquired what the roots were and whence they came ; and having learned that they were *cibo di maiali*, or pigs' food, you would have cast him forth, and the truffles after him. For such is the wisdom of this world, and so is man deluded! But as for the bran boiled in water, whether it be pigs' broth or not, 'tis the specific for your illness."

"Ah well, my dear Virgilio," replied the Emperor, "in future serve me up as many pigs' dainties and give me as much pigs'-doctor stuff as you please, provided that all be as good as truffles, or the medicine bran broth. It is foolish to be led by mere fancies : a pig or a peasant may know as well as a prince what is pleasant for the palate or good as a cure. *Evviva Virgilio !*"

In this merry tale I have followed to the letter an undoubted original, which was in every detail new to me ; and this is the more remarkable since there is in it decidedly the stamp and expression of a kind of humour and philosophy which seems to be peculiar to individual or literary genius. The joke of pigs' dainties, pigs' remedies, the calling the cook a pig, and the final reduction of the Emperor to a degree below that animal, is carried out with great ingenuity, yet as marked simplicity.

The best truffles in Italy are sold as coming from *Norcia*, and Nortia, who was an old Etruscan goddess, known to the original Virgil, is in popular tradition in Tuscany the Spirit of Truffles, to whom those who seek them address a *scongiurazione*, or evocation, which may be found in my "Etrusco-Roman Remains." In Christian symbolism the truffle is associated with St. Antony and his pig. When the saint had resolved to die by hunger, the pig dug up and brought to him a number of truffles, the saint seeing in this an intimation by a miracle that he should eat and live, which thing would seem to be poetically commemorated in the *saucisses aux truffes*, or Gotha sausages, in which pork and truffles are beautifully combined.

The most remarkable variety of the truffle is one found in the United States, south of Pennsylvania. It is called *tuckahoe*, or Indian bread, and, with most things American, is remarkable for bigness at least, since it weighs sometimes fifteen pounds and hides at a depth of fifteen feet underground. Like California fruit, it is far more remarkable for size or weight than excellence. An incredible quantity of so-called truffles, which appear thinly sliced or in small bits in dishes even in first-class hotels or restaurants all over Europe, are nothing but burned potatoes, or similar vegetable carbon, flavoured sometimes with extract of mushrooms, but much oftener are simply tasteless soft coal. Very good truffles, equal to the French, for which they are sold, are found in the South of England. The truffle is, like raw meat, caviare, and oysters, strongly stimulating food, and as a *purée* or paste is beneficial for anæmic invalids.

BALSÀBO.

There once lived in Florence in the days of King Long-Ago or Queen Formerly a signore who went beyond all the men who ever sinned, in making evil out of good and turning light into darkness. For, under cover of being very devout and serving the saints, he well-nigh outdid many a devil in making all about him unhappy. He had six children, three boys and three girls, all as fine young folk as there were in Tuscany. For he was severe in punishing and slow in rewarding, always reviling, never giving a kind word. Once when his eldest son saved him from drowning at the risk of his own life, he abused and struck the youth for tearing his garment in so doing. And in his family there was ever the wolf at the table with such a hunger that one could see it,* while all save himself went so sorrily clad that it was a shame to behold, and if anyone made a jest or so much as smiled there came abuse and blows. And to offend and grieve and insult was so deeply in him that it became a disease.

However, evil weeds must fade as well as flowers; everything dies except Death, and the longer time he takes to sharpen his scythe, the more keenly will it cut. So it came to pass that one day this good man, but very bad parent, came suddenly to his death-bed, while his children stood round with eyes as dry as the Arno in August, which, though it may shine here and there, never runs over.†

Now, by chance there stood by the dying man the great magician Virgilio, who indeed had much love and pity for these young people. And at the same minute, but seen only by him, there came floating in, like a bit of gold-leaf on a light feather, borne on the current of air, a certain *folletto*, or devil, who had been drifting about in the world for a thousand years, and in all that time had only learned more and more that everything is naught, or nothing of much consequence, and that good or evil stand for one

* "Egli ha la lupa" (*i.e.*, fame); also "Ho una fame ch'io la veggio."
—"Proverbi Italiani da Orlando," Pescetti, 1618.
† In the Italian MS.: "I figlii erano al letto del padre che sapevano alla fine, ma non una lacrima sortiva dal loro ciglio."

another, according to circumstances. And as the dying
man was one who, above all people living, made the
meanest trifle a thing of vast importance, so this devil,
whose name was Balsàbo, went beyond all his own kind of
diavoli pococuranti in being unlike the great Signore di
Tribaldo (as the dead man was called), he being a *diavolo
a dirittura*, a devil in a straight line, or directly forward.
And this demon being invisible to all save Virgil, the
master said to him secretly :

"Art thou willing to enter this man's body and act as his
soul, and become father of a family ?"

"As ready for that as for anything. No doubt I will
find fun in it," answered Balsàbo.

Then Virgil said :

> "Spirito di Belsàbo,
> Io ti scongiurò
> Che per comando mio
> Tu lasci una vita sfrenata
> Come 'ai tenuto per il passato
> E dentro il corpo di Tribaldo
> Tu possa entrare e divenire
> Un capo di famiglia
> Fino a ordine mio.
> E tutti quei
> Fanciulli educherai (*sic*)."

> "Spirit of Belsàbo,
> I now conjure thee
> That by my command
> Thou shalt leave the lewd life
> Which thou did'st lead of old,
> And enter into this body
> Of Di Tribaldo, and become
> Head of a family,
> And educate his children."

So into the body he went, as the spirit of Di Tribaldo
went out, like the toy which shows the weather in which
one puppet pops forth as the other goes in. So there he
lay for a minute, all the children around in silent amazement that he had departed without cursing them. When
all at once up leaped Balsàbo, as gay as a lark, crying like
a *Scaramuccio* :

"Whoop, pigs ! here we are again !"

Hearing which, the dear children, understanding that he
had come to life again, did indeed weep bitterly, so that

Di Tribaldo, had he stopped a little longer, might have been amazed. But he had no sooner gone out of his body than a great grim devil, a kind of detective demon, who was on the look-out for souls, whipped him up, gave him a couple of cuffs to keep him quiet, and, putting him into a game-bag, drawing the cords tight, and then rolling them round and tying them, flew off to give the prey up to the proper authorities, and what disposition they made of this precious piece of property I know not, nor truly do I much care. All that can be said is that 'twas a good riddance of bad rubbish, and that we may all rejoice that he comes no more into this story.

But what was the amazement of the well-nigh bereaved children when their solemn parent made a leap half-way to the ceiling, and then, while imitating with his mouth a *zufolo*, or shepherd's pipe, to perfection, began to dance with grace a wild *coranto*, and anon sang :

> "Chi ben vive, ben muore,
> Io lo credo in mio cuore ;
> Oggi vivo, in figura,
> E doman in sepoltura,
> Ho scappato ben il orco,
> Morto io, morto il porco !" *

> "He who lives well may well depart,
> As I believe with all my heart.
> To-day alive, and all in bloom,
> To-morrow buried in the tomb ;
> But I've escaped, and don't care why !
> If I were dead the pig might die !
> The pig might die, the world be burned !
> And everything to ashes turned !"

Which pious song being ended, he asked them why they were all staring at him like a party of stuck pigs, and bade them scamper and send out for a good supper, with flowers and wine ; and on their asking what he would have, he replied, still singing :

> "Everything to please the palate,
> Venison, woodcocks, larks, and sallet,
> Partridges both wild and tame,
> And every other kind of game,

---

* "Morto io, morto il porco." Latin : "Me mortuo terra misceatur incendio" (Suetonius in "Vitâ Neronis")—"When I shall be dead, the devil may take everything !"

Buttered eggs and macaroni,
Salmagundi, rice and honey,
Mince-pies and oyster too,
Lobster patties, veal ragoût,
Beef, with mushrooms round the dish,
And everything that heart could wish."

Whereupon, being told by his eldest daughter, who was of opinion that he had gone mad, that such a supper would cost twenty crowns, he replied that it could not be done for the money, and that he should always expect such a meal every day, and a much better one when guests should come. Wherein he kept his word, and amazed them all by urging them to stuff and cram to their hearts' desire, but especially by pressing them to drink ; and whereas it had been of yore that they had been scolded like beasts if they so much as begged for a second glass of sour, half-watered wine, they were now jeered and jibed as duffers and sticks for not swigging off their bumpers of the best and strongest like men.

And they also noted a great change in this, that while the late Signore Tribaldo had ever been as severe in manner and conversation as any saint, and grim as an old owl, the Signore Balsàbo during the meal cracked one joke after the other, some of them none too seemly, and roared with laughter at their frightened looks. But as 'tis easy to teach young cats the way to the dairy, they began to slowly put out one paw after the other, and be of the opinion that on the whole their dear papa had been much improved by his death and revival. And some word having been said of games, he suddenly whipped out a pack of cards and proposed play. At which his eldest son replying that it would be but a thin game with them who had hardly a *quattrino* apiece, Balsàbo sent for his strong-box, which was indeed well-lined, and gave them each a hundred crowns in gold, swearing it was a shame that such a magnificent family as his should go about like poor beggars, because handsome youth and beautiful girls needed fine clothes, and that in future they were all to spend what they liked—and bless the expense at that !—for as long as there was twopence in the locker, half of it should be theirs.

Then they sat down to play, and Gianni, the eldest son, and Bianca, the eldest daughter, who had aforetime learned to play a little on the sly, thought they would surely win.

But Balsàbo in the end beat them all, and when they marvelled at his luck roared with laughter, and said 'twas no wonder, for he had cheated at every turn; and then, sitting down again, showed them how 'twas done, but bade them keep it all a family secret. " For thus," said he, " we can among us cheat all the gamesters in Florence, and ever be as rich as so many Cardinals."

And then he said to them, as in apology: " Ye have no doubt, my dear children, marvelled that I have this evening been somewhat strict and austere with you, which is not to be blamed, considering that I have been dead and am only just now alive again; but I trust that in future I shall be far more kind and indulgent, and lend you a helping hand in all your little games, whatever they be; for the only thing which can grieve me is that there shall be any fun or devilry going on, and I not have a hand in it. · And as it is becoming that children should obey their parents, and have no secrets from them, I enjoin it strictly on you that whatever you may be up to, from swindling at pitch-and-toss, up to manslaughter or duels, ye do nothing without first taking counsel with me, because I, being more experienced in the ways of this wicked world, can best guard you against its deceptions. And so, my beloved infants, go in peace, which means go it while you are young, and as peacefully as you can, and merrily if you must!"

Now, the eldest son, Gianni, had longed well nigh to being ill, and even to tears, to wear fine clothes (in which Bianca and the others were well up with him), and have a gallant horse, like the other youths of his rank in Florence. But kind as Balsàbo had been to him, he hardly dared to broach the subject, when all at once his father introduced it by asking him why he went footing about like a pitiful beggar, instead of riding like a cavalier; and learning that it was because he had no steed, Balsàbo gave a long whistle and said:

" Well, you are a fool of forty-five degrees! Why the devil, if you thought I would not approve it, did you not buy a horse on post-obit credit, and ride him on the sly? However, 'tis never too late to mend. But such a goose as you would be certainly cheated in the buying. Come with me."

And Gianni soon found that his saint of a father was well up to all the tricks of the horse trade, the end being that he had the best steed in Florence for half of what it would have

cost him. And from this accomplished parent he also
learned to ride and fence, and in the latter he taught his son
so many sly passes and subtle tricks, crafty glissades and
botte, that he had not his master in all the land.

And now a strange thing came to pass : that as all these
young people, though willing enough to be gay and well
attired, were good at heart and honest, as they day by day
found that their father, though really bad in nothing, had,
on the other hand, no more conscience or virtue than an old
shoe or a rag scarecrow, so it was they who began to ser-
monize him, even as the late Signore Tribaldo had lectured
them, the tables being quite turned. But what was most
marvellous was that Signore Balsàbo, far from taking any
offence, seemed to find in this being scolded for his want of
heart, morals, and other crimes, a deep and wondrous joy, a
sweet delight, as of one who has discovered a new pleasure
or great treasure. This was especially the case when he
was brought to book, or hauled over the coals, by his
daughter Bianca, who was gifted with the severe eloquence
of her other father, which she now poured forth in floods on
his successor.

Now, you may well imagine that an old devil-goblin who
had been kicked and footed about the world for a thousand
years between the back-kitchen of hell unto the inner courts
of the Vatican, including all kinds of life, but especially the
bad, thus having a family to support and beloved daughters
and sons to blow him up, and, in fact, the mere having any
decent Christian care enough for him to call him a soulless
old blackguard, was like undreamed-of bliss. He had been
in his time exorcised by priests in Latin through all that
grammar and vocabulary could supply, and cursed in
Etruscan, Greek, Lombard, and everything else ; but the
Italian of his daughter had in it the exquisite and novel
charm that there was real *love* mingled with it and gratitude
for his profuse kindness and indulgence, so that 'twas to him
like the pecking of an angry and dear canary bird, the which
thing acted on him so strangely that he at times was fain to
look about him for some stray sin to commit, in order to get
a good sound scolding. For he had fallen so much into
decent life and ways by living with his dear children that it
often happened that he did nothing wrong for as much as
three or four days together. .

And truly it was a brave sight to see him, when reprimanded, cast down his eyes and sigh : " Yes, yes ! 'tis too true : *mea culpa ! mea maxima culpa !* It was indeed wicked!" when all the while he hardly knew where the sin was or wherein he had done wrong or right or anything else. Now, it may seem a strange thing that so old a sinner should ever come to grace ; but as ye know that in old tombs raspberry or other seeds, hard and dry, a thousand years old, have been found which, however, grew when planted, so Balsàbo began to think and change, and try, even for curiosity's sake, what being good meant.

Meanwhile it was a marvel to see how well—notwithstanding all the expenditure, to which there was no limit, save the consciences of the children—Balsàbo kept the treasury supplied. And this was to him a joke, as all life was, save, indeed, the children, in whom he began to take interest, or for whom he felt love ; for, what with knowing where many an old treasure lay hidden, or the true value of many a cheap estate, and a hundred other devices and tricks, he ever gained so much that in time he gave great dowers to his daughters, and castles and lands, with titles, to his sons.

Now, it came to pass—and it was the greatest marvel of all—that Bianca, by her reproving and reforming Balsàbo, had her own heart turned to goodness, and gave herself up to good works and study and prayer ; and unto her studies Balsàbo, curiously interested, gave great aid. Then she learned marvellously deep secrets of magic and spirits, but nothing evil ; and it came to pass that in her books she found that there were beings born of the elements, creatures appointed to live a thousand years or more, and then pass away into air or fire, and exist no longer. Furthermore, she discovered that such wandering spirits sometimes took up their abode in human bodies, and that, being neither good nor bad, they were always wild and strange, given up of all things to quaint tricks and strange devices, as ready unto one thing as another.

And it came to her mind, as she noted how Balsàbo knew all languages, and spoke of things which took place ages before as if he had lived in them, and of men long dead as if he had known them, that he who was her father aforetime was ignorant of all this as he was of gentleness or kindness or good nature, all which Balsàbo carried to a fault, not caring to take the pains to injure his worst enemy or to do a good turn to his best friend, unless it amused him, in which

case he would kill the one with as little sorrow as if he were
a fly, and give the other a castle or a thousand crowns, and
think no more of it than if he had fed a hawk or a hound.
And all such good deeds he played off in some droll fashion,
like tricks, as if thinking that sport, and nothing else, was
the end and aim of all benevolence. However, as regarded
Bianca and her brothers and sisters, he seemed to have other
ideas, and to her he appeared to be as another being, in love
and awe obeying her as a child and striving to understand
her lessons.

So this went on for years, till at last one day Bianca, full
of strange suspicions, which had become well nigh cer-
tainties, went to Virgilio and said:

"Tell me in truth who is this being whom thou didst send
us as my father, for that he is not the Di Tribaldo of earlier
days, I am sure. Good and kind he hath been, but too strange
to be human; wild hart is he, not to be measured as a man."

Virgil replied:

"Thou hast guessed the riddle, and yet not all; for he is
a spirit of the elements, and his appointed time is drawing
near to an end, and, being neither good nor evil, he would
have passed away in peace into the nothing which is the
end of all his kind. But thou hast awakened in him a
knowledge of love and duty, so that he will die in sorrow,
for he has learned from thee what he has lost."

Then Bianca asked:

"Can he not be saved?"

And Virgil replied:

"If anyone would give his or her life, then by virtue of
that sacrifice, when the thousand years of his existence
shall be at an end, the two lives shall be as one in the
world where all are one in love for ever."

Bianca replied:

"That which I have begun I will finish. Having opened
the bud, I will not leave the flower; having the flower, I
will bring it to fruit and seed; the egg which I found and
saved, I will hatch. She who hath said ' A ' must also say
' B,' till all the letters are learned.

> "'Who such a course hath once begun,
>   To the very end must run.'

And so will I give my life to give a soul to this poor spirit,
even as the Lord gave His to save mankind."

Then Bianca departed, and many days passed. On a time Virgilio saw Balsàbo, who greeted him with a sad smile.

"My sand is well-nigh run out, oh master," said the spirit. "Yet another day, and the sun which is to rise no more will go down behind the mountain-range of life. *Il sole tramonta.*"

"And art thou pleased to have been for a time a man?" asked Virgil.

"It was not an ill thing to be loved by the children," replied Balsàbo. "There I had great joy and learned much—yea, far too much for my own happiness, for I found that I was lost. When I was ignorant, and only a poor child of air and earth, fire and water, I knew nothing of good or evil, or of a soul or a better life in eternity; now I have learned all that by love, and also that it is not for me."

"Wait and see," replied Virgilio. "He who has learned to love has made the first step to immortality."

And after a few days, news was brought to Virgilio that Balsàbo, whom men called Di Tribaldo, was dying, and that Bianca also could not live long; and that night the master, looking from his tower beyond the Arno on the hill, that which is now called the San Gallo, or the Torre di Galileo, saw afar in the night a strange vision, the forms of a man and of a young woman, divinely beautiful, sweetly spiritual, in a golden, rosy light, ever rising higher and higher, while afar there was a sound as of harps and voices singing:

> "They walked in the world as in a dream,
> For nothing they saw as it now doth seem;
> And all they knew of care and woe
> Is now but a tale of the long ago;
> And they will walk in the land on high
> Where flowers are blooming ever and aye,
> And every flower in its breath and bloom
> Sings in the spirit with song perfume,
> And the song which it sings in the land above,
> In a thousand forms, is eternal love."

And as they rose Virgilio saw falling from them, as it were, a rain of rose-leaves and lilies, and every leaf as it fell faded, yet became a spirit which entered some new-born babe, and the spirit was its life.

"Sweetly hast thou sung, oh Spirit of God," said Virgilio,

as the last note was heard and the sight vanished. "The poorest devil may be saved by Love."

The idea that a soul or spirit, human or other, can enter into a dead body and revive it is to be found in the legends of all lands, from those of ancient Egypt, as appears in that of "Anpu and Bata," which has been nine times translated into English, down to several of these Italian tales. It is a fancy which need not be traditional or borrowed; it would occur to man as soon as the Shaman pretended to go out of his body while in a trance.

After the foregoing was written out, including the allusion to seeds found in tombs a thousand years old which grew again, and which were, of course, Roman or Etruscan, as the only kind known in Italy—I never having read of any such thing save as regards corn found in Egypt—I met with the following passage in "The Sagacity and Morality of Plants," by Dr. J. E. Taylor:

"Seeds have been found in Celtic tumuli . . . which, after an interval of perhaps two thousand years, have germinated into plants, and similar successful experiments have been made with seeds found in ancient Roman tombs."

As regards the original of this story, it was so imperfect, brief, and trifling that I have, as it were, well-nigh reconstructed it, and might as well claim to be its author as not, as I should have done were I an earlier Italian novelist, who without scruple appropriated popular stories with as little conscience as Robert Burns did old ballads. Bishop Percy amended them, and owned it, and all that he got thereby was much abuse and ridicule. But it is of little consequence when the legend is not offered as a mere tradition, and this is only a scrap of tradition *réchauffé*.

The character of Balsàbo belongs closely to the class which includes Falstaff, Panurge, Punch, Belphegor, and many other types who are "without conscience or cognition" of right or wrong, neither adapted to be banned or blessed, genially selfish, extravagantly generous, good fellows and bad Christians, yet who have ever been pre-eminently popular. But I am not aware that it ever entered into a mortal head to dream of their being reformed, any more than their cousins Manfred and Don Giovanni, for which reason I consider this tale of Balsàbo as decidedly original. Sinners we have had repentant by thousands, but this is really the only history of the conversion of Nothingarian.

Paracelsus was the first writer, following the Neo-Platonists and popular traditions, to make a mythology of elementary spirits and define their nature.

"There dwell," he says, "under the earth semihomines, or half-human beings, who have all temporal things which can be enjoyed and desired. They are called 'gnomes,' though properly the name should be sylphs or pygmies. They are not spirits, yet may be compared to them . . . between them and the devil is a great difference, because he does not die and they do, albeit they are very long-lived. And they are not *spirits*, because a spirit is immortal."

This gave birth in later days to the "Entertainments" of the Comte de Gabalis, and the exquisite "Undine" of La Motte Fouqué. Of late years exact science, by its investigations into zoology and botany, has approached Paracelsus by discovering incredible developments in *instinctive* intelligence, as distinguished from self-conscious reason, in all that exists.

Since the foregoing tale, with the comment on it, was written, even to the last word, I met with and read a novel entitled " Entombed in the Flesh," by Michael Henry Dziewicki,* which, both as regards plot and many details, bears such an extraordinary, and yet absolutely accidental, resemblance to the story of " Balsàbo " that, unless I enter a protest to the contrary, I can hardly escape the accusation of having borrowed largely from it.   In it a demon, neither angel nor devil, enters into the body of a man just dead, and has many marvellous and amusing adventures, being, of course, involved in the fate of a girl whom Lucifer wishes to destroy.   The end is, however, very different, because in the novel Phan-tasto, the spirit, is set free, and the maiden rescued by the latter going into a Salvation Army meeting and being moved by hearing the name and teaching of Jesus.   In " Balsàbo " the demon has immortality conferred on him by Bianca's giving her own *life* to effect it.   This is, I think, more ingenious than any other sacrifice could be, because in the tale, though it be rudely expressed, there is the exquisite conception that an immortal existence can take in, include with it, and identify a minor intelligence or raise it to a higher sphere.

That I have somewhat enlarged the original tale or written it up will be evident to everyone, but I have omitted very little which is in the text, save an incanta-

* Published by William Blackwood and Sons, Edinburgh, 1897.

tion at the end which Virgil addresses to the unborn souls who are to enter into the bodies of the children born of the rose-leaves. But I have inadvertently missed one point, to the effect that, after having been kicked out of hell, Balsàbo got down so low in morality as to be finally expelled from the Vatican. The literal translation of the passage is as follows:

"But poor Balsàbo, who had been kicked out of the kitchen of hell, . . . and even from the Vatican (felt honoured) . . . when Bianca scolded him like a child, and said: '*Vergogna !*'—'For shame!'"

VIRGIL, MINUZZOLO, AND THE SIREN.

"Caperat hic cantus *Minyas* mulcere, nec ullus
Præteriturus erat Sirenum tristia fata
Iam manibus remi exciderant stetit uncta carina."
ORPHEUS : *Argonauticis.*

[Virgil had a pupil named Minuzzolo, who was very small indeed, but a very beautiful youth, and the great master was very fond of his disciple.]

They undertook a long journey round the world, since Virgil wished that his little Minuzzolo should learn all the wonders which are hidden in the earth.

So he said to him one day:

"Know, Minuzzolo, that we are going on a long journey which may last for years, and thou must be right brave, my boy, for many are the perils through which we must pass, and dire are the monsters which we shall meet."

So they went forth into the world, far and wide, and little Minuzzolo showed himself as brave as the biggest, and as eager to learn as a whole school with a holiday before it when it shall have got its lesson.

All things he learned: how to resist all sorceries and evil spells; he could call the eagle down from the sky, and the fish from the sea; but one thing he did not learn from his master.

One day Virgil gave him a book wherein was the charm

against the Song of the Siren, the words which protect him who knows them against the music of the Voice. But two leaves stuck together like one, so that Minuzzolo skipped two pages, and never knew it.

Virgil had gone forth, and Minuzzolo, seated in a hut in the forest where they lived, began to sing. Then he heard in the wood a girl's voice, which seemed to come from a torrent, singing in answer; and it was so sweet that all his soul and senses were captured, he forgot all duty and desire, his master and everything, all in a mad yearning to follow the sound. So he went on and on, led by the song; day and night were unnoticed by him. The Voice went with the torrent, he followed it to a river, and the river to the sea, where the waves rolled high in foam and fog; he followed the song, it went deep into the sea, but he gave no heed, but went ever on.

Then he found himself in a very beautiful but extremely strange old city—a city like a dream of an ancient age. And as eve came on, the youth asked of this and that person where he could pass the night, and all said that they knew of no place, for into that city no strangers ever came. However, at last one said to him : "I know where there dwells a witch, and she often hath strange guests; perhaps she will give thee shelter."

"I will go to her," replied Minuzzolo.

"Better not," was the reply. "I did but jest, and I would be sorry if so fair a youth should be devoured by some monster."*

"Little fear of that have I," replied the young magician. "He who has harmed no one need fear none, and in the name of my Master I am safe."

So he went to the house and knocked, and there came to his call an old woman of such unearthly ugliness, that Minuzzolo saw at once that she was a sorceress. So when she asked what he wanted, he replied :

> "In the name of him whom all
> Like thee obey, and heed his call,
> And tremble at his lightest word,
> VIRGIL, my master and thy lord,
> I bid thee give me food and rest,
> Whate'er thou canst and of the best !"

---

* *Male a far ti mangiare da qualche orco*—*Orco* is from *Orcus*, the Spirit of Hell.

And she answered :

> " Whate'er is asked in that dread name,
> I'm sworn to answer to the same."

So the youth stayed there and was well served. And in the morning he thanked the old woman, and asked her where he could find Virgil. She replied :

" Do not seek him in the forest where thou didst leave him. Since then thou hast passed over half the world, for she who called thee was a Siren, whom none can resist unless they learn the spell which thy master, foreseeing that thou wert in danger, gave thee, and which thou didst not learn. However, I will give thee a ring which will be of use, but do not seek its help until thou shalt be in dire need. And then thou shalt say to it :

> " ' In nome del gran Mago,
> In nome di Virgilio,
> A chi sara buono !
> Questo anello sara mia sposa !' "

> " In the name of the great magician !
> In the name of Virgil !
> To whom be all good,
> This ring shall be my spouse !"

" Well shall I remember it," replied Minuzzolo. So he went on to the land and by the strand ever on, till he came to a great and fine ship, and pausing as he looked at it, he thought he would like to be a sailor. Therefore he asked the captain if a boy was wanted. And the captain, being much pleased, took him and treated him very kindly, and for three years Minuzzolo was a mariner.

But one night there was a great storm, and there came in an instant such a tremendous wave and gale of wind that Minuzzolo was blown afar into the sea and wafted away a mile ere he was missed. However, he gained a beach and scrambled ashore, where he lay for a long time as if asleep. Yet it seemed to him, while thinking of the captain and his mates, that he were being borne away and ever on, as if in a dream, and indeed, when he awoke, he found himself in what he knew must be another country, in another clime.

And being very hungry, and seeing a fine garden wherein delicious fruit was growing, he approached a tree to pluck a pear ; when all at once there sprang out a man of terrible form, with eyes like a dragon, who threatened him with death.

But Minuzzolo drew the ring from his pocket and repeated the charm, and as he did this the sorcerer fell dead. And then he heard the voice of the Siren singing afar, and it drew nearer and nearer, till a beautiful girl appeared. And when she saw the hideous sorcerer lying dead, she exclaimed with joy: "At last I am free! This the great Master Virgilio has done; over land and sea and afar off he has put forth his power. Blessed be his name!"

Then she explained to the youth that she and others had been enslaved and enchanted, and compelled to become a Siren and bewitch men. But Virgilio, knowing that she was lurking near to charm his pupil, had given him the book to read, but that her master by his power had closed the leaves, so that Minuzzolo had yielded to her song. But Virgilio had put forth a greater power, and brought it to pass that the Siren was herself enchanted with love, and in the end the sorcerer was defeated.

Then Virgilio appeared and blessed the young couple, who were wedded and lived ever after happily. Such things did Virgilio.

This strange story, in which classic traditions are blended with the common form of a fairy-tale, was sent to me from Siena, where it had been taken down from some authority to me unknown. It begins very abruptly, for which reason I have supplied the introductory passage in parenthesis.

Minuzzolo, led strangely afar over the sea, drawn by the voice of the Siren, suggests that the Argonauts were called *Minii*, because they were descended, like Jason, from the daughters of *Minia*. There may be here some confusion with Minos, of whom Virgil says that "he holds in his hand an urn and shakes the destiny of all human beings, citing them to appear before his tribunal," "Quæsitor Minos urnam movet." In the Italian legend Minuzzolo, or Minos, has a ring which compels all who hear his charm to obey.

Minuzzolo wins his Siren by means of a ring, and it is remarkable that Hesychius derives the name *Siren* from σείρη, *scire*, a small ring. Moreover, the sirens in the old Greek mythology did not of their own accord or will entice sailors to death. " The oracle," says Pozzoli (Dizionario Mit.) " had predicted that they should perish whenever a single mortal who had heard their enchanting voices should escape them." Therefore they were compelled by a superior power to act as they did.

Confused and garbled as it all is, it seems almost certain that in this tale there are relics of old Græco-Latin mythology.

The names of the three Sirens were Aglaope, Pisinoe, Thexiopia; according to Cherilus, Thelxiope, Molpe and Aglaophonos. *Clearchus*, however, gives one as Leucosia, another as Ligea, the third as Parthenope. " Aglaope was sweetest to behold, Aglaophone had the most enchanting voice." Therefore we may infer that Aglaope, or Aglaophone, was the heroine of this tale. It is remarkable that *Aglaia*, a daughter of Jupiter, was the fairest and first of the three Muses, as Aglaope was of the Sirens.

It would seem evident that Edgar A. Poe had the Siren Ligea in mind when he wrote :

> " Ligeia, Ligeia,
> My beautiful one,
> Whose harshest idea
> Will to melody run . . .
> Ligeia ! wherever
> Thy image may be,
> No magic shall sever
> Thy music from thee ;
> Thou hast bound many eyes
> In a dreamy sleep,
> But the strains still arise
> Which thy vigilance keep."

Most remarkable of all is the fact that the Sirens, who were regarded as evil witches or enchantresses of old, are in this story, which was written by a witch, indicated as women compelled by fate to delude mariners, which has escaped all commentators, and yet was plainly enough declared by the Oracle.

LAVERNA.

> ' One day a fox entered a sculptor's shop,
> And found a marble head, when thus he spoke:
> ' O Head ! there is such feeling shown in thee
> By art—and yet thou canst not feel at all !' "
> *Æsop's Fables.*

It happened on a time that Virgil, who knew all things hidden or magical, he being a magician and poet, having heard an oration, was asked what he thought of it.

And he replied :

" It seems impossible for me to tell whether it is all introduction or conclusion.   It is like certain fish, of whom one is in doubt whether they are all head or all tail, or the goddess Laverna, of whom no one ever knew whether she was all head or all body, or both."

Then the Emperor asked him who this deity might be, for he had never heard of her.

And Virgil answered :

" Among the gods or spirits who were of the ancient times there was one female, who was the craftiest and most knavish of all.   She was called Laverna ; she was a thief, and very little known to the other deities, who were honest and dignified, while Laverna was rarely in heaven or in the country of the fairies.   She was almost always on earth among thieves, pickpockets, and panders ; (she lived) in darkness.   Once it happened that she went to a great priest, in the form of a very beautiful, stately priestess, and said to him :

" ' Sell me your estate.   I wish to raise on it a temple to (our) god. I swear to you on my body that I will pay thee within a year.'*

"Therefore the priest gave her the estate. And very soon Laverna had sold off all the crops, grain, cattle, and poultry. There was not left the value of four farthings. But on the day fixed for payment there was no Laverna to be seen. The fair goddess was far away, and had left her creditor in the lurch—*in asso*.

"At the same time Laverna went to a great lord, and bought of him a castle, well-furnished, with much land. But this time she swore *on her head* to pay in full in six months. And she did as she had done by the priest; she stole and sold everything—furniture, cattle, crops; there was not left wherewith to feed a fly.

"Then the priest and the lord appealed to the gods, complaining that they had been robbed by a goddess. And it was soon found that the thief was Laverna. Therefore she was called to judgment before all the gods. And she was asked what she had done with the property of the priest, unto whom she had sworn by her body to make payment at the time appointed. And she replied by a strange deed, which amazed them all, for she made her body disappear, so that only her head remained, and it cried:

"'Behold me! I swore by my body, but body have I none.'

"Then all the gods laughed.

"After the priest came the lord, who had also been tricked, and to whom she had sworn by her head. And in reply to him Laverna showed to all present her whole body, and it was one of the greatest beauty, but without a head, and from the neck there came a voice which said:

> "'Behold me, for I am Laverna, who
> Have come to answer to that lord's complaint
> Who swears that I contracted debt with him,
> And have not paid, although the time is o'er,
> And that I am a thief because I swore
> · Upon my head; but, as you all can see,
> I have no head at all, and therefore I
> Assuredly ne'er swore by such an oath!'

"Then there was indeed a storm of laughter among the gods, who made the matter right by ordering the head to

---

* Swearing by the body or any part thereof implied the destruction or forfeiture of it, *i.e.*, death or slavery in case the oath should be broken."

join the body, and bidding Laverna pay up her dues, which she did.

" Then Jove spoke and said :

" ' Here is a roguish deity without a duty, while there are in Rome innumerable thieves, sharpers, cheats, and rascals—*ladri, bindolini, truffatori e scrocconi*—who live by deceit. These good folk have neither a church nor a god, and it is a great pity, for even the very devils have their master Satan. Therefore I command that in future Laverna shall be the goddess of all the knaves or dishonest trades-men, and all the rubbish and refuse of the human race, who have been hitherto without a god or devil, inasmuch as they have been too despicable for the one or the other.'

" And so Laverna became the goddess of all dishonest people. Whenever anyone planned or intended any knavery or aught wicked, he entered her temple and invoked Laverna, who appeared to him as a woman's head. But if he did his work badly and maladroitly, when he again invoked her he saw only the body. But if he was clever, then he beheld the whole goddess, head and body.

" Laverna was not more chaste than she was honest, and had many lovers and many children. It is said that, not being bad at heart, she often repented her life and sins ; but do what she might she could not reform, because her passions were so inveterate. And if a man had got any woman with child, or any maid found herself *incinta*, and would hide it from the world and escape scandal, they would go every day to invoke Laverna.* Then, when the time came for the suppliant to be delivered, Laverna would bear her in sleep during the night to her temple, and after the birth cast her into slumber again, and carry her back to her bed. And when she awoke in the morning she was ever in vigorous health and felt no weariness, and all seemed to her as a dream.

" But to those who desired in time to reclaim their children Laverna was indulgent, if they led such lives as pleased her and faithfully worshipped her. And this is the manner of the ceremony and the incantation to be offered to Laverna every night :

" There must be a set place devoted to the goddess, be it a room, a cellar, or a grove, ever a solitary place. Then

---

* The same was believed of Diana. I have omitted here much needless verbiage and repetition, and abbreviated what follows.

take a small table of the size of forty playing-cards set
close together, and this must be hid in the same place, and
going there at night. . . .

"Take the forty cards and spread them on the table,
making of them, as it were, a close carpet on it. Take of
the herbs *paura** and *concordia* and boil the two together,
repeating meanwhile :

> "'Fo bollire la mano della concordia,
> Per tenere a me concorde.
> La Laverna, che possa portare a me
> Il mio figlio e che possa
> Guardarmelo da qual un pericolo !
>
> "'Bollo questa erba ma non bollo l'erba.
> Bollo la *paura†* che possa tenere lontano
> Qualunque persona, e se le viene,
> L'idea a qualchuno di avvicinarsi,
> Possa essere preso da paura,
> E fuggire lontano !'"

> "I boil the cluster of *concordia*
> To keep in concord and at peace with me
> Laverna, that she may restore to me
> My child, and that she, by her favouring care,
> May guard me well from danger all my life !

> "I boil this herb, yet 'tis not it which boils ;
> I boil the *fear* that it may keep afar
> Any intruder, and if such should come
> [To spy upon my rite], may he be struck
> With fear, and in his terror haste away !"

"Having said this, put the boiled herbs in a bottle, and
spread the cards on the table, one by one, saying :

> "'Batezzo queste quarante carte
> Ma non batezzo le quarante carte.
> Batezzo quaranta dei superiori
> Alla dea Laverna che le sue
> Persone divengono un vulcano
> Fino che la Laverna non sara
> Venuta da me colla mia creatura.
> E questi dei dal naso dalla bocca,
> E dall' orecchie possino buttare
> Fiammi di fuoco e cenere,
> E lasciare pace e bene alla dea
> Laverna, che possa anche essa
>   Abbracciare i suoi figli,
>   A sua volunta !'"

---

* I conjecture that this is wild poppy.
† A play on *paura* (fear) and the name of the plant.

" I spread before me now the forty cards,
 Yet 'tis not forty cards which here I spread,
 But forty of the gods superior
 To the deity Laverna, that their forms
 May each and all become volcanoes hot,
 Until Laverna comes and brings my child.
 And till 'tis done, may they all cast
 Hot flames of fire and coals from their lungs,
 And leave her in all peace and happiness,
 And still embrace her children at her will."

The character of Virgil is here clearly enough only an introduction by the narrator, in order to make a Virgilian tale or narrative. But the incantation, which I believe to be *bonâ fide* and ancient, is very curious and full of tradition. The daring to conjure the forty gods that they may suffer till they compel Laverna to yield is a very bold and original conception, but something like it is found very often in Italian witchcraft. It is of classic origin. In the witchcraft manufactured by the Church, which only dates from the last decade of the fifteenth century, it never occurs. The witches of Sprenger and Co. never lay any of the Trinity under a ban of torture till a desire is accomplished, nor are they ever even invoked.

La femme comme il faut, or " the only good woman," is a very ungallant misogamic corner tavern sign once common in France. It represents a headless woman. Perhaps she was derived from some story like this of Laverna. It recalls the inhuman saying: " The only good (Red) Indian is a dead Indian."

Laverna is in this tale another form of Diana. There are also traces of Lucina in the character.

VIRGIL AND THE UGLY GIRL.

> " Though her ugliness may scare,
> Money maketh all things fair."
>
> *Proverb.*

" *Gelt—wie lieb'ich Dich.*"—How truly I love thee ! or, " Money—how I love thee !"—*German Jest.*

There was once in Rome an ugly young lady; yes, the ugliest on earth ! And, as if this were not enough, she was ill-tempered and spiteful, and in his whole course the sun did not shine on a more treacherous being. She was a true devilkin, being as small as a dwarf. However, devil or not, she was worth millions, and had the luck to be betrothed to the handsomest young man in Rome, who was, indeed, poor.

One day a certain Countess said to Virgil :

" I cannot understand how it comes to pass that such a splendid fellow is allied to such a horrid little fright—*un tal spauracchio !*"

Virgil said nothing, but he went home and took two scorpions, and by his magic art turned them into gold, and of these he made two ear-rings and sent them to the Countess, who was delighted with them, and when Virgil asked her if she liked them, answered : " *Tanta, tanta, sono molto belli*"—" Very much, they are so beautiful !"

" You said to me a little while ago," replied Virgil, " that you did not see what the handsomest man in Rome finds to admire in the ugliest girl. It is gold, Signora Contessa, which does it all—gold which makes scorpions so charming that you wear them in your ears, and call them beautiful !"

The Countess laughed, and said : " Thou speakest truth—

> " ' Gold like the sun turns darkness to nigh',
> And fear or hatred to love and delight.
> Gold makes raptures out of alarms,
> Gold turns horror to beautiful charms,
> And gives the beauty of youth to the old.
> On earth there's no magic like that of gold.' "

VIRGIL AND THE GEM.

> " Cil une mouche d'arain fist,
> Que toutes mouches qui estoient.
> Celle approchier ne povoient;"
>
> RENARS CONTREFAIS, A.D. 1318.

> " Et fist une mousche d'arain,
> De quoi encor le pris et ain.
> A Naples cele mousche mist
> Et de tel maniere la fist,
> Que tant com la mousche fu la
> Mousche dedenz Naples n'entra,
> Mais je ne sai que puis devint,
> La mousche, ne qu'il en avint."
>
> ADENÈS LI ROIS : *Roman de Cleomadès.* *XIIIth Century.*

" There were at that time near the city many swamps, in consequence of which were swarms of *flies*, which caused death. And VIRGIL . . . made a fly of gold, as large as a frog, by virtue of which all the flies left the city."—*La Cronaca di Partenope*, 1350.

" Trovasi chi egli fece una moscha di rame, che dove la posa niuna moscha apariva mai presso a due saettate che incontanente non morissi."

ANTONIO PUCCI, *XIVth Century.*

Once there came to the Emperor a merchant with many gems and jewels, and begged him to purchase some.

The Emperor asked of Virgil, who was present :

" Which is the very best of all these stones ?"

Virgil replied :

" Let them all remain for a time in the light of the sun, and I will tell you which is the gem of them all."

This was done, and after a time a fly alighted on one.

" This is the gem of greatest value," said Virgil.

" But it is really hardly worth a crown," replied the merchant.

" And yet it is worth all the rest put together," answered Virgil ; " for it increases marvellously the intellect or under-standing, and thereby one can win with it the love of whom he will."

" Very well," said the Emperor, " I will buy it, and find by experience whether it can increase wit whereby we gain hearts."

He did so, and finding that the stone had the virtue which Virgil ascribed to it, said to the sage one day :

" How was it that thou didst find out and understand the value of that gem ?"

" I knew it, because I saw that there was in the stone a very small fly (*moschettina*—gnat), and I knew that flies are very quick and gay, and have great cleverness, as anyone can see if he tries to catch them, and they make love all the time."

" Truly thou art à devil, oh Virgil," replied the Emperor ; "and for reward I hereby make thee Emperor or Pope over all the flies. There are, by the way, far too many of them, and a perfect plague—they spoil all the meat in the shops. I would that thou couldst banish all thy subjects from Rome."

" I will do it," answered Virgil.

Then, by his magic, he summoned the Great Fly—Il Moscone, the King of all the Flies—and said to him ·

" Thy subjects are far too many, and a sore plague to all mankind. I desire that thou wilt drive them all out of Rome."

" I will do it," replied the Moscone, " if thou wilt make a fly of gold as large as a great frog, and put it in my honour in the Church of Saint Peter. After which, there will no more flies be seen in Rome."

Then Virgil went to the Emperor and told him what Il Moscone had said, and the Emperor commanded that the fly should be made of many pounds of gold, and it was placed in the Church of Saint Peter, and so long as it remained there no fly was ever seen within the walls of Rome.

I have another version of what is partially the same story, but with a curious addition, which is of greater antiquity and most unconsciously really Virgilian, or the old tale of the bull's hide.

THE FLIES IN ROME.

It happened one summer in Rome that people were sadly afflicted with flies. Nothing like it had ever been seen ; they swarmed by millions everywhere, they blackened the walls, the meat on the butchers' stands was hidden under masses of them. And the poor suffered in their children, many of whom died, while all kinds of food was poisoned and corrupted everywhere.

Then the Emperor said to Virgil:

" Truly, if thou hast indeed the art of conjuring, now is the time to show it, by conjuring away this curse, for I verily believe that all the flies of Egypt are come here to Rome."

Virgil replied:

" If thou wilt give me so much land as I can enclose in an ox's hide, I will drive all the flies away from Rome."

The Emperor was well pleased to get so much for so small a price, as it seemed to him, and promised that he should truly have as much land as could be enclosed or covered* in the skin of an ox.

Virgil summoned Il Moscone, the King of the Flies, and said to him:

" I wish that all flies in Rome leave the city this very day!"

Il Moscone, the King of the Flies, replied:

" Cause me to become by magic a great fly of gold, and then put me in the Church of Saint Peter, and after that there will be no more insects in the city."

Then Virgil conjured him into the form of a fly of gold, and it was placed in the church, and at that instant all the flies left Rome. At which the Emperor was well pleased.

Then the Emperor asked Virgil where the land lay which was to be taken in the ox-hide.

" Come to-morrow and you shall see," answered the sage.

So the Emperor came with all his Court, and found Virgil mounted on horseback, bearing a great bundle of leather cord, like shoe-strings, and this had been made from the skin of the ox. And beginning at one gate and letting fall the cord, he rode around the city until all Rome was surrounded.

" Your Highness will observe," said Virgil, " that I have taken exactly as much land as could be enclosed in an ox's hide, and as Rome stands on the ground, therefore all Rome is mine."

" And what wilt thou take for this bit of earth—houses, people and all?" inquired the Emperor.

" I ask what to me is its full value, oh my Emperor, for I have long loved your beautiful niece! Give her to me

* Quaintly spelled *quo prire* in the original MS.

with one hundred thousand crowns in gold, and I will restore to you your city."

The Emperor was well pleased to grant this, and so it came to pass that all Rome was bought and sold in one day for a purse and a princess, or for a woman and one hundred thousand crowns.

It will be observed by many readers that in the first tale here narrated there are combined two of the older Virgilian legends, one being that of the Gem which has within it a mysterious power, and which is thus told in "The Wonderful History of Virgil the Sorcerer."*

"Soon after, the Emperor having his crown-jewels laid out before him, sent for Virgilius, and said: 'Master, you know many things, and few are hid from your ken. Tell me now, if you be indeed a judge of gems, which think you is the best of these?' The Emperor having pointed out one gem of peculiar brilliancy, Virgilius laid it, first in the palm of his hand, then to his ear, and said: 'Sire, in this stone there is a worm.' Forthwith the Emperor caused the stone to be sawn asunder, and lo, in the centre was found a worm concealed! Amazed at the sagacity of Virgilius, the Emperor, at the charge of the country, raised his allowance to a whole loaf per diem."

The story of the fly is told in almost all the collections. The reader will bear in mind the following frank and full admission, of which all critics are invited to make the worst, that in many cases I had already narrated these Virgilian tales to my collector, as I did here—a course which it is simply impossible to avoid where one is collecting in a speciality. If you want fairy-tales, take whatever the gods may send, but if you require nothing but legends of Red Cap, you must specify, and show samples of the wares demanded. But it may here be observed, that after I had com-

* London, D. Nutt, 1844, price 1s., Mediæval Legends, No. II.

municated these tales, they all returned to me with
important changes. In the older legends the fly made
by Virgil is manifestly—like the leech which he also
fabricated—simply an *amulet* or talisman formed under
the influence of the planets, or by astrology. In the
version which I give there is an altogether different,
far more ancient and mysterious motive power described. This is the direct aid of *Moscone*, the King of
the Flies, suggestive of *Baal tse Bul*, or Beelzebub
himself. The reader may find a chapter on this
mystical being, who is also the god of news, in the
" Legends of Florence," Part II. According to my
story, the Golden Fly is not a *talisman* made by
planetary influences, but a tribute of respect to a
demon, which he demands shall be set up in Saint
Peter's. Here the *witch*, ever inimical to orthodox
faith, appears in black and white—so true is it, as I
have before remarked, that even where my assistant
has been asked to re-tell a tale, it always returned
with darker and stranger colouring, which gave it an
interest far greater than existed in the simple narrative.
The tale of the fly, as a mere amulet, is of almost no
importance whatever, beyond its being an insignificant
variant ; but as a legend of the chief of the flies, or
Beelzebub, claiming honour and a place in the great
Christian Church, it is of extraordinary novelty.

Amber, in which insects are often found, especially
small flies or midges, was anciently regarded as a gem,
and is classed as one in the *Tesoro delle Goie. Trattato
curioso*, Venice, 1676.

It may be observed that something like this story of
the gem with an insect in it occurs not only in the
early legends of Virgil, but also in the oldest *novelle*, as

may be seen in Roscoe's "Italian Novelists." In fact, there is probably not one of the old Neapolitan Virgilian stories which is not, like this, of Oriental origin.

THE COLUMNS OF VIRGIL AND HIS THREE WONDERFUL STATUES.

> "En sic meum opus ago,
> Ut Romæ fecit imago
> Quam sculpsit Virgilius,
> Quæ manifestare suevit
> Fures, sed cæsa quievit
> Et os clausit digito."
>
> DE CORRUPTO ECCLESIÆ STATU: XVIIth Century. Virgilius
> the Sorcerer (1892).

The reader who is familiar with "The Legends of Florence" will remember that, in the second series of that work,* there are several tales referring to the Red Pillars of the Baptistery, of which, as Murray's "Guide Book" states, "at each side of the eastern entrance of the Battisterio di San Giovanni there is a shaft of red porphyry, presented by the Pisans in 1117." To which I added:

"Other accounts state that the Florentines attached immense value to these columns, and that once when there was to be a grand division of plunder between Florence and Pisa, the people of the former city preferred to take them, instead of a large sum of money, or something which was apparently far more valuable. And the Pisans parted from them most unwillingly, and to deprive them of value passed them through a fire. Which is all unintelligible nonsense, but which becomes clear when we read further.

"I had spoken of this to Mr. W. de Morgan, the distinguished scholar, artist, and discoverer in ceramics, when

----

* "Legends of Florence," collected from the people, etc., by Charles Godfrey Leland. London, David Nutt, 1896.

he informed me that he had found, in the 'Cronaca Pisana' of Gardo, a passage which clearly explains the whole. It is as follows:

" In the year 1016, the Pisans brought the gates of wood which are in the Duomo, and a small column, which is in the façade, or above the gate of the Duomo. There are also at the chief entrance two columns, about two fathoms each in length, of a reddish colour, and it is said that whoever sees them is sure in that day not to be betrayed. And these two columns which were so beautiful had been so enchanted by the Saracens,* that when a theft had been committed the face of the thief could be seen reflected in them. And when they had scorched them they sent them to Florence, after which time the pillars lost their power; whence came the saying, *Fiorentini ciechi*, or ' blind Florentines.'†

" Unto which was added, *Pisani traditori*, or ' treacherous Pisans.' Those pillars were, in fact, magic mirrors which had acquired their power by certain ceremonies performed when they were first polished, and which were lost."

A German writer on witchcraft, Peter Goldschmidt, states that there was once in olden time in Constantinople a certain Peter Corsa, who, by looking in two polished stones or magic mirrors, beheld in them proof that his wife, then far away, was unfaithful to him. It is possible, or probable, that this refers to the same pillars, before they had been brought to Pisa, even as the column of the Medicis in the Piazza Annunciata was sent from the East to Florence.

What renders this the more probable is the following

---

* This is certain proof that the columns had been brought from the East.

† This is mentioned by many writers. I read it last in a very curious old manuscript History of Florence, written apparently about 1650, which —though it was in good condition, and well bound in parchment—I purchased for four *soldi*, or twopence, from an itinerant dealer. Finding by a note that the work belonged to the library of the Liceo Dante, I restored it to that institution. I also found in this manuscript an account of the miracle of the blooming of the elm-tree of San Zenobio.

passage by Comparetti, given in his "Virgilio nel Medio Evo":

"In a History of the Pisans, written in French in the fifteenth century and existing in manuscript in Berne, there is mention of two columns made by Virgil, and which were then in the cathedral of Pisa, on the tops of which one could see the likeness of anyone who had stolen or fornicated." See De Sinner, "Catal. Codicum MSS. Bibl. Bernensis," II., p. 129; Du Meril, "Mélanges," p. 472.

It is most unlikely that the Pisans had *two* pairs of columns, in each of which appeared the forms or phantoms or *simulacra* of criminals, for which reason we may conclude that those in the Battisterio of Florence are quite the same as those which were said to have been made by Virgil. And it is also probable that the belief that they were made by Virgil went far to give them the great value which was attached to them. They should be called the columns of Virgil.

It may be observed that the Berne manuscript cited mentions that it was on the *top* of the pillars that the visions were seen, and that the tops of the columns of the Battisterio have been knocked away, possibly by the Pisans, in order to deprive them of their peculiar value.

Virgil is also accredited with having made a statue which, like Mahomet's coffin, hung free in mid-air, and was visible from every part of Rome, or in fact from every door and window. And it had the property that no woman who had once beheld it had, after that, any desire to behave improperly, which thing, according to the plainly-speaking author of "Les Faicts Merveilleux de Virgille," was a sad affliction to the Roman dames, *qui aymoyent par amour*, since they could not put foot out of doors without seeing "that nasty image" which prevented them from having *soulas de leurs amours.* So they all complained bitterly to Virgil's wife, who promised to aid them. Therefore, one day when her husband was absent, she went up the bridge or ladder which led to the statue and threw down the latter. "So, from that time forth, the *dames de Rome firent à leur volonté et a leur plaisance, et furent bien ayses de lymage qui fut abbatu.*" Truly the Ibsenite and other novelists of the present day, but especially the lady realists of our time, have great cause to be thankful that no such statues are stuck up in the public places of our cities, for if such were the case their occupation would be gone for ever—or until they had overturned them.

Virgil would appear, however, to have been somewhat inconsistent in this matter of statues, or else desirous of demonstrating to the world that he could go to opposite extremes, since he made another, which is thus delicately hinted at in a footnote by Comparetti : *

"In contradizione con questo racconto in cui Virgilio apparisce come protettore del buon costume, trovasi un altro racconto, secondo il quale . . . egli avrebbe fatto una donna pubblica artificiale. Cosi Enenkel nel suo 'Welt-buch'; vede V. J. Hagen, 'Gesammtten Abenteuer,' II., 515; Massmonn, 'Kaiser Chronik,' III., 451. Una leggenda rabbinica parla anch' essa di una statua destinata a quell' uso ed esistente in Romæ. Vede Praetorius, 'Anthropodemus Plutonicus,' I., 150, e Liebrecht nella 'Germania di Pfeiffer,' X., 414."

* It is worth noting *en passant* that, according to Max Nordau, one of the Ibsenites, modern Illuminati or Naturalists—I forget to which division of the great body of reformers he belongs—has seriously proposed this creation of *donne artificiale. Vide* Nordau, "Degeneration."

The passage in Enenkel referred to is given with the rest of the "Weltbuch" by Comparetti, and is as follows :

> "Virgilius der selbe man,
> Begunde nu ze Rôme gân,
> Und versuocht 'sain maisterschaft,
> Ob es wær' wár der teuvel kraft,
> Er macht' ze Rôm' ain stainein Weib
> Von Künste den het ainen Leib
> Swann' ain Schalk, ain boeser Man
> Wolte ze ainem Weibe gân,
> Daz er gie zu dem Staine,
> Der boese, der unraine,
> Das im was bei des staines Leib
> Recht als ob er wær im Weib,
> Nicht vür baz ich en sagen sol
> Main mainung 'witzt ihr alle wol."

Bonifacius, in his "Ludicra," Ravisius Textor ("Officina"), and Kornmann ("Curiosa") have brought together all the instances in special chapters of men who have fallen in love with statues. I observe that in a late popular novel this device of the *donna artificiale* is described in a manner which leaves actually nothing to be desired to the lovers of indecency, vileness, blasphemy, or "realism"—*c'est tout un.*

It may be observed that in another tale collected by me, Virgil has for his Egeria a statue called Pæonia, which comes to life when he would confer with her, and which I regard, on what is at least startling coincidence if not full proof, a tradition of Minerva-Pæonia and Esculapius.

The tale in question declares that the magician Virgil, who had a marked fancy for making statues love, or turning women into stone—ever petting or petrifying among the petticoats—had a third favourite, a Pæonia, who was marble when not specially required for other purposes than ornament. These three ladies suggest the Graces :

> " Aglaia, Euphrosyne que Thaliaque splendida
> Clara letitiæ matres !"

It is probably by mere coincidence or chance that in Keats' "Endymion" the habitual friend and comforter of the hero is :

> " *Peona*, his sweet sister ; of all those
> His friends, the dearest, . . .
> Whose eloquence did breathe away the curse.
> She led him like some midnight spirit-nurse."

But that Peona, through all the poem, plays the part which Pæonia has with Virgil is unquestionable. It would seem as if there is, if not a spiritual, at least an æsthetic influence in names. *Nomen est omen*. "All Bobs are bobbish," said a farmer, "and all Dicks dickies."

VIRGIL AND ADELONE.

> " Who would have ever said that amid the horrors of prison I would find a true friend to console me ?"—Boethius *to* Patricius.

> " All by prayer and penitence
> May be at length forgiven."
> *Ballad of Sir Tannhäuser.*

There once lived in Florence a young man who was not really bad at heart, but utterly selfish, especially to his relations, and was without heed or feeling as to the sufferings of others. And, it being in his power, he wasted all the income of the family on sport, letting his brothers and sisters endure great privations ; nor would he have cared much had they starved. He was like all such people— frivolous and capricious. If he met a poor child in the street, he would give it a gold crown, and then let all at home hunger for days.

One day his suffering mother went to Virgilio, and, telling

him all about her son, begged the master, if it were possible, to reform him.

Virgilio said to her : " I will indeed do something which will bring thy son to his senses."

The young man was named Adelone, and Virgilio, meeting him the next day, said :

" If thou wouldst fain see a strange thing indeed—such as thou hast erewhile prayed me to show thee by my art— then be to-night at twelve in the cloister of Santa Maria Novella, where thou wilt see and learn that which it is most needful for thee to know. But to behold and bear the sight thou must be bold, for a faint heart will fail before it."

Then Adelone, who, to do him justice, was no coward, did not fail to be in the cloister of Santa Maria Novella at the appointed hour. And as the last stroke of twelve was heard, Adelone saw before him the spirit of a young man named Geronio, who had died one year before, and who had been, as one like him in all respects, his most intimate friend. They were always together, and what one did the other joined in ; both were reckless wasters of money, and selfishly indifferent to their families. And as Adelone looked at Geronio he saw in the face of the latter such an expression of awful suffering, that it was a torture to behold him. And Geronio, seeing this, said :

" Depart now, for it is time ; but this night I will come to thee and remain with thee till morning."*

And Adelone was glad to have seen Geronio once more, but greatly grieved at finding him in such suffering.

That night he was in his room, which was on the ground, and at the appointed hour the spirit came. And, looking with awe at his friend, Adelone said :

" I see that thou art in pain beyond all belief."

" Yes," replied Geronio ; " I suffer the greatest agony, such as no mortal could endure. But I pray you come with me."

Then the two sunk softly down into the earth, ever deeper and deeper in silent darkness, until Adelone saw that they were in an immense cavern, all of gray ice, dimly lighted, with dripping icicles hanging from the roof, and all the floor was covered with dirty, half-freezing water, under

---

* This is finely conceived to give an idea of the great effect of the agony expressed in the face of the spectre. Adelone would naturally be so deeply impressed by it as to be unable to maintain the interview.

which was a bed of stinking mud, and over all was an air of sadness and wretchedness beyond description.

" This is my home," said Geronio; " but it is as nothing compared to what I suffer in my soul—which is a thousand times more terrible than anything which mortals can imagine, for they have no idea of what spiritual torture is like, because they always think of pain as bodily. But know that I had rather be beaten or burned in fire for a year than suffer for an instant the remorse which I endure."

" Can anything be done to help you ?" asked Adelone.

" Yes, all can be done ; and you can save me and not only give me peace, but do as much for thyself, and thereby escape what I have suffered. If thou wilt lead a good and loving life—good and kind to all, especially to thy family and friends, no longer wasting money and life on selfish follies, no longer neglecting duty and acting as an egoist— thus thou canst give me peace, and rescue me from this inferno. But woe unto thee, shouldst thou promise this and fail to keep thy word. For when thy time cometh, as come it will, thou wilt suffer as I do—yea, with redoubled remorse."

Then Adelone, looking about him, saw many sad shades of men and women wandering or wading through the icy water ; all people who had lived for themselves alone, all waiting till someone as yet alive should, by good conduct, save them. And none spoke, for they were doomed to silence. So they looked at one another, and passed on, and such looks were the only thing like comfort allowed them.

Then Adelone fell, as it seemed to him, asleep, and when he awoke he was in his own room, but he well knew that it was no dream which he had beheld. And from that hour he was another man, becoming as good as he had been bad, living to make all others happy, and devoted in every way to his family. And thereby he became for the first time truly contented.

Six months passed, and one night at twelve o'clock, on awaking, he saw before him Geronio, who no longer seemed to suffer as before, though there was still in his eyes something terrible.

" How is it with thee ?" asked Adelone.

" Far better. Come with me."

Then Adelone found himself in a great castle, which

seemed like a free prison, which was grim and without comfort. Many souls were in it, but they were walking about together, or resting and conversing, apparently in no suffering. It was a joyless place, but not one of torture, nor was it filthy.*

" We do not suffer so much here," said Geronio. " We have still much remorse, but at least we have the consolation of being able to converse one with another, and enjoy sympathy in sorrow."

" What do you talk about ?" asked Adelone.

" Chiefly about the people whom we hope will set us free. I talk of thee, because all my hope is in thee. I think of nothing else by day or night."

Then Adelone returned to his home. After six months he beheld Geronio again. Again he found himself in a castle, but the spirits were conversing happily, many were singing hymns, they had guitars and mandolins, and here and there were vases of flowers which gave forth delightful perfume.

Geronio said to him :

" Here we are happier still, and, believe me, friend, if thou canst in this life make others as good as thou art, to love their relations and friends, and cease to be selfish, thereby everyone can save another soul, and win great reward for himself."

Adelone replied :

" I truly will do all I can to content thee."

From that day he did all that he could, not only to do good himself, but to cause others to act like him. Six months after this Geronio came to him and said :

" Now that I know that thou art truly good, learn that I am at peace. And as thou hast been the means of giving it to others, know that in future all good spirits will aid thee !"

It is not enough not to be a sinner. He who does not take care and pains and labour earnestly to make others happy will be punished as an evil-doer. He who does not love (us) is an enemy.

It is to be remarked in this, as in all the other tales from the same sources, when a moral end or plot is to

* E ne un luogo sporco.

be worked out, it is done without benefit of clergy or
aid of priest, or the Church. For these are legends of
the witches and wizards, who have ever been the foes,
and consequently the hated and afflicted, of the
orthodox. It is a curious reflection that as it has been
said that the last savage in America will die with the
last Indian, so the *strega*, or witch, will remain to the
end a heathen. And I find curious emotion in the
thought that what I have gathered, or am gathering,
with such care, is the last remainder of antique
heathenism in Europe. Superstitions there are everywhere, but in this kind Italy is alone.

VIRGIL AND DORIONE, or THE MAGIC VASE.

I have a vase in which I daily throw
All scraps and useless rubbish—oh that I
Had one wherein to cast away all thoughts,
Imaginations, dreams and memories
Which haunt and vex the soul, to disappear
For ever, lost in fast forgetfulness !
That were a vase indeed, and worth far more
Than that which forms the subject of this tale.

Many centuries ago there was in Naples a young man
named Dorione, who studied magic, and his master was a
great sorcerer named Virgil. One evening Dorione found
himself in company with friends, and there was present
another wizard named Belsevo.* Now, there was not bread
enough in the house for supper for all.

"Never mind," remarked Belsevo. "He who hath art
will find his bread in any part. Observe me."

Taking a large vase, he turned it upside down and said :

Viene pane !
Abbiamo fame ;
Dimmi o Cerere del pane !
Se questa grazia mi farai,
Sempre fedele a te sarai."

----

* Evidently the Belsàbo of a preceding tale.

" Come, bread, to me,
  For hungry are we !
  Oh, Ceres, give us bread !
  Grant me this grace benign,
  And I will be ever thine !"

Then he removed the vase, and there were on the table eight small loaves.

Then Belsevo said to Dorione :

" Canst thou not give us wine for the bread, O scholar of the grand master Virgil ?"

But Dorione, being only a beginner in magic, could not effect such a miracle, and was much ashamed because all laughed at him.

The next morning Dorione told what had happened to Virgil.

" Well didst thou deserve," replied the master, " to be thus scoffed at and jeered, for a young magician should never play tricks at a table like a juggler to amuse fools. But thou hast been sufficiently punished, and to please thee I will give thee a fine present. And if thou canst not make bread come, thou shalt at least have the power to make it and other things disappear. I will give thee this vase of bronze. It is but small, as thou seest, but tell any object, however large, to disappear in it, then the vase will swallow it. Thou shalt keep for thyself in secret a house somewhere, and whatever the vase may swallow thou wilt find it in the house, however distant thou mayst be from it. Only say, ' Go into the vase !' and by the vase it will be swallowed up. But thou shalt never use it to steal, or for any dishonest purpose. So long as thou art honest it will serve, and none shall rob thee of it. And if that should come to pass, call to it and it will return to thee."

Then Dorione took the vase, and thanked the grand master Virgil. After a time the scholar went on a long journey. Dorione possessed a small castle in a remote place in the mountains of Tuscany, and in it was a secret vault. " There," he said, " I will send all that the vase may swallow. Many a thing may be come by honestly, if one knew how to send it away and where to put it.

" ' He who hath a cage, I've heard,
    In time will surely get a bird.' "

It came to pass that he became the secretary of a certain

lord, who, like many of the brave gentry of his time, was ever at war with somebody, plundering or being plundered, every one in his turn, as fortune favoured.

> "Up on the top of the hill to-day,
> Down in the dale to-morrow;
> Oft in the morning happy and gay,
> After a night of sorrow;
> For some must fall that others may rise,
> And the swallow goes chirping as she flies."

One evening his master heard a trumpet afar, and, looking forth, seemed suddenly startled, like a man in great alarm. Pointing to a splendid suit of armour, he said :

"Seest thou that armour, Dorione? It is worth ten thousand crowns, and I would give ten thousand it were this instant in hell. I took it in a raid from the Grand Duke, and he will be here in ten minutes with all his men. If he finds the armour I shall lose my head. And there, too, is an iron chest full of gold and jewels—all plunder, and all in evidence against me."

"If you will give it to me," answered Dorione, "I will make it all vanish in an instant."

"Yea, I give it with all my heart; but be quick about it, for the Grand Duke and his soldiers are at the gate, and I feel the rope round my neck !"

Then Dorione brought his vase in a minute, and uttered the conjuration :

> "Vattene via! Vattene via!
> Roba bella, cosa mia!
> Vai nell' istante al mio castello!
> Apri la bocca, vaso bello !"

> "Hasten away! Begone! begone!
> All ye fine things which are now mine own,
> Fly to my castle—never pause;
> Beautiful vase, now open thy jaws."

And in an instant the armour and chest went flying into the vase and disappeared.

Just as they vanished the Duke and his men entered, but though they sought in every cranny they found nothing; and so, having come for a bargain of wool, went away shorn,* as the proverb says.

---

* In the MS. : "'Many are deluded, or get a thumb at the nose,' says the proverb." "Maxima sero delusi, ho sia con un palma di' naso cosi, dice il proverbio." This expressive sign of the thumb is represented in an Irish Gospel of St. Mark of the sixth century.

"Thou hast saved my life," said the Signore. "God only knows how you ran away with the things, but you are welcome to them. Truly I was glad to get them, but a thousand times better pleased to see them go."

One day the Signore and Dorione found themselves in a battle together, sore beset and separated from all their troop. They were in extremest danger of being killed.* When all at once there came an idea to Dorione, who had his vase slung to his side like a canteen. He pronounced the spell, ordering all the arms in the hands of the enemy to fly through the vase to his castle. In an instant swords and spears, daggers and battle-axes, had left their owners, who stood unarmed and amazed. So the two were saved.

The Signore took a great deal of booty, and rewarded Dorione very liberally, the more so because he was greatly delighted to see the gifts disappear in the vase—no matter what, all was fish to that net, and all the sheep black—and Dorione liked to please his kind master, especially in this way. Yes, to amuse him he would often wish away a gold-hilted and jewelled sword or helm from an enemy, and was pleased to hear the brave old knight laugh to see the things fly.

The generosity of the lord stopped, however, at a certain point. He had a beautiful daughter whom Dorione loved, *alla follia*, to distraction, but the father would not consent to bestow her on him. But it came to pass that one day the castle was besieged by a vast force, which spared neither man, woman nor child, and it seemed plain that the besieged must yield. The lord bade Dorione to cause the arms of the enemy to vanish.

"This time," replied his secretary, "I cannot do it. The fame of my vase or of my power has spread far and wide, and the enemy have had their arms enchanted by a mighty sorcerer, so that I cannot take them."

They fought on until of all the garrison only Dorione, with the lord and his daughter, were left alive. They were in extremity.

"And now," thought Dorione, "something must be done, for there is many a wolf at the door. Let me see

---

* This superlative is rendered in the original manuscript by the very original expression: "They were so near being killed, that they were almost at the point of death."

whether I cannot make the young lady go into my vase, and then her father." So, bringing them together, he said :

> "Signora bella, signora mia !
> La più bella che su questa terra sia !
> Ti prego—subito, subito,
> Di qua vattene via !
> Vai nell istante al mio castello,
> Vi troverai un vaso bello,
> Che la sua bocca aprira,
> E li dentro ti salvera !"

> " Lovely lady, lady mine own,
> The fairest whom earth has ever known ;
> Fly in a hurry, oh, fly away !
> Leave the castle—flit while you may,
> And off to my distant shelter flee !
> The beautiful vase is ready for thee,
> Who will open her mouth to take you in.
> Safe you will be when once within !"

In a second, ere the eye could follow, the young lady was whirled away mysteriously, and, the conjuration being repeated, then her father. After which Dorione prayed to the spirit of the vase, who was no other than Saint Virgil himself,* to save him also. And in an instant he felt himself swallowed up like a bean in the mouth of a horse. And as soon he found himself in the vault of the castle with the lady and her father. And they were amazed, in looking about, to see what wealth was there gathered up, for Dorione had been very industrious in many a battle in sending arms and booty to his home.

Then all three, joining hands, danced and sang for joy to find themselves safe, Dorione and the lady doing the most rejoicing, because the lord had promptly said :

" After this you may get married." And they had the wedding that night.

The good lord, as a proof of affection and esteem for Dorione, pronounced an oration of regret as a penance on himself for not having sooner consented to the nuptials, ending with these words : " And now let everyone here present drink a cask of wine, and get as drunk as a tile, or four fiddlers."†

---

* " Lo spirito del vaso che era quel santo Virgilio." Here Virgil is for once fairly sainted or canonized.

† " Bevve un barile pieno di vino, e divenne ubbriaco come un tegolo o quattro suonatori di violini." This recalls "tight as a brick " (Manuscript).

*VIRGIL AND THE LADY OF ICE AND WATER.**

> " And truly at that time it came to pass
> That Virgil, by the power of sorcery,
> Made a fair lady, who did shine like glass
> Or diamonds with wondrous brilliancy,
> Whom to the Emperor he did present,
> And who therewith, I trow, was well content."
>
> VIRGILO II. MAGO (MS.).

It happened on a time that the Emperor, coming from Rome to Florence, was guest in the Duke's palace, and treated so magnificently and in a manner so much after his own heart, that he was indeed well content.

Now, in those days there was in Florence no Signore who, when he gave an entertainment, did not invite Virgil, not only because he was the greatest poet in Italy, but because he always played some admirable trick or jest, which made men merry and was always new.

So at the first great feast the Emperor was greatly delighted at the endless jokes, as well as by the genius of the distinguished guest.

Therefore, when the Emperor, before his departure, gave in turn a great entertainment to all the nobles of Florence, as well as of Rome, who were in the city, he sent the first invitation to Virgil, requesting him at the same time to invent for the occasion a jest of the first magnitude.

So unto this for such occasion the magician gave all his mind. And that the Emperor should really "*catch the fly*," he resolved that the jest should be one at the Imperial expense—*e lo scherzo voleva farlo a lui medesimo.*

After long meditation he exclaimed, " *Ecco, l' ho trovato!* I've got it! I will give him a girl made of water!"

Forthwith he wrote to the Emperor that he would not fail to be at the festival, but also begged permission to bring with him a beautiful young lady—his cousin.

The Emperor, who was very devoted to the fair sex, inferred from this directly that the jest was to be of a kind which would please all free gallants—that is to say, the being introduced to some easy and beautiful conquest—either wedded or a maid. And, delighted at the thought

* "Virgiglio e la Donna di Diaccio" (Title in MS.).

that the trick would take this turn, he replied to Virgil that he had *carta biancha*, or full permission to bring with him whomever he pleased.

Then the magician made a woman of ice and light and water, clear as the light of day he made her, and touched her thrice with his wand, and lo! she became beautiful—but such a beauty, indeed, that you would not find the like in going round the world; the sun or moon ne'er shone upon her like, for she was made of star-rays and ice and dewdrops, so that she looked like all the stars swimming in a burnished golden sky, and shining like the sun, so resplendent in her beauty that she dazzled the eyes.

When Virgilio arrived at the palace, all the guests were there before him, and they were so overwhelmed with blank amazement at the sight of the sorcerer with such a beauty, that they, in silence and awed, drew apart on either side, leaving open space through which Virgilio passed to the Emperor. And the latter was himself for a minute stupefied at the sight of such brilliancy and beauty, when, recovering himself, he gave his arm to the fair cousin, and asked her name. To which she replied: "*La Donna di Diaccio*" (ice).

"*Donna di Fuoco!* (Our Lady of Fire),* rather," cried the Emperor, "since all hearts are inflamed at thy beauty. Truly, I had no idea that the great poet had such a lovely cousin!"

The dance began, and the Emperor would have no other partner than this lady, who outshone the rest as the moon the stars, and yet surpassed them even more by her exquisite grace in every movement, and by her skill as a dancer, so that one seemed to see a thousand exquisite statues or studied forms of grace succeeding to one another as she moved. Nor was she less fascinating in her language than in her beauty, and no wonder, for Virgilio had called into the form one of the wittiest and most gifted of all the fairies to aid the jest.

So the dance swept on, and the Emperor, utterly enchanted, forgot Virgilio and his promised jest, and the time, and the court, and all things save the beauty beside him. Finally he withdrew with her to a side-room, where,

---

* In allusion, probably, to the "Madonna del Fuoco," whose festival is annually celebrated at Forli, in the Toscana Romagna. The writer of this story was from the neighbourhood of Forli. "The Madonna del Fuoco is probably Vesta" (*vide* "Etrusco-Roman Legends," by C. G. Leland).

sending for refreshment, he sat pouring forth wine into himself and love into the ears of the lady by turns.

Virgil, indeed, wishing the Emperor to have a fine time of it for awhile, did nothing to disturb the splendid pair. But as daybreak would soon appear, he spoke to one and another, saying that he had promised the Emperor a merry jest to make them all laugh. Whereupon there was a general cry for the diversion, and by one consent the gay company invaded the room where the fond couple sat.

Then Virgil, with the greatest politeness and a laughing air, said:

"Excuse me, your Highness, but it seems that my fair cousin here has so engrossed you that you have forgotten that you laid an absolute command on me that I should prepare and play some rare jest, the like of which you had never seen, and I fear, should I forget it, you may ne'er forgive me."

Then the Emperor, good-natured and grateful to the poet for his fair cousin's sake, excused the intrusion, and begged for the jest, expressing a hope that it would be a thoroughly good one.

Then Virgil said to the Emperor:

"Take my cousin upon thy lap, and let her arms be round thy neck!"

"*Per Bacco!*" cried the Emperor, "the jest begins well!"

"And now embrace her firmly!" exclaimed Virgil.

"Better and better!" quoth the Emperor.

Then Virgil spoke solemnly to the lady, and said:

"What is thy name?"

"Donna di Diaccia," was her reply.

"Then, Lady of Ice," replied the wondrous man, "in the name of my magic power, I summon you to return to the ice from which you sprung, and to the water from which you were born!"

Then little by little, as she sat in the Emperor's lap, the beautiful girl became a brilliant block of ice, and truly the great man, as his fingers and all his person began to freeze, was fain to place the image on the sofa, where they saw it presently thaw—features and feet and all dispersing, and running away in a stream, till every trace had flown, and the Emperor and the company understood that they had been admiring a Woman of Water.

5

There was a pause of utter bewilderment, as of awe, at this strange ending, and then a roar of laughter, in which the Emperor himself finally joined, crying : " *Viva Virgilio !* Long may he flourish with his magic art !" And so the feast ended with the clattering of cups, laughter, and merry cheers.

[So the Donna di Diaccio was a spirit ? Certainly—the Spirit of Ice-water. If there is spirit in vermouth, why should there not be one in the iced water which you mix with it ?]

This story may remind the reader of " Our Lady of the Snow," or Byron's " Witch of the Alps," or Shelley's " They all seem to be Sisters," or else suggest " Frozen Champagne," and " Philadelphia Frozen Oysters."

VIRGIL THE MAGICIAN, OR THE FOUR VENUSES.

> " Maint autres grand clercs ont estè
> Au monde de grand poesié
> Qui aprisrent tote lor vie,
> Des sept ars et le astronomie,
> Dont aucuns i ot qui a leur tens,
> Firent merveille par lor sens ;
> Mais cil qui plus s'en entremist,
> Fu Virgile qui mainte enfist.
> Pour ce si vous en conterons
> Aucune dont oi avons."
>
> *L'Image du Monde* (1245).

Virgilio was as great a magician as he was a distinguished poet. And of the great works which he did when alive many are yet remembered here in Florence, and among other things his skill was such that by means of it he made statues sing and dance.

Ecco come avenne—behold how it came to pass ! It chanced one day that when walking alone in the environs of Florence, he found himself in a place where there were four very beautiful Venuses.* And looking at them with great admiration, and observing their forms, he said:

"Truly they all please me well; and if they could converse I hardly know which I would choose for a companion. *Ebbene!* I will make them all talk and walk, live and move, and can then see if anyone of them will show any gratitude for the gift of life."

Then he took human fat, and anointed with it all the statues, and then of the blood of a wild boar, and rubbed it very thoroughly over them, and when this was done he waved his magic wand, and said:

"In the name of my magic art and power I order you to speak and move and live!"

And with this they all awoke, as it were, from a long dream, and stepping down from their pedestals, they walked about, seeming far more beautiful than before. And they gathered round Virgil, for truly they were enchanted with him as well as by him, in more ways than one, and embraced and kissed him with a thousand caresses and endearments, and each and all wished him to select her as his mate.

Then Virgilio, laughing, said:

> "I know not which to choose among the four;
> I cannot make all four into a wife;
> But to determine who shall be the first,
> Do ye go forth and seek each one a gift,
> And come to-morrow evening to my house,
> And she who brings the gift which I prefer
> Shall be the fair one first preferred by me."

And on the following eve the first who came was the Venus Agamene; thus was she called who brought the first gift, and this was a splendid diamond. Virgilio received it with admiration, but said that he must wait to see what the others would bring before he could decide.

Then the second was announced, whose name was Enrichetta, and she presented a marvellous garment, richly embroidered and adorned. And this too was admired; but to her also Virgilio said he would await what was to come.

The third, whose name was Veronica, brought such a wonderful bouquet of flowers that the magician was more

---

* Four antique marble statues of women. Any ancient female statue is commonly called a *Venus* by the people at large in Italy.

pleased with it than he had been by the diamond or the
robe.

Then there came the fourth, called Diomira, and she
brought a splendid crown of ——.* And Virgil preferred this
to all, and gave the prize to Diomira. So he bade them all
come the next evening to a grand festival. And when they
came, it was indeed a wonderful assembly, for there were
present, and in life, all the statues from all the palaces.
They came down from their pedestals and danced in the
house of Virgilio—nor did they return until the early dawn ;
and so it came to pass that on that night all the statues
spoke and danced.

> " They danced so merrily all the night,
> Till the sun came in with a rosy light,
> And touched the statues fair,
> When in an instant every one
> Was changed again to marble stone.
> Per Bacco !   I was there !"

It is not remarkable that there should be so many
tales in Italy of statues speaking or coming to life.
They abounded among the Romans, and are to be
found in later literature.   Bonifacius, in his " Ludicra,"
as I have said, collects instances of men who have
loved statues, and Zaghi, whom I shall quote again
directly, does the same.   But the idea of images speaking is so natural that we need not have recourse to
tradition to account for its existence.

Among the archaic and very curious traditions in this
tale we are told that Virgil rubbed the statues with
human fat and the blood of a wild boar. Both of these
occur not only in witchcraft, but also in the wild science
of the earlier time, as potent to give or take life.   For
the blood of a boar that of a bull is equivalent.   In the
recipes for preparing the celebrated poison of the
Borgias one or the other is presented.   That of the

---

* Here there is a hiatus, or blank in the manuscript. By crown is
here meant a fillet or tiara, as will be shown anon.

boar still exists in the poisoning common in Germany caused by eating *Blutwurst*. In the " Selva di Curiosità," by Gabriel Zaghi, 1674, there is a chapter (xx.) devoted to showing that bull's blood—*sangue di toro*—is a deadly poison ; to prove this he cites Plutarch, Pliny, Dioscorides, and others, from which it appears that the idea is ancient. That it gives life to statues in the tale is quite in keeping with the strange and rude homœopathy which is found in Paracelsus, and all the writers on mystical medicine of his time, from which Hahnemann drew his system, *i.e.*, that what will kill can also cure, or revive.

It is very remarkable that in this tale Agamene brings a diamond. According to Hyginius (" Astronom.," II., 13, *vide* Friedrich, " Symbolich der Natur.," p. 658), Aega (or Agamene) nursed the youthful Jupiter. In another legend (No. 1) Virgil is the son of Jove. " Aega was a daughter of the Sun, and of such brilliancy that the Titans, dazzled by her splendour, begged their mother *Gäa*, or Gea, to hide her in the earth." This clearly indicates a diamond. Jupiter transformed her into a star.

It is simply possible, and only a conjecture of mine, that in Diomira we find the name of Diomedea, the *Diomedea necessitas* of Plato (" De Repub," lib. 6), who carried all before her. Diomira conquers all her rivals in this legend. She is the *Venus Victrix*.

I cannot help believing when we find such curious instances of tradition as that of Aega, or Agamene, surviving in these tales, that there is a possibility that the whole story may, more or less, be of classic or very ancient origin. We are not as yet able to *prove* it, and so there are none who attach much value to these fragments. But a day will come when scholars will think more of them. That there still survives a great deal of Græco-Latin lore which was not recorded by classic writers has become to us a certainty. Therefore it is possible, though not now to be proved, that these statues of Virgil had a common origin with the image of Selostre, or *Testimonium luminis*, described by Pausanius, which spoke when the sun rose or at the Aurora.

If it be possible, and it certainly is conjectural, that Diomira is the same with Diadumena, we have beyond question a very remarkable illustration of old tradition surviving in a popular tale ; for Diadumena, or " She who binds her forehead with a fillet," or band, was the name of one of the most beautiful statues of Polycletus. According to Winkelmann ("Ist. dell Acte," lib. 6, cap. 2), this statue was very frequently copied and familiarly known. A statue in the Villa Farnese is believed to be an imitation of it. Were this conjecture true, the gift brought by Diomira would be the fillet which Virgil wears by tradition, as typical of a poet. An ornament, fillet, or tiara is, effectively, a crown. Therefore, the meaning of the myth is that a true poet is such by necessity ; he cannot help it—*poeta nascitur, non fit.*

VIRGIL, THE LADY, AND THE CHAIR.

"Now the golden chair wherein Juno was compelled to sit, by the artifice of Vulcan, means that the earth is the mother of riches, and with it that part of the air which cannot leave the earth, Juno being air."—
NATALIS COMITIS : *Mythologia*, lib. ii., 79 (1616).

> "Thou wolt algates wete how we be shape !
> Thou shalt hereafterward, my brother dere,
> Come wher thee needeth not of me to lere,
> For thou shalt by thine own experience
> Conne in a chaiere rede of this sentence
> Better than Virgile while he was on live
> Or Dante also."
>
> CHAUCER : *The Frere's Tale.*

There once lived in Rome a very great, rich, and beautiful Princess, but she was as bad at heart as could be, and her life was of the wickedest. However, she kept up a good appearance, and was really at last in love with a fine young man, who returned her affections.

But Virgil, knowing all, and pitying the youth, said to him that the woman would certainly be the cause of his ruin, as she had been of many others, and told him so many terrible things of her, that he ceased to visit the Princess.

And she, first suspecting and then learning what Virgil had done, fell into bitter hatred, and swore that she would be revenged on him.

So one evening she invited the Emperor and many nobles, among them Virgil, to a splendid supper.

And being petty and spiteful by nature, the Princess had devised a mean trick to annoy Virgil. For she had prepared with great craft a chair, the seat of which was of paper, but which seemed to be of solid wood. It appeared to be a handsome seat of great honour.

But when the great man sat on it, there was a great crash, and he went down, indeed, but with his legs high in the air. So there was a peal of laughter, in which he joined so heartily and said so many droll things over it, that one would have thought he had contrived the jest himself, at which the lady was more angry than ever, since she had hoped to see him angry and ashamed. And Virgil, taking all the blame of the accident on himself, promised to send her in return a chair to pay for it. And he requested leave to take the proper measure for it, so that she might be fitly taken in.

Which she was. For, having returned to his home, Virgil went to work and had a splendid chair made—*con molto artifizio*. With great art he made it, with much gold inlaid with pearls, studded with gems. It was all artificial.*

And having finished it, Virgil begged the Emperor to send it to the Princess as a gift.

The Emperor did so at the proper time, but there was in it a more cunning trick than in the one which she had devised. For there were concealed therein several fine nets, or snares, so that whoever sat in it could not rise.

Then the Princess, overjoyed at this magnificent gift, at once sent an invitation to her friends to come to a supper where she could display it; nor did she suspect any trick, having no idea that she had any enemy.

And all came to pass as Virgil planned. For the lady, having seated herself in great state, found herself caught, and could not rise.

Then there was great laughter, and it was proposed that everyone present should kiss her. And as one beginning leads to strange ending, the end thereof was that they treated her *senza vergogna*, saying that when a bird is once caught in a snare, everybody who pleases may pluck a feather.

The classical scholar will find in this tale a probable reminiscence of the chair made by Vulcan wherein to entrap Juno, in which he succeeded, so that she was made to appear ridiculous to all the gods. It is worth noting in this connection that such chairs are made even to the present day, and that without invisible nets or any magic. One is mentioned in a book entitled "The Life of Dr. Jennings the Poisoner" (Philadelphia, T. B. Peterson, Bros.). If any person sat in it, he or she fell back, and certain clasps closed over the victim, holding him or her down perfectly helpless, rendering robbery or violence easy. Since

---

* "Tutto era artificiale," meaning very artistic or æsthetic.

writing the foregoing, I have in a recent French novel read a description of such a chair, with the additional information that such seats were originally invented for and used by physicians to confine lunatic patients. A friend of mine told me that he had seen one in a house of ill-fame in New York.

The legend of the Lady and the Chair suggests a very curious subject of investigation. It is very probably known to the reader that, to make a mesmerized or hypnotized subject remain seated, whether he or she will or not, is one of the common experiments of the modern magicians. It is thus described by M. Debay in his work " Les Mystères du Sommeil et Magnetisme."

The operator asks the subject, " Are you asleep ?"
" No."
" Rise from your chair." (*He rises.*) " Tell all present that you are not asleep."
" No. I am wide awake."
The operator takes the subject by the hand, leads him to different persons present with whom he is acquainted, and asks him if he knows them. He replies:
" Certainly I know them."
" Name them."
He does so.
" All right. Now sit down." (*The subject obeys.*) " And now I forbid you to rise. It is for you impossible—you cannot move !"
The subject makes ineffectual efforts to rise, but remains attached to the chair as if held fast by an invisible power.
The operator then says:
" Now you may rise. I permit you to do so. Rise—I order it !"
The subject rises from the chair without an effort.

I have frequently had occasion to observe that, in all of these legends which I have received from witches, the story, unlike the common fairy tale or *novella* of any kind, is only, as it were, a painted casket in which is enclosed the jewel of some secret in sorcery, generally with an incantation. Was not this the case with many of the old myths? Do they not all, in fact, really set forth, so far as their makers understood them, the mysteries of Nature, and possibly in some cases those of the wonder-works or miracles of the priests and magicians? There was a German—I forget his name—who wrote a book to prove that Jupiter, Juno, and all the rest, were the elements as known to us now, and all the wonders told of all the gods, with the "Metamorphoses" of Ovid, only a marvellous poetic allegory of chemical combinations and changes. That hypnotism was known to Egyptians of old is perfectly established—at least to his own satisfaction—by Louis Figuier in his "Histoire du Merveilleux dans les Temps Modernes," Paris, 1861; and it is extremely possible. Therefore it may be that Juno in the chair is but the prototype of a Mademoiselle Adèle, or Angelique Cottin, or Marie Raynard, or some other of the "little Foxes," who, by the way, are alluded to in the Old Testament.

VIRGIL AND THE GODDESS OF THE CHASE.

"*Images*, though made by men, are the bodies of gods, rendered perceptible to the sight and touch. In the images are certain spirits brought by invitation, after which they have the power of doing whatever they please ; either to hurt, or to a certain extent to fulfil the desires of those persons by whom divine honours and duteous worship are rendered unto them. . . . Do you not see, O Asclepias, that *statues* are animated by sense, and actually capable of doing such actions?"—HERMES TRISMEGISTUS, AP. AUGUSTINE, C. D., viii. 23.

> " And there withall Diana gan appere
> With bowe in hand, right as an hunteresse,
> And saydé, ' Daughter—stint thin heavinesse. . . .'
> And forth she went and made a vanishing."
> CHAUCER : *The Knighte's Tale.*

There was in the oldest times in Florence a noble family, but one so impoverished that their *giorni di festa*, or feast-days, were few and far between. However, they dwelt in their old palace, which was in the street now called the Via Citadella, which was a fine old building, and so they lived in style before the world, when many a day they hardly had anything to eat.

Round this palace was a large garden in which stood an ancient marble statue of a beautiful woman, running very rapidly, with a dog by her side. She held in her hand a bow, and on her forehead was a small moon ; it seemed as if, instead of being in a garden, she was in a forest hunting wild game. And it was said that by night, when all was still and no one present, and the moon shone, the statue became like life, and very beautiful, and then she fled away and did not return till the moon set, or the sun rose.

The father of the family had two children, a boy and a girl, of nine or ten years of age, and they were as good as they were intelligent, and like most clever children, very fond of curious stories.

One day they came home with a large bunch of flowers which had been given to them. And while playing in the garden the little girl said :

" The beautiful lady with the bow ought to have her share of the flowers."

" Certainly," answered her brother, " because I believe that she is as good as she is beautiful."

Saying this, they laid flowers before the statue, and made a wreath, which the boy placed on her head.

Just then the great poet and magician Virgil, who knew everything about the gods and *folletti*, whom people used to worship, entered the garden, and said, smiling :

" You have made the offering of flowers to the goddess quite correctly, as they did in old times ; all that remains is to make the prayer properly, and it is this.   Listen, and learn it."   So he sang :

> " Bella dea dell arco !
> Bella dea delle freccie !
> Della caccia e dei cani !
> Tu vegli colle stelle
> Quando il sole va dormir,
> Tu colla Luna in fronte,
> Cacci la notte meglio del di
> Colle tue Ninfe al suono
> Di trombe—sei la regina
> Dei cacciatori,
> Regina della notte !
> Tu che siei la cacciatrice
> Più potente di ogni
> Cacciator—ti prego
> Pensa un poco a noi !"

> " Lovely Goddess of the bow !
> Lovely Goddess of the arrows !
> Of all hounds and of all hunting ;
> Thou who wakest in starry heaven
> When the sun has gone to sleep ;
> Thou with moon upon thy forehead
> Who the chase by night preferrest
> Unto hunting by the day,
> With thy nymphs unto the sound
> Of the horn—thou Queen of Hunters !
> Queen of night, thyself the huntress,
> And most powerful, I pray thee,
> Think, although but for an instant,
> Upon us who pray unto thee !"

Then Virgil taught them the *Scongiurazione*, or spell to the goddess Diana :

> " Bella dea dell' arco del cielo,
> Delle stelle e della Luna.
> La regina più potente
> Dei cacciatori e della notte ;
> A te riccoriamo,
> E chiedamo il tuo aiuto

> Che tu possa darci
> Sempre la buona fortuna !"

> " Fair goddess of the rainbow !
> Of the stars and of the moon !
> The queen all-powerful
> Of hunters and the night,
> We beg of thee thy aid
> To give good fortune to us !"

Then he added the conclusion :

> " Se la nostra scongiurazione,
> Ascolterai,
> E buona fortuna ci darei,
> Un segnale a noi lo darei !"

> " If thou heedest our evocation,
> And wilt give good fortune to us,
> Then give us in proof a token."

And having taught them this, Virgilio departed.

Then the children ran to tell their parents all that had happened, and the latter impressed it on them to keep it all a secret, nor breathe a word or hint of it to anyone. But what was their amazement, when they found early the next morning before the statue a deer freshly killed, which gave them good dinners for many a day—nor did they want thereafter at any time game of all kinds.

There was a neighbour of theirs, a priest, who held in hate all the idolatry of the olden time, and all which did not belong to his religion,* and he, passing the garden one day, beheld the statue crowned with roses and (other) flowers. And in a rage, seeing in the street a decaying cabbage, he rolled it in the mud, and threw it, all dripping, at the face of the statue, saying :

" Ecco male bestia d'idolo, questo e l'omaggio che io ti do, gia che il diavolo ti aiuta !"—(Behold, thou vile beast of an idol, this is the homage which I render thee, and may the devil help thee !)

Then the priest heard a voice in the gloom where the trees were thick, which said :

> 'Bene bene—tu mi hai fatto
> L' offrande—tu avrai
> La tua porzione
> Di caccia.   Aspetta !"

---

* " Alla *sua* religione."

" It is well—since thou hast made
Thy offering, thou'lt get thy portion
Of the game—but wait till morning !"

All that night the priest suffered from horrible fancies
and fears, and when at last, just before three, he fell
asleep, he soon awoke from a nightmare, in which it
seemed as if something heavy rested on his chest. And
something indeed fell from him and rolled on the ground.
And when he rose and picked it up, and looked at it by the
light of the moon, he saw that it was a human head, half
decayed.*

Another priest who, hearing the cry which he had uttered,
entered his room, said :

" I know that head. It is of a man whom I confessed,
and who was beheaded three months ago at Siena."

And three days after this the priest who had insulted the
goddess died.

In a single incident this tale recalls that of Falkenstein, one of the synonyms* of the wild huntsman in
Germany, of whom it is said that as he passed by, a
reckless fellow wished him luck, whereupon he heard
the words, "Thou hast wished me luck; thou shalt
share the game;" whereat there was thrown to him a
great piece of carrion. And soon after he died.† But
the true plot of this narrative is the conduct of the
goddess Diana, who rewards the children for their
worship and punishes the priest for his sacrilege.

And, noting the sincere spirit of heathenism which
inspires many of these legends, the belief in *folletti* and
fate, and curiously changed forms of the gods of Græco-
Roman mythology, still existing among the peasants,
it is worth inquiring whether, as the very practical
Emperor Julian believed, a sincerely religious and

---

* ' La testa d'un uomo piena di vermi e puzzolente," a parody of the
decayed cabbage.
† I may here note that the ruined castle of the dreaded Falkenstein is
in sight of the rooms where I am now writing in Homburg-les-Bains.

moral spirit, under any form, could not be adapted to
the progress of humanity? The truth is that as the
heathen gods are one and all, to us, as something
theatrical and unreal, we think they must have been
the same to their worshippers. Through all the Renaissance to the present day the pretended appreciation
and worship of classic deities, and with them of classic
art and mythology, reminds one of the French billiard-
player Berger, who, when desirous of making a very
brilliant exhibition of his skill, declared that he would
invoke the god of billiards! They may seem beautiful,
but they are dead relics, and the worst is that no one
realizes now that they ever really lived, moved, and
had a being in the human heart. And yet the Italian
witch still has a spark of the old fire.

Diana Artemis is known to poets and scholars in
certain varied characters thus summed up by Browning:

> " I am a Goddess of the ambrosial courts,
> And save by Here, Queen of Pride, surpassed
> By none whose temples whiten this the world.
> Through Heaven I roll my lucid moon along;
> I shed in Hell o'er my pale people peace;
> On Earth, I, caring for the creatures, guard
> Each pregnant yellow wolf and fox-bitch sleep,
> And every feathered mother's callow brood,
> And all that love green haunts and loneliness
> Of men; the chaste adore me."

But to her only believers and worshippers now left
on earth—such as Maddalena—Diana is far more than
this, for she is the queen of all witchcraft, magic,
sorcery, the mistress of all the mysteries, of all deep
knowledge, and therefore the greatest of the goddesses
—all the rest, in fact, except Venus and Bacchus, who
only exist in oaths, being now well-nigh forgotten and
unknown to them.

VIRGIL AND THE SPIRIT OF MIRTH.

" 'Tis an ancient tale that a boy for laughing at Ceres was turned into a stone.   For truly too much merriment hardens us all."—*Comment on L. M. Brusonii ' Facetie.'*

In ancient times there lived in Florence a young lord who was very beautiful, and ever merry—and no wonder, because he was *Il Dio della Allegria*—the God of Mirth—himself.

He was greatly beloved, not only by his friends, but by all the people, because he was always so joyous, kind-hearted, and very charitable.

Every evening this spirit-lord went with his friends to the theatre, or to his parties (*al circolo*), and the name by which he was known was Eustachio.   All awaited with impatience his arrival, for with it the merriment began, and when he came there was a joyous shout of " Evviva il Dio dell' Allegria !"

It came to pass that in a theatre Eustachio met with a girl, a singer, of such marvellous beauty and wit, that he fell, like one lost, in love with her ; which love being reciprocated, he took her to himself, and kept her in a magnificent home, with many fine attendants, and all that heart could desire.   In those days every signore in Florence thus had an *amante*, and there was great rivalry among them as to who should keep his favourite in the best style—*con più di lusso.*   And this lady so beloved by Eustachio, was not only the most beautiful, but the most magnificently entertained of any or all in the city.

Now, one evening there was a grand festival in a *palazzo*, where there was dancing and gay conversation, Eustachio being as usual present, for all his love for his lady did not keep him from the world, or making mirth for all.   And as they diverted themselves or sung to music, there entered a group of young lords, among whom was Virgilio, the great poet.*

Then Eustachio rose and began to clap his hands and cry, " *Evviva !*   Long live the great poet !" and those who were at table ceased to eat, and those who were dancing

---

* Singer or minstrel, one who sings his poems, and not merely a writer of poems, is understood by *poeta* in all these legends.

left the dance with their partners, and all in welcome cried, "*Evviva il gran poeta!*"

Then Eustachio begged Virgilio to sing, and the poet did so, for there was no one who would have refused anything to Eustachio, so winning were his ways.

So Virgil made him the subject of his song, telling in pleasing verse how free he was from care, ever laughing like sunshine, ever keeping himself free from thought, which kills joy and brings sorrow.

And Eustachio, singing and laughing, said that it was because he was ever among friends who banished thought, and so kept away melancholy.

Then Virgil, still softly singing, asked him whether, if he should lose his lady-love, he would not be melancholy for a time, despite the consolations of friends and relations.

Eustachio replied that he would indeed regret the loss, and it would make him sad for a time, but not as a settled grief or incurable sorrow, for that all things pass away, every night hath its morning, after every death new life, when the sea has sunk to its lowest ebb then it rises, and that he who knows this can never know trouble.

Virgil ended the dialogue of song by saying that he who believes he can never be sad knows not what sorrow and trials are, that grief must come some time or other to all, even to the God of Mirth himself, and offered to make a wager of a banquet for all present, if he could not within two weeks' time cause Eustachio to know what grief, and a melancholy which should seem incurable, was like.

Eustachio assented, and said he would add a thousand gold crowns to the bet.

There was a statue named Peonia to whom Virgil had given life; and going to her, who was now as other women, he said:

"I can give life to a statue, but how to change a human being to marble is beyond my power; I pray thee, tell me how I may turn into an image, such as thou wert, this beautiful girl whom Eustachio adores."

And Peonia, smiling, replied: "Before thou didst come hither I knew thy thought and thy purpose. Lo! here I have prepared a bouquet of flowers of such intense magic perfume that it will make Eustachio love to madness, as he never did before; but when his mistress inhales the perfume she will become a statue."

6

And as she bid he did, and placed the bouquet in the lady's chamber, and when she smelt at it she became a statue, and sat holding the flowers. And Eustachio seeing her sitting there in the dim twilight, knew not the truth, but also smelt of the perfume, and became more in love than man can dream, but when he found that the lady was petrified he was well-nigh mad with grief, nor could anyone console him. And this passed into an iron-like melancholy, nor would he leave the room where the statue sat.

Now, the friends of all, though they well knew that Virgilio had done this, still remembered that he had mighty and mysterious power, and then, thinking over the wager, concluded that he had been in some manner in the affair. So they went to him, praying that he would do something to keep Eustachio from madness or death.

Then Virgilio, the great master, went to the room where Eustachio sat in profound grief by the statue, and said, with a smile, "*Caro giovane* (My dear youth), I have won my wager, and expect to see thee this evening in the hall at the banquet and dance, bringing the thousand crowns."

"Dear Virgilio," answered Eustachio, "go to my parents or friends, and receive thy gold, and assemble them all to banquet or to dance; but do not expect me, for from this room I never more will stir."

Then Virgilio, gently removing the magic bouquet from the hand of the statue, stepped to the window and threw it down into the street—when lo! the lady flushed into life, and with a laugh asked them what they were all doing there? And then Eustachio burst out laughing for joy, and they danced in a circle round Virgilio. Eustachio paid down the thousand crowns, which Virgil gave as a wedding present to the bride—for of course there was a wedding, and a grander banquet than ever. But though he was the God of Mirth himself, Eustachio never declared after this that he would or could never mourn or think of grief.

What is remarkable in this tale is the confusion between the conception of the hero as a spirit, or the God of Mirth, and his social condition as a young Italian gentleman about town. It is this transition from the god to the popular hero, a mere mortal, which forms the subject of Heine's "Gods in Exile."

There is another Florentine legend, in which this god appears by the more appropriate name of *Momo*, evidently *Momus*, in which a young lord who had never laughed in his life is made merry for ever by having presented to him the image of a laughing goblin, which one of his peasants had dug up in a ruin. Whenever he looks at it, he bursts into a roar of laughter, which has the effect of changing his character very much for the better.

What is perhaps most significant in this tale is the name *Peonia*. Pæonia in classic mythology was Minerva, as a healing goddess. As such, alone, she bears the serpent. Esculapius is termed by Claudian the *Pæonio*—dragon or snake. In reference to which I find the following in the " Dizionario Mitologico " :

" *Peonia*, an additional name of Minerva, worshipped . . . as guardian of health. Therefore she has for a tribute the serpent, as emblem of the art of healing. *Peonico* was a surname of Apollo."

When medicine was synonymous with magic, Peonia Minerva would naturally appear as one familiar with occult arts. The changing to a statue and being revived from a statue to life is a very evident symbol of raising from death to life. Æsculapius, who was the male equivalent of Peonia, revived corpses. As Minerva and other deities were familiar to the people as statues, in which there was believed to be a peculiar spirit or life, we can readily understand how any image of a goddess was supposed to be at times revived.

Peonia in our story works her miracle by means of flowers. This, if we are really dealing with an archaically old Italian tradition, is marvellously significant.

The *pæonia*, or peony, or *rose de Nôtre Dame*, was believed in earliest Roman times to be *primus inter magnos*, the very first and strongest of all floral amulets, or to possess the greatest power in magic. This was due to its extreme redness, this colour alone having great force to resist the evil eye and sorcery. The most dreaded of all deities among the earliest Etrusco-Latin races was Picus, who appeared as a woodpecker, to which bird he had been changed by Circe. "Nam Picus, etiam rex, ab eadem Circe virga tactus, in volucrem picum evolavit," as Tritonius declares. When people dug for treasure which was guarded by this dreaded bird, he slew them unless they bore as a protecting amulet the root of the peony. But there is a mass of testimony to prove that the *pæonia*, or peony, was magical. Many classic writers, cited by Wolf in his work on amulets, 1692, declare its root drives away phantasms and demons. It was held, according to the same writer, that the same root protected ships from storms and houses from lightning. It is true that this writer evidently confuses the peony with the poppy, but the former was from earliest times strong in all sorcery.

It is also curious that, in old tradition, Pygmalion the sculptor is represented as indifferent to women. Venus punishes him by making him fall in love with a statue. Eustachio, the Spirit of Mirth, declares that the death of his love would not cause him deep grief and for this Pæonia and Virgil change the lady into a marble image. It is the very same story, but with the plot reversed.

Peonia, or peony, regarded as the poppy, since the two very similar plants were beyond question often confused, had a deep significance as lulling to sleep—a synonym for death, a reviving force—and it was also an emblem of love and fertility (Pausanias, II., 10). Peonia lulls the lady to sleep with flowers, that is, into a statue.

I do not regard it as more than *probable*, but I think it possible that in this story we have one of the innumerable *novelle* or minor myths of the lesser gods, which circulated like fairy-tales among the Latin people, of which only a small portion were ever written down. That there were many of these not recorded by Ovid, and other mythologists, is very certain, for it is proved by the scraps of such lore which come to light in many authors and casual inscriptions. It requires no specially keen imagination, or active faculty of association, to observe that in this, and many other legends which I have collected and recorded, there are beyond question very remarkable relics of old faith and ancient tradition, drawn from a source which has been strangely neglected, which neglect will be to future and more enlightened antiquaries or historians a source of wonder and regret.

A certain Giovanni Maria Turrini, in a collection of odds and ends entitled "Selva di Curiosità," Bologna, 1674, declares that "the peony, if patients be touched with it, cures them of epilepsy, which results from the influence of the sun, to which this plant is subject, the same effect resulting from coral." Here we also have the restoring to life or reason, as if from death; that is to say, from a fit or swoon. Truly, the ancients did not know botany as we do, but there was for them far more poetry and wonder in flowers.

Some time after all the foregoing was written I

found—truly to my great astonishment—that in a
novel by Xavier Montepin there is a student named
Virgil, who has a mistress named Pivoine—the title
of the book—which word is in Latin *Pæonia*. This,
according to the kind of criticism which is now exten-
sively current, would settle the whole business, and
determine "the undoubted original." I believe it to
be a mere chance coincidence of names—strange,
indeed, but nothing more. For, in the first place, I
am sure that my collector or her informants are about
as likely to have read the *Sohar*, or "Book of Light,"
or Hegel's "Cyclopædia," as any novel whatever.
But the great part of what is curious in my narrative
is not that Virgil loves Pæonia, but that Pæonia-
Minerva depresses people to, or *raises them from, death
by means of flowers*. Very clearly in the Italian tale,
as in others, Virgil is a physician, and Pæonia is his
counterpart, of all which there is no hint in the French
novel.

So it once befell that in a very strange Italian tale
of Galatea, the Spirit of the White Pebble, there was a
narrative agreeing in *names* with one in a romance by
Eugene Sue. But on carefully examining the account
of the Virgins of Sen, given by Pomponius Mela
(Edition 1526, p. 34, for which purpose I expressly
purchased the book), I found that the legend, as known
to Maddalena, and also to an old woman whom she
did not know, contained the main element as given by
Mela, which is *not* to be found in the French story,
namely, the transmigration of the soul or metamor-
phosis into different forms. The Latin writer states
that such enchantresses are called Gallicenas. Now,
there was at one time a great infusion of Celtic blood

into Northern Italy, and if it was in correspondence with the Gauls, it *may* possibly be that the story of Sen and Galatea of the White Stone passed all round.

It may be observed, however, that there may linger among French peasants some legend of Virgil and Pivoine, or Pæonia, which Montepin had picked up, and should this be so, doubtless there is some folk-lorist who can confirm it. This is far more likely than that my authority took the names from a French novel.

The Spirit of Mirth in this story has really nothing in common with Momus, who was, in fact, the God of Sneering, or captious, petty criticism of the kind which objects to great and grand or beautiful subjects, because of small defects. The Virgilian spirit is that of the minor rural gods, or the daughters of the dawn, who were all smiling sub-forms of the laughing Venus. These play the principal part in the mythology of the Tuscan peasantry. This spirit differs from that of Momus as an angel from a devil.

Psellus held that there was a soul in all statues.

That the God of Mirth, or Laughter, is in this tale also a gay young cavalier in Florentine society is paralleled or outdone by Chaucer in the "Manciple's Tale," in which Apollo is described as follows:

> " Whan Phebus dwelled here in erth adoun,
> As oldé bookes maken mentioun,
> He was the mosté lusty bacheler
> Of all this world, and eke the best archer. . . .
> Thereto he was the semelieste man
> That is or was sithen the world began."

That is, this "flour of bacheleric as well in fredom as in chivalric" was simply human while here below, having "a wif which that he loved more than his lif." Chaucer wrote this evidently with conscious humour of the naïve paradox by which those of his age could thus confuse gods and common mortals, even as a Red Indian vaguely confuses the great beaver or wolf with a human being. It is a curious reflection that, at the present day in Italy, there are believers in the old gods who regard the latter in the same way, as half divine and half like other folk.

NERO AND SENECA.

" This Seneka, of which that I devise,
  Because Nero had of him swiché drede,
  For he fro vices wold him ay chastise
  Discretely, as by word, and not by dede.
  ' Sire,' he wold say, ' an Emperor mote nede
  Be vertuous, and haten tyrannie.'
  For which he made him in a bathe to blede
  On both his armès till he mustè die."
                    CHAUCER : *The Monke's Tale : Nero.*

" Già tra le infamie delle regie sale
  Due uomini vedevansi soltanto
  A cui volera orribilmente male,
  Questo amatore delle stragi, e pianto,
  Uno di questi è Seneca, ch' eguale
  In Roma non aver per nobil vanto
  Nelle dottrine di filosofia,
  E nel fare una bella poesia. . . .
  Nerone che non vuol d'ogni folliá,
  Avere appreso un rigido censore,
  Fece morir, con modi scellerati,
  Tanto costui, che Seneca, svenati !"
      Storia di Nerone : A Florentine Halfpenny Ballad.

"Alteri vivere oportet si vis tibi vivere."
" Thou must live for others if thou wouldst live for thyself."—
                    SENECA : *Epistolæ.*

There was once in Rome a young Emperor named Nerone. As a boy, he was by no means badly inclined, and it seemed for a long time as if he would grow up into a great and good man.

He had a tutor or teacher named Seneco,* who was

* So given in the text for Seneca.

benevolent and wise beyond all the men of his time, and he had such influence on the young Nerone, that for two years the youth behaved well and did no harm to anyone.

But little by little he was led astray by courtiers who flattered and corrupted him, and who of course did all they could to injure Seneco in his esteem, saying that the sage was really an old knave, and that he was engaged in plots with the design of becoming Emperor himself. And the end of it all was that Nerone believed them.

So he sent a letter to Seneco, in which he declared that the time had come for the old man to die; but that he might choose his own manner of death by suicide.

Seneco, having read it, said: "What an evil youth is this, of what a corrupted heart! Well, infamous as the command is, I will die! But I will leave him a legacy which shall be his ruin."

Thus he wrote to Nerone:

"I will die this very day, but I leave you a gift which is more than a fortune. It is a book of magic and necromancy. If you wish for anything, be it the love of a woman or the death of a man, or his disaster, or to destroy all Rome, you will find in the book spells by which it may be done."

And when he knew that Nerone had the book, he went at once into a hot bath, and said to his surgeon:

"Open my veins, so that I may bleed to death. I will die, but I know that the Emperor will soon follow me."

So he died, and all Rome wept.*

Then Nerone read the book, and it seemed as if it were poisoned, for while reading it he perceived as it were an exhalation † from hell.

He read in the book how to commit all crimes and sins, how to seize on fortunes, or rob whom he would, and learned from it all the secrets of licentiousness—*tutte cose voluttiose*—and having finished it, he became a veritable devil.

He collected many lions and tigers, and all kinds of terrible wild beasts, and then drove among them all the Christians and saints in Rome, and they were devoured by the beasts. Then he took the fortunes of all the rich men,‡ and decreed that all the women in the city were his wives. After which he every day debauched them in the open streets before their husbands, and likewise ordained that all

* "Così moriva e tutta Roma piangeva."   † *Vampa.*
‡ *Capitalisti*, bankers.

men and women should do the same openly.   And he committed even more infamous deeds in public places, with an
orchestra, saying it was best to make love to the sound or
accompaniment of music.

And one day, to make a scene in an opera, he (set fire to
and) burned all Rome.

Then the people made a revolution, and drove him out
of his palace.   It is said that this palace was all gilded.
(*Era tutto dorato.*)

In a public square was a statue of Seneco, and it was of
marble.   So the people in a rage drove Nerone before them
until, utterly weary and exhausted, he fell down at the foot
of the statue of Seneco.   And beholding the image of his
tutor, Nerone cried:

"*Tu mi vincesti, tu mi imperasti*—Thou hast conquered, O
Seneco; thou hast prevailed over me, and had thy revenge!
And accursed be the day in which thou didst send me
the book which gave me the power to have all which I
desired!"

And all who were present were astonished when they
heard the statue reply:

"I am avenged, and thou art punished."

Then a butcher struck him heavily; he gave him a death-
wound with an axe, and Nerone, dying, said:

"If thou hast no shame for having killed an Emperor,
thou shouldst at least blush at having put to death the
best actor in Rome!"

Then the ground opened, and there came forth the flame
and thunder of hell, with many devils who howled. . . .

And so did Nero die, who was the most infamous king[*]
who ever lived in this world since it was a world.

Though there are so many authentic traits of the
Emperor Nero in this tradition, the reader is not to
infer from them that she who wrote it has had access
to a copy of Suetonius.   There is a "halfpenny
dreadful," or *sou* shocker, entitled the "Life of Nero"
—*Vita di Nerone*—published by Adriano Salani, the
Catnach of Florence, Via Militare, No. 24 (No. 107 on

---

[*] " Il più grande birbone."

his catalogue), to say nothing of other halfpenny classical works, such as the "Story of the Proud Emperor," "The Empress Flavia," and the "Tale of Pyramus and Thisbe," which, as they are to be found on many open-air stands, may account for a great deal of such learning in the popular mind. One may meet daily in Italy with marvellous proof in many forms of what a strange, curious, confused mass of old Latin lore still lingers among the people, and the marvellous contrast which it presents to what the common folk read and reflect over in other lands. But Nero would be most likely to be remembered, because he is frequently mentioned or described in popular Lives of the Saints as a great maker of martyrs, and caster of them unto lions.

This does not belong to the cycle of Virgilian tales, but it was sent to me as one from Siena. To my collector it was all one, so that it referred to a magician, and had the idea occurred to the writer, the name of Virgilio would have been substituted for that of Seneca. Doubtless in their time, since they began life in India, or Egypt, or Arabia, these legends have borne many names, and been as garments to the memory of many sages—even as Buddha in his Jatakas was the first of a line which has ended in the heroes of European nurseries.

The halfpenny, or *soldo*, or *sou* ballad of Nero, to which I have referred, is too curious as illustrating the remarkable knowledge of classical antiquity still current among the Italian people, to be lightly passed by. Its title-page is as follows :

"Storia di Nerone, dove si narrano, le Stragi, i Delitti, le Persecuzioni e gli Incendi commessi da questo infame Tiranno in Roma"—"History of Nero ; in which is told the Murders and Crimes committed by this Infamous Tyrant in Rome."

This poem and others of the same stamp are quite as barbarously classic-mediæval or Romanesque as anything in any of these stories of Virgilio, and if I cite it, it is to give a clear idea of the remarkable degree to which strange traditions, and very ancient legends or "learning," have lingered among the people. I really cannot understand why this marvellous survival of old Latin romance, and this spirit of the Dark Ages among the people, attracts so little attention among literary people, and especially Italians. For it certainly indicates to any thinking mind the survival of a great deal of classic tradition which has never been recorded.

VIRGIL AND CICERO.

> " Magic is genius most mysterious,
> And poetry is genius passed to form,
> And these allied give birth to Eloquence ;
> For never yet was there an orator
> Who did not owe his best to Poetry."—C. G. L.

There was once a young man named Cicero, who was a student with Virgil, and who, being poor, served the great magician in all things.

When Christmas came, with the New Year, Virgil, being well pleased with his fidelity, resolved to make a handsome gift to Cicero, and so said :

" *Che vuoi?* What wilt thou have ?"

" I would like," replied young Cicero, " to be master of the art of speech "—*Il dono di parlar bene.*

" Would you not prefer wealth ?" asked Virgil.

" He who hath a ready tongue can have his will mid old or young," answered Cicero ; " and as the proverb says :

> " Chi ha eloquenza,
> Ad ogni cosa ha pretenza."

> " He who hath but eloquence
> Hath unto everything pretence."

" But do not forget," remarked Virgil, "that amiable speech is courteous and refined. And remember to always speak well of women—everywhere."

> " If it be false, or if it be true,
> Speak gently of women, whatever you do."

After a while Cicero, wanting change of life or to try his fortune, left Virgil and Rome, going first to Florence and then to Ravenna, where his parents dwelt.

So ever travelling on afoot, he came one night to a solitary place among rocks in a forest, where he saw at some distance a ruined castle. And entering, hoping to find a place to sleep, he was astonished to perceive a light, and going further, came into a spacious hall, where, seated at a table, were six gentlemen and a lady, all of them far more beautiful and magnificent in every respect than ordinary mortals, especially the lady, who, as Cicero thought, surpassed all women whom he had ever seen, as the moon outshines the stars.

"*Salve Domine!*" exclaimed the scholar; "and excuse my intrusion, since I did not expect to find company here, though I would have indeed come many a day's journey, had I known of it, to behold such handsome and brilliant cavaliers, and such a marvel of beauty as yon lady, as all the world would do."

"Thou hast a smooth tongue and a sweet gift of speech," replied the lady, with a smile; "and I not only thank thee for the whole company, but invite thee to sup with us, and lodge here, and be most welcome."

So they supped gaily; and Cicero, who from the company of Virgil and his friends and the court was familiar with the world, was amazed, and wondered who these marvellous people could be. At last he chanced to ask:

"What day of the week is this?"

"Truly you can here take your choice," replied the lady, with a laugh. "But of all the days of the week, which do you prefer?"

"Friday," replied Cicero; "because it is the only one which bears a woman's name or that of Venus. *Evviva Venere, evviva le donne!*

> "Hurrah for Venus, whate'er befall!
> Long life unto love, and to ladies all!"

" This youth has a tongue of gold and honey," said the lady. "And what do you think of the other days of the week?"

"Other people do not think much about them in any way," replied Cicero. " But that is not the case with me. To me they are all saints and gods. *Domenica* is a holy name, which praises the Lord. *Giovedi* (Tuesday) is the day of Jove, and that is a glorious name. *Evviva Giove!* So it is with them all; and were I rich enough, I would build a temple to the days of the week wherein to worship them."

" That money shall not be wanting, O thou happy man!" replied the lady. " Knowest thou who we are ? We are the Seven Days of the Week; and for what thou hast said of me, every Friday thou shalt find a hundred gold crowns under thy pillow. And when thou needest any special favour, then pray to us all."

And as he heard the last word Cicero fell asleep. When he awoke he was alone in the ruin, but by him was a purse with one hundred crowns in gold.

Then in time Cicero built the temple, as he had promised, to Venus, and in it he placed all the images of the seven gods. Then whoever wanted a favour invoked those deities, as indeed did Cicero when he needed aught; and those gods were the seven youths, and those youths whom he had found in the hall were the days of the week.

Then for a time Cicero lived in happiness. But something came to disturb it, for one morning he saw at a window near by a young lady of such marvellous beauty that he was as if enchanted, nor was she less pleased with him.

" Tell me, thou splendid star," said Cicero, " the very truth now passing in thy mind. Dost thou love me?"

" In very truth," she replied, " I do love thee. O Cicero, but thou lovest only to lose, for this day I am to leave Rome never to return, unless thou canst by some miracle so manage it as to prevent the journey, and keep me here!"

Then Cicero went to the Temple of the Days and conjured them thus:

> " Lunedi e Marte ! (Martedi.)
> Fai che la stella mia non parta !
> Mercurio e Giove !
> Fai che la stella non mova !"

" Monday and Tuesday,
  I pray you cause my love to remain !
  Wednesday and Thursday,
  Let her not move !
  Venus, thou who art the fairest day,
  The one whom I most adore !
  Thou who hast put me in the way of wealth,
  And unto whom I truly built a temple,
  As I did promise in the bygone time,
  And as thou thyself didst promise,
  That if I needed aught, and came to thee,
  My wishes should be granted, now I pray
  To Venus and to Saturn—Saturday,
  That as I have no peace, and none can know,
  Till I have won the maid, give her to me !
  And thou, O Sunday, when the wedding comes,
  I pray thee give her to me with thy hand !"

Then a voice from the depth of the temple replied :

" Because thou hast spoken so well,
  What thou hast asked is granted ;
  She whom thou lovest
  Is not of the race of men ;
  She is an enchantress,
  Born of Venus, who loves her,
  Venus, who bent her to love thee ;
  The grace is granted :
  Wed and be happy !"

This pretty and fanciful, or strange, tale recalls that in the " Pentamerone " of Gianbattista Basile, the Neapolitan, in which a young man meets the Twelve Months in human form, and pleases March by speaking well of him. In this story the hero is a famed orator, who not only possesses the *gaber*—or " gift of the gab " —but of whom we are told how he came by it, namely, from Virgil, whose verse has indeed for ages wakened eloquence in many hearts.

The days of the week in English are derived as follows:

Sunday	-	- Sun day.
Monday	-	- Moon day.
Tuesday	-	- Tuisco's day.
Wednesday	-	- Woden or Odin's day.
Thursday	-	- Thor's day.
Friday	-	- Frey's day.
Saturday	-	- Seater's day.

According to this, Friday is the luckiest day, because Frey was the god who gave good fortune, and Freya, his female counterpart, was the Northern Venus. The Italian names with their gods correspond to ours, as the deities of the North resembled those of the Latin pantheon. As this is an interesting subject, I take from the Italian Historical-Mythological Dictionary the following:

> "*Settimana* is a time composed of seven days. Dion Cassius asserts that the Egyptians were the first to divide time into periods of seven days, and that it was suggested by the seven planets. However, the ancients in this did not follow the rule, since in that case we should have had Saturn, Jupiter, Mars, the Sun, Venus, Mercury, and the Moon. Saturday, Sabato, is derived from Saturn, who ruled the first hour."

It was, in fact, from the disposition of the *hours* that the days of the week received their names; hence the transposition of names, as is very ingeniously worked out by the author.

It is almost amusing to observe that in this, as in all tales coming from a witch source, the incantations, though not at all necessary to the story, are given with scrupulous care.

To the reader who would seriously study Cicero, yet in a deeply interesting form, I commend "Cicero and his Friends," by Gaston Bussier (London : A. D. Innes and Co., 1897). According to this genial and vigorous French writer, there is a great deal of mystery as to the manner in which the noble orator acquired the money to purchase estates and villas, when he was notoriously devoid of income. It is true that a great deal of public money was passing through his hands just then, but as he was as incorruptible and pure as an average American senator, of course *this* cannot account for his acquisitions. Here the legend comes to our aid and meets the difficulty. Having the Seven Days to draw upon, which probably means infinite extension of time and renewal of his notes, the great Roman, borrowing, like his friend Cæsar, by millions, got along very comfortably. In fact, they borrowed so much that all Rome was interested in their prosperity, and helped to make them rich that they might pay.

VIRGIL AND THE GODDESS VESTA.

" Put out the light, and then—put out the light !"

" Ut inquit Hecateus in Genealogiis : Enim vero cùm *duæ* essent Vestæ, per antiquiorem Saturni matrem ; terram ; at per juniorem ignem purum ætheris significarunt."—*Mythologia Natalis Comitis*, A.D. 1616.

Many centuries have passed since there was (worshipped) in Florence a goddess who was the great spirit of virtue and chastity, (yet) when a maid had gone astray she always devoted herself to worship the beautiful Avesta, as this deity was called, and the latter never failed in such case to get her devotee out of the difficulty. Her temple was that building which is now called the Baptistery of Saint John, and she was the goddess of light, as of candles, torches, and all that illuminates. And Avesta was, as I have said, known as the deity of virtue, albeit many of the people shrugged their shoulders when they heard this, being evidently strongly inclined to doubt, but they said nothing for fear of punishment.

For it was rumoured that Avesta had many lovers, and that in the rites of her religion there were secrets too dark to discover, and that as everything in her worship was involved in mystery and carried on occultly, it followed, of course, that it involved something wrong. And it was observed that once a month many women who worshipped her met in her temple by night, and that they were accompanied by their lovers, who with them adored the goddess in the form of a large lighted lamp. But that when this rite was at an end and the multitude had departed, there remained unnoted a number, by whom the doors were closed and the light extinguished, when a general orgy ensued, no one knowing who the others might be.* And it was from this came the saying which is always heard when two lovers are seated together by a light and it goes out, that Avesta did it.†

There was in Florence a young lord who loved a lady of great beauty. But she had a bitter rival, who to cross their love had recourse to sorcery or witchcraft, and so " bound " or cast on him a spell which weakened his very life, and made him impotent and wretched, that his very heart seemed to be turned to water.

And this spell the witch worked by taking a padlock and locking it, saying :

> " Chiudo la catena,
> Ma non chiudo la catena,
> Chiudo il corpo e l'anima
> Di questo bel signor ingrato,
> Chi non ha voluto,
> Corrispondermi in amore,‡
> Ha preferito un' altra a me,
> E questa io l'odio
> Come odio la signorina,
> Pure catena che incateni
> Tanti diavoli tieni !
> Tengo incatenata questo signor
> Fino a mio comando
> Che nessuno la possa disciogliere
> E incatenato possa stare,
> Fino che non si decidera
> Di sposarmi. . . ."

> " Now here I close the lock,
> Yet 'tis not a lock which I close ;
> I shut the body and soul
> Of this ungrateful lord,
> Who would not meet my love,
> But loves another instead,
> Another whom I hate,
> Whom I here lock and chain
> With devil's power again.

---

* " E cosi tutti facevano l'amore nel buio, senza sapere chi era quello che facevano. . . ."

† *Vide* " Etrusco-Roman Remains."

‡ By inadvertence or a blunder in the original manuscript, the wizard or witch is made male and female, and the victim alternately the young lady and the lover. It would make no difference as regards the plot.

> I hold this man fast bound
> That none shall set him free
> Until I so command,
> And bound he shall remain
> Till he will marry me."

One day Virgil was passing the Piazza del Duomo, when he met with the young man who had thus been bound or bewitched, and the victim was so pale and evidently in terrible suffering, that the great poet and magician, who was ever pitying and kind, was moved to the heart, and said:

"Fair youth, what trouble have you, that you seem to be in such suffering?"

The young man replied that he, being in love unto life and death, had been bewitched by some malignant sorcery.

"That I can well see," replied the sage, "and I am glad that it will be an easy thing for me to cure you. Go thou into a field which is just beyond Fiesole, in a place among the rocks. There thou wilt find a flat stone bearing a mark. Lift it, and beneath thou wilt find a padlock and chain. Take this golden key: it is enchanted, for with it thou canst open any lock in the world of door or chain.* Keep the lock, open it, and then go to the Temple of Vesta and return thanks with prayer, and wait for what will come."

So the young man did as Virgil had told him, and among the rocks found the stone and the padlock, and went to the Temple of Avesta, where he opened the lock and made the prayer to the goddess, which having done, he fell asleep, and no one beheld him.

And while he was there the young lady entered the Baptistery to worship Avesta, to offer her devotions, which being ended, she sat down and also fell into a deep sleep, and no one observed her.

But later in the night, when the doors were closed and the light extinguished, and the worshippers who remained were calling "Avesta!" the two sleepers who were side by side were awakened by a rustling of silk, and this was caused by the dress of the goddess, who roused them. And the young man found himself restored to vigorous health and unwonted passion, and quickly noting that a lady was by him, and carried away by feelings beyond his control,

---

* "Serratura o luchetta."

embraced and kissed her—nor did she indeed resist, for the will of Avesta was on them both. But noting that the lady had a silk handkerchief* partly out of her pocket, he adroitly stole it, putting in its place his own, and so with a kiss he left her, neither knowing who the other was. But on awaking, as if it were from a dream or a delirium, the lady was overcome with shame and grief, and could only think that madness or magic had overcome her reason, to cause her to yield as she had done. For this morning she felt more passionately in love with her betrothed than she had ever done before, and this was because the spell which had bound her was broken with the opening of the padlock.

But what was the astonishment of the lover, who was also restored to all his health and strength, when in the morning he looked at the handkerchief which he had carried away and found embroidered on it the arms and name of his love! So he went to visit her, and his greeting was :

" Signorina, have you lost a handkerchief ?"

" Not that I know of," replied the lady, amazed.

" Look at the one in your pocket, and then at *this*," was his laughing reply.

She did so, and understanding all in an instant, cried out in shame and horror, while she became at first like blood and then milk. Then the gentleman said :

" It seems to me, Signorina, that we must by mistake have exchanged handkerchiefs last night in the dark, and no wonder, considering the fervency of our devotions. And since we have begun to worship and pray so devoutly, and have entered on such a good path, it were a pity for us to turn back, and therefore it were well for us to continue to travel on it hand in hand together. But I propose that instead of changing pocket-handkerchiefs, we exchange rings before the altar and get married."

The lady laughed and replied :

" I accept with great pleasure, Signore, the handkerchief ; just as the women in Turkey do when it is thrown to them. And you know the proverb :

> " ' La donna chi prende
> Tosto si rende
> E poi si vende.' "

---

* Florentine *folar*, or *follo*, from *foglio*, a leaf. I conjecture that this is the original of the English slang *vogel*, a silk handerchief, and not the German *vogel*, a bird.

"She who will take will give herself away,
And she who gives will sell herself, they say."

"Even so will I sell mine for thine; but you must take the bargain on the nail, and the ball on the bound in the game of love."

"Yes," replied the young man; "I do so with all my heart. But as for our handkerchiefs, I now see that it is true that the peasant does not always know what it is that he carries home in his bag from the mill. Thanks be to Avesta that we found such good flour in our sacks!"

"To Vesta and to Virgil be all praise!" replied the lady. "But I think that while we continue our daily worship in the temple, we will go there no longer by night. *Vi sono troppo donne devote nel buio*"—There are too many lady devotees there in the darkness.

As a mere story this legend were as well left out, but it is one of a hundred as regards curious relics of mythologic and other lore. Firstly, be it observed that a secret doctrine, or esoteric as opposed to exoteric teaching, was taught in all the mysteries of the gods. Diana, who is identical with Vesta, Avesta, or Hestia, as a goddess of light by night and also of chastity, had her lovers in secret. What further identifies the two is that in this tale girls who have got into trouble through love, pray to Vesta, even as Roman maids did under similar circumstances specially to Diana.

There is no historical proof whatever that the Baptistery was ever a temple of Vesta, but there is very remarkable circumstantial evidence to that effect which I have indicated in detail in an article in the *Architectural Review*. Both Vesta and Saint John were each in her or his religion the special deities or incarnations of Light or Fire, and Purity or Chastity. The temples of Vesta were like those of Mars, and Mars alone, either round, hexagonal, or square, to indicate the form attributed with variations to the world. The early tradition of all writers on Florence speaks of the Baptistery of Saint John as having been a temple of Mars, which legend the priests naturally endeavoured to deny, thinking it more devout and "genteel" to attribute its erection to a Christian Empress.

The binding and rendering impotent by means of a padlock, and forty other devices, to render married folk miserable, or lovers languid, was so common two centuries ago, that there is almost a literature, occult, theological, and legal, on the subject. The Rabbis say it was invented by Ham, the son of Noah. The superstition was generally spread in Greece and Rome. It is still very commonly believed in and practised by witches all over Europe, and especially by gipsies and the Italian *strege*.

What is above all to be remarked in this tale is that it recognises a double nature in Vesta—one as a chaste goddess of fire, the other of a voluptuous or generative deity, signified by extinguishing the lights. And this is precisely what the oldest writers declared, though it was quite forgotten in later times. As Natalis Comes declares, " There were *two* Vestas, one by the first wife of Saturn, another by the younger one, meaning the earth, the other fire," as Ovid witnesses, " Fastorum," lib. 6. In fact, there was a double or second to every one of the Greek or Etruscan gods. And this belief which was forgotten by the higher classes remained among the people. And it may be specially noted that the second Vesta was called the mother of the gods, as Strabo declares, and she was in fact the Venus of the primitive or Saturnian mythology.

THE STONE FISH, AND HOW VIRGIL MADE IT EATABLE.

"Virgille plus fu sapïens
Plus clerc, plus sage et plus scïens.
Que nul a son temps vesquist,
Et plus de grans merveilles fist
Pour voir il fist de grans merveilles ;
Homs naturels ne fist pareilles."

RENARS CONTREFAIS, A.D. 1319.

In the old times, when things were so different from what they are now—the blue bluer, the red redder, when the grains of maize were as big as grapes, and grapes as big as pomegranates, and pomegranates as big as melons, and the Arno was always full of water, and the water so full of fine large fish that everybody had as many as he wanted for nothing, and the sun and moon gave twice as much light—there was, not far from Via Reggio, a castle, and the signore who owned it was a great bandit, who robbed all the country round, as all the gentlemen did in those times when they could, for it is true that with all the blessings of those days they had some curses !

One day there passed by a poor fisherman with an ass, and on it was a very large, wonderfully fine fish, a tunny, which was a load for the beast, and which was intended for the good monks of an abbey hard by, to whom the man hoped to sell it, partly for money and partly for blessings. When lo ! he was met by Il Bandito, as the signore was called, and, as you may suppose, the gentleman was not slow to seize the prey, which fell as it were like a roasted lark from heaven into his mouth. And to mock the poor fellow, the signore gave him a small bottle of wine to repay him.

Then the fisherman in his despair cursed the Bandito to his face, saying :

" May God forget and the devil remember thee, and as thou hast mocked my poverty, mayest thou pass centuries in worse suffering than ever was known to the poorest man on earth.

" Thou shalt live in groans and lamentations, thou accursed of God and despised by the devil ; thou shalt never have peace by day or night !

" Thou shalt be in utter wretchedness till thou shalt
see someone eat this fish.

> " ' In pietra cambiato
> E in pietra sarai confinata.' "

> " Thyself a stone, as thou shalt find,
> And in a stone thou'lt be confined,
> And the fish likewise a stone shall be
> Till someone shall eat it and set thee free ! "

And as the poor man prophesied, it came to pass: the
fish was changed into a stone, and the signore into a statue.
And the latter stood in a corner of the dining-hall, and
every day the fish was placed at dinner on the table, but
no one could eat it.

So three hundred years passed away, and the lord who
had inherited the castle had a beautiful daughter, who was
beloved by a young signore named Luigi, who was in
every way deserving of her, but whom the father disliked
on account of his family. So when he asked the father for
her hand, the latter replied that he might have it when he
should have eaten the stone fish, and not till then. So the
young man went away in grief.

One day, when this young gentleman was returning from
the chase bearing two fine hares, he met Virgilio, who
asked him to sell him one. Whereupon the young man
replied : " Oh, take your pick of them, and welcome ; but
say nothing about payment. Perhaps some day you may
do as much for me."

" Perhaps," replied Virgilio, " that day may be nearer
than you think. I never make my creditors wait, nor let
my debts run into arrears. What is there on earth which
you most desire ?"

" Truly it is something, signore, which I trow that neither
you nor any man can render possible, for it is to eat the
stone fish in the castle up there."

" I think that it can be managed," replied Virgil, with a
smile. " Take this silver box full of salt, and when the
fish is before you, sprinkle the salt on it, and it will grow
tender and taste well, and you can eat it. But first say
unto it :

> " ' Se tu pesce sei fatto
> Da un uomo, pel suo atto,
> Rimane sempre come sei,
> Ma se tu sei scongiurato,

O vere scongiurato,
Non restare pietra—ritorna come eri.' "

" Fish, if once a man thou wert,
Then remain e'en as thou art !
But if a fish, I here ordain
That thou become a fish again."

Then Luigi went to the castle, and was with much laughter placed before the fish, and the signore asked him if he would have a hammer to carve it with.

"Nay, I will eat it after my own fashion," he replied. "I do but beg permission to use my own salt, and say my own grace."

Then he sprinkled the salt and murmured the incantation, when the fish became soft and savoury, as if well cooked, and Luigi ate of it, till the signore of the castle was satisfied, and admitted that he had fulfilled the conditions—when lo! the fish became whole as before, and a stone again.

Then an old statue which was in the hall, in a corner of the wall, spoke and said:

"Now I am at peace, since the fish has been eaten.

" ' Dacche il pesce ha stato mangiato,
Io non sono più confinato.' "

And saying this, there went forth from the image a spirit-form, which vanished.

Then Luigi wedded the young lady of the castle, and Virgilio, who was present, promised the pair a happy life. And he said:

"Thou wilt be, O Luigi, the beginner of a family or race which, like the Holy Church, will have been founded on a stone, and while the Church lasts thy name shall endure."

The concluding paragraph refers to *pietra*, a stone, and to the text, well known to the most ignorant Catholic, " Petrus es et super hanc petram edificabo ecclesiam meam," whence it has been said that the Roman Church was founded on a pun, to which the reply might be, "And what if it was?" since there was no suspicion in early times that the pun, as a poetical form, might not be seriously employed in illustration. Dr. Johnson made the silly assertion

that a pun upon a proper name is the lowest kind of
wit, in which saying there is—as in many of his axioms
—more sound than sense ; nor is it altogether reverent
or respectful, when we reflect that both Christ and
Cicero used the despised figure of speech.   In one of
the tales in this collection the Emperor of Rome
speaks of a wheat-bran (*tisane*) which had been ordered
as " pigs' broth," which was exactly the term by which
Cicero alluded to the Verrine law, which also bears
that meaning.   As his adversary was a Jew, and the
query was, " What has a Hebrew to do with pig-broth,
or pork-soup ?"—*i.e.*, the law of Verres—the joke, with
all due deference to the law-giver Samuel, may be fairly
called a very good one.*

VIRGILIO AND THE BRONZE HORSE.

" The horse of brass."—MILTON.

" But evermore their moste wonder was
About this horse, since it was of brass.
It was of faerie as the peple seemed,
Diverse folk diversely han deemed."
CHAUCER : *The Squiere's Tale.*

One day Virgilio went to visit the Emperor, and not
finding him in his usual good temper, asked what was the
matter, adding that he hoped it would be in his power to do
something to relieve him.

Then the Emperor complained that what troubled him
was that all his horses seemed to be ill or bewitched,
behaving like wild beasts, or as if evil spirits were in them,
and that which grieved him most was that his favourite white
horse was most afflicted of all.

" Do not vex yourself for such a thing," replied Virgil.
" I will cure your horses and all the others in the city."

Then he caused to be made a beautiful horse of bronze,

* It may be noted that any clever modern juggler could perform the
miracle of the fish as here described.

and it was so well made that no one, unless by the will of Virgil (*senza il volere di Virgilio*), could have made the like. And whenever a horse which suffered in any way beheld it, the animal was at once cured.

All the smiths and horse-doctors in Rome were greatly angered at this, because after Virgil made the bronze horse they had nothing to do. So they planned to revenge themselves on him. And they all assembled in a vile place frequented by thieves and assassins, and there agreed to kill Virgil. Going to his house by night, they sought for him, but he escaped; so they, finding the bronze horse, broke it to pieces, and then fled.

When Virgil returned and found the horse in fragments he was greatly grieved, and said:

" The smiths have done this. However, I will yet do some good with the metal, for I will make from it a bell; and when the smiths hear it ring, I will give them a peal to remember me by."

So the bell was made and given to the Church of San Martino. And the first time it was tolled it sang:

> " Io ero un cavallo di bronzo.
> Dai nemici son' stato spezzato.
> Ma un amico che mi ama,
> In campana, mi ha cambiato
> E la prima volta che faro
> *Dindo, dindo!* dichiarero
> Chi e becco a caprone."

> " I was a horse of bronze, and tall.
> My enemies broke me to pieces small.
> But a friend who loves me well
> Had me made into a bell.
> Now here on high I proudly ring,
> And as I *dindo! dindo* sing,
> I tell aloud, as I toll and wave,
> Who is a *wittol* and a knave."

And all the smiths who had broken the horse when they heard the bell became as deaf as posts. Then great remorse came over them and shame, and they threw themselves down on the ground before Virgil and begged his pardon.

Virgil replied:

" I pardon you; but for a penance you must have six other bells made to add to this, to make a peal, and put them all in the same church."

This they did, and then regained their hearing.

This same story is told of Virgil in Comparetti's collection; but the present tale in the original has about it a smack or tone of the people which is wanting in the older version. Thus, the song of the bell is a peculiarly quaint conception, and probably an adaptation of some popular jest to the effect that bells proclaim the name and shame of certain persons. I have found that, with rare exception, the legends which I have given, as preserved by a class to whom tradition has a special value, are more complete in every respect than the variants drawn from other sources.

VIRGILIO AND THE BALL-PLAYER.

" Ima subit, resilit.   Ventosi prælia vento,
Exagitant juvenes : pellunt dextra atque repellunt,
Corruit ille iterùm ; levisque aere truditur aer ;
Ictibus impatiens obmurmurat ; altaque rursus
Nubila metitur cursu ; si forte globosa
Excipiant miserata globum patiturque repulsam."
P. CAR. DE LUCA, l. 19, EX. J. B. GANDUTIO : *Harpastum Florentinum ; or, On the Florentine Game of Ball* (1603).

" Jamque calent lusorum animi ; color ardet in ore
In vultu sanguis rubet, omnesque occupat artus ;
Præcipites hinc, inde ruunt, cursuque sequaci
Atque oculis sphæræ volucri vigilantibus justant."
PILÆ LUDUS : *The Game of Ball.   Auctor Incertus.
XVIth Century.*

" Now the playing at *ball* is allowed to Christians, because, like chess, draughts, billiards, bowls, *trucca*, and the like, it is a game of skill and not of chance, which latter makes illicit the most innocent play."— *Trattato di Giochi*, etc., *Rome*, 1768.

There was once upon a time a grand signore in Florence who had a clever servant, a young man, who, whether he had a fairy god-mother or a witch grandmother is not told ; but it is certain that he had such luck at playing ball as to always win and never lose.   And his master so arranged it with him as to bet and win immense sums.
One day Virgilio, being present at a match in which this

young man played, observed that there sat upon his ball a tiny invisible goblin, who directed its course as he pleased.

" Beautiful indeed is thy play," said Virgilio to the youth, "and thy ball—*ha tutta la finezza dell' arte*—hath all the refinement of its art ; but 'tis a pity that it is not an honest ball."

" Thou art mistaken," replied the young man ; but he reddened as he spoke.

" Ah, well," answered Virgil, " I will show thee anon whether I have made a mistake or told the truth. *A carne di lupo dente di cane*—A dog's teeth to a wolf's hide. My young friend and his old master need a bite or two to cure them of their evil ways."

There was in Florence the next day a great fair, or *festa*, and Virgil, passing where young people were diverting themselves, saw a very beautiful, bold-faced girl, who looked like a gipsy, or as if she belonged to some show, playing ball. Then Virgil, calling a goblin not bigger than a babe's finger,* bade it go and sit on the girl's ball, and inhabit and inspire it to win. It did so, and the girl won every time. Then Virgilio said to her :

" Come with me, and I will show you how to win one hundred crowns. There is a young man who carries all before him at playing ; thou must drive him before thee ; *e render la pariglia*— pay him back in his own money. Then shalt thou have one hundred crowns."

So they went together to the castle, and Virgilio said to the old signore :

" I have found a young girl who plays ball so well, that I am anxious to try her game against that of your young man."

" What will you bet on her ?" asked the old signore.

" A thousand crowns," replied Virgilio.

" Done !" was the response.

But when they met on the ground the youth and the girl fell in love at first sight to the last degree, and not being much troubled with modesty, told one another so—*schiettamente e senza preamboli*—plainly, without prelude, preamble, or preface, as is the way and wont of professionals or showpeople, wherein they showed their common sense of the value of time, which is to them as money.

* The original reduces this to a minimum—"Non più grande del dito mignole di un' bimbo di nascita."

Then they began to play, and it was in the old fashion, with two balls at once, each player tossing one to the other with the drum.* And it came to pass that in the instant that the two goblins beheld one another from afar they also fell in love. And as fairies and *folletti* do everything, when they will, a thousand times more rapidly than human beings, and as neither could or would conquer in the game, they both cried :

" Let us be for ever united in love."

So the two balls met with a bump half-way in their course and fell to the ground as one, while the fays embraced ; and at the same instant the youth and the girl, unable to suppress their feelings, rushed into one another's arms and began to kiss, and Virgilio and the old signore roared with laughter, the latter having a second attack of merriment when Virgilio explained to him the entire trick and plot.

Then, as it was a drawn game, the thousand crowns were by common consent bestowed on the young couple, who were married to their hearts' content, having one *festa* after another, at which all the guests went from bottle to bottle, even as the ass of a dealer in pottery goeth from door to door, or as the pig of Saint Antonio went from house to house. Amen !

Singularly enough, though this story comes from a witch source, there is in it no incantation addressed to a ball to make it always win for its owner; and, oddly enough, I recall one for that purpose, taken from an American burlesque of " Der Freyschütz," in which the demon-hunter calls on Zamiel the fiend to give him a magic ninepin or skittle-ball.

> " Sammy-hell, a boon I beg !
> By thy well and wooden leg !
> We ask for that 'ere bowling ball
> Wot'll knock down one and all.
> Give us all the queer ingredients,
> And we'll remain your most obedients !"†

---

* This is exactly like a small tambourine, but more strongly made.
† *The Boston Comic Annual,* 1828.

The idea of enchanted dice which always throw sixes and the like, forms the subject of stories possibly wherever dice are thrown or cards played, inasmuch as all gamblers who live or lose by chance are naturally led to believe that fortune can be invoked or propitiated. Hence the majority of them carry charms, fetishes, or amulets.

— —

VIRGIL AND THE GENTLEMAN WHO BRAYED.

" Braire comme des Asnes en plain marché."
Cf. LEROUX DE LUICY : *Facetieux Réveille-matin,*
pp. 103, 171. *XVII. Siècle.*

" Ha, Sire Ane, ohé !
Belle bouche, rechignez !
Vous aurez du foin assez
Et de l'avoine à-plantez !"
Chanson, XII. Siècle.

There were once assembled at the table of the Emperor many friends of Virgilio, who praised him highly. But there was also one who abused him bitterly, and called him an ass; and the word went forth to all the city, and much was said of it, and there was a great scandal over it.

When Virgil heard of it he smiled, and said that he thought he would ere long be even with the gentleman who had jackassed him ; and those who knew him were of the same opinion, for certainly the means of retaliation were not wanting to him.

Now, the Emperor had given to Virgilio an ass to ride, and the poet said to his patron that, if he would order that the animal might go or come wherever he pleased, he would show him some time a merry jest. To which the Emperor right willingly assented.

So one day there were many lords seated at the imperial table, and among them were Virgilio and his enemy. But what was the amazement of all save the magician when the servants, flying in, said that the ass of the Signore Virgilio had entered the door, and insisted on coming into the banqueting-hall.

" Admit him instantly," said the Emperor.

The ass came in as politely as an ass could. He bowed down before the Emperor and kissed his hand.

" He has come to visit his dear brother," remarked the enemy of Virgil.

" *That is true*," replied the ass ; and walking up to the gentleman, he stared him in the face, and said : " Good brother, good-day !"

The signore, bursting into a rage, tried to utter something, but only brayed—and such a bray, the King of the Asses himself could not have equalled it. There was a roar of laughter long and loud, revived again with each succeeding roar. At last, when there was silence, Virgil said :

" But tell me, Ciuchino, donkey mine, which of us three is the *real* ass ? For thy brother there says that I am one, and thou callest him brother, and yet from thy appearance I should say that thou art truly ' the one.'"

And the ass replied :

" Trust not to looks in this world, for in outward seeming there is great deceit. By their *voice* shall ye know them ; by their song, which is the same in all lands. For many are the languages of mankind, but there is only one among asses, for we all bray and pray in the same tongue."

" Truly," replied Virgilio, " thou almost deservest to become a Christian, and I will help thee to it." Saying this, he touched the donkey's nose with his wand, and his face became as the face of the gentleman, on whom there now appeared a donkey's head.

" Now we are indeed beginning to look more like ourselves," quoth the ass.

" *A un-ky—aunky—aunky—ooooh !*" brayed the gentleman.

" That, my lords," explained the donkey, " when translated into *volgare* from our holy tongue, is my brother's confession of faith, wherein he declares that he is the very Ass of Asses—the *summa summarum*, and the *somaro dei somari.*"

" That will do," exclaimed Virgilio ; and touching the ass and the signore, he restored to each his natural form and language. And the signore rushed out in a blind rage, but the ass went with proper dignity, first saluting the company, and then bowing low before the Emperor ere he departed.

" *Per Bacco !*" exclaimed the Emperor ; " the ass, it seems to me, hath better manners and a finer intellect than his brother."

" 'Tis sometimes the case in this world, your Imperial Highness, that asses appear to advantage—even at court."

VIRGIL AND THE GIRL WITH GOLDEN LOCKS.

> " And they had fixed the wedding day,
> The morning that must wed them both,
> For Stephen to another maid
> Had sworn another oath ;
> And with this other maid to church
> Unthinking Stephen went—
> Poor Martha, on that woeful day,
> A pang of pitiless dismay
> Into her soul was sent."
> WORDSWORTH : *Poems of the Imagination : The Thorn.*

There was once in Florence a wealthy widow lady of noble family, who had a son who was all that a parent could have wished, had he not been somewhat reckless and dissipated, and selfish withal, which he showed by winning the love of girls and then leaving them ; which thing became such a scandal that it caused great grief to the mother, who was a truly good woman. And so the youth, who was really a devoted son, seeing this, reformed his ways for a long time.

But as the proverb says, he who has once drunk at this fountain will ever remember the taste, and probably drink again. So it came to pass that in time the young gentleman fell again into temptation, and then began to tempt, albeit with greater care and caution—'tis so that all timid sinners go, resolving the next step shall be the last—till finally, under solemn promise of marriage, he led astray into the very forest of despair a very poor and friendless maid, who was, however, of exquisite beauty, and known as " the girl of golden locks," from her hair. It might be that the young man might have kept his word, but at an evil time he was tempted by the charms of a young lady of great wealth and greater family, who met him more than half-way, giving him to understand that her hand was to be had

8

for asking; whereupon he, who never lost a chance or left a fruit unplucked, asked at once and was accepted, the wedding-day being at once determined on.

Then the girl with the golden hair, finding herself abandoned, became well-nigh desperate. Ere long, too, she gave birth to a child, which was a boy. And it was some months after this, indeed, ere the wedding of the youth to the heiress was to take place, when one day, as the young unmarried mother was passing along the Arno, she met the great poet and sorcerer Virgil, who saw in her face the signs of such deep suffering, and of such a refined and noble nature, that he paused and asked her if she had any cause of affliction. So with little trouble he induced her to confide in him, saying that she had no hope, because her betrayer would soon be wedded to another.

" Perhaps not," replied Virgil. " Many a tree destined to be felled has escaped the axe and lived till God blew it down. On the day appointed we three will all go to the wedding."

And truly when the time came all Florence was much amazed to see the great Virgil going into the Church of Santa Maria with the beautiful girl with the golden hair and bearing her babe in his arms. So the building was speedily filled with people waiting eagerly to witness some strange sight.

And they were not disappointed. For when the bride in all her beauty and the bridegroom in all his glory came to the altar and paused, ere the priest spoke Virgil stepped forward, and presenting the girl with golden locks, said:

" This is she whom thou art to wed, having sworn to make her thy wife, and this is thy child."

Then the infant, who had never before in his life uttered a word, exclaimed, in loud, sweet tones:

> " Thou'rt my father, I'm thy son;
> Other father I have none."

Then there was a great scene, the bride being as one mad, and all the people crying, " *Evviva*, Virgilio! If the Signore Cosino* does not wed the girl with golden hair, he shall not escape us!" Which he did indeed, and that not so unwillingly, for the sight of the girl and the authority of

* Signore Cosino, or Cosimo. This name appears here for the first time in the story.

Virgil, the cries of the people, his own conscience, and the marvellous occurrence of the babe's speaking, all reconciled him to it.

So the wedding was carried out forthwith, and every soul in Florence who could make music went with his instrument that night and serenaded the newly-married pair.

And the mother was not a little astonished when she saw her son, who had gone forth with one bride, return with another. However, she was soon persuaded by Virgil that it was all for the best, and found in time that she had a perfect daughter-in-law.

I had rejected this story as not worth translating, since it presents so few traditional features, when it occurred to me that it indeed very clearly and rather curiously sets forth Virgil as a benevolent man and a sympathizer with suffering without regard to rank or class. This Christian kindness was associated with his name all through the Middle Ages in literature, and it is wonderful how the form of it has been preserved unto these our times among the people.

There is a tale told by one Surius, " In Vita S. Anselmi," cited by Kornmann in his work " De Miraculis Vivorum " in 1614, which bears on this which I have told. A certain dame in Rome not only had a child, *ex incestu*, but magnified her sin by swearing the child on the Pope, Sergius. The question being referred to Saint Anselm, he asked the babe, which had never spoken, whether his papa was the Pope. To which the infant answered, " Certainly not," adding that Sergius "*nihil cum Venere commercium habere*"—Anselmus, as is evident, being resolved to make a clean sweep of the whole affair and whitewash the Holy Father to the utmost while he was about it. Salverté would, like a sinner, have said that Anselm was perhaps a ventriloquist—*es kann sein !*

But let us not discuss it, and pass on, just mentioning that since I wrote the above I found another legend of an Abbot Daniel, of whom Gregory of Tours and Sophronius relate that he, having prayed that a certain lady might become a mother, and the request being complied with, some of Daniel's enemies suggested that other means as well as prayer, and much more efficacious, had been resorted to by the saint to obtain the desired result. But Daniel, inquiring of the babe when it was twenty-five days of age, was, *coram omnibus*, fully acquitted, the *bambino* pointing to his true father, and saying, with a nod, "*Verbis et milibus*"—*That's* the man! And the same happened to a Bishop Britius.   But Saint Augustine beats the record by declaring that, "It hath sometimes happened that infants as yet unborn have cried out *ex utero matris*—which is indeed a marvellous thing!" ("De Civitate Dei," III., c. 31).

And yet it seems to me that Justinus, Procopius, and several others, have done as well, if not better; for it is related by them that a number of orthodox believers who had their tongues cut out by Socinians, or Unitarians (whom the zealous Dean Hole declares are all so many little ungodly antichrists, or words to that effect), went on praying and preaching more volubly than ever.   The same is told by Evagrius of some pious women, but I do not offer this as a miracle, there being in it nothing improbable or remarkable.

That the Arians, or Unitarians, or Socinians have set tongues to wagging—especially the tongues of flame which play round the pyres of martyrdom—is matter of history — and breviary.   But that they have been the cause of making dead and tongueless Trinitarians talk, seems doubtful.   However, as the Canadian said of the ox: "There is no knowing what the subtlest form of Antichrist *may* do." *Passons !*

VIRGIL AND THE PEASANT OF AREZZO.

"Optuma tornæ
Forma bovis, cui turpe caput, cui plurima cervix,
Et crurum tenus a mento palearia pendent ;
Tum longo nullus lateri modus ; omnia magna,
Pes etiam, et camuris hirtæ sub cornibus aures.
Nec mihi displiceat maculis insignis, et albo,
Aut juga detrectans, interdumque aspera cornu,
Et faciem taurs propior, quæque ardua tota,
Et gradiens ima verrit vestigia cauda."
VIRGILIUS : *Georgics*, lib. iii.

"Annescis, pinguem carnibus esse bovem ?"
Epigrams by FRIED. HOFMANN (1633).

"*Fallium non facit philosophum nec
Cucullus monachum——*"

"Dress if you will
A knave in silk, he will be shabby still."

This legend, with several others, was gathered in or near Arezzo.

In the old times people suffered in many things far more than they now do, firstly from the signori, who treated them worse than brutes, and as if this were not enough, they were tormented by witches and wizards and wicked people who went to the devil or his angels to revenge them on their enemies. However, there were good and wise men who had the power to conquer these evil ones, and who did all they could to untie their knots and turn back their spells and curses on themselves, and the greatest of these was named Virgilio, who passed all his life in doing good.

Now, it is an old custom in Arezzo that when men take cattle to a fair, be it oxen or cows or calves, the animals are tricked out or ornamented as much as possible, and there is great competition as to this among the peasants, for it is a great triumph for a contadino when all the people

say that his beasts made the finest show of any in the place;
so that it is said a man of Arezzo will spend more to bedeck
his cattle for a fair than he will to dress his daughters for
a dance.

Now, there was a very worthy, honest man named Gianni,
who was the head or manager under the proprietor of a
very fine estate near Arezzo, and one day he went to the
fair to buy a yoke of oxen.   And what he cared for was to
get the best, for his master was rich and generous, and did
not much heed the price so that he really got his money's
worth.

But good as Gianni was, he had to suffer the affliction
which none can escape of being envied and hated.   For
wicked and spiteful souls find something to hate in people
who have not done them any wrong, and whom they have
not the least motive to harm—*nessunissimo motive*.

So the good Gianni found at the fair a pair of oxen which,
so far as ornament was concerned, were a sight to behold.
For they were covered with nets, and adorned with many
bands of red woollen stuff all embroidered with gold, and
bearing in gold the name of their owner, having many cords
and tassels and scarfs of all colours on their heads.   And
these cords were elaborately braided, while there hung a
mirror on the forehead of each animal, so that the elegance of
their decoration was the admiration of all who were at the fair.

Then Gianni, seeing the oxen, drew near, but before
making an offer, complimented the owner on their beautiful
appearance.   And this done, he said :

"All very fine, but in doing business for my patron I set
aside all personal friendship.   Your cattle are finely dressed
up, but how are the beasts themselves?   That is all that
I care to know, and I don't wish to have them turn out
as it happened to a man who married a wife because he
admired her clothes, and found, when she was undressed,
that she was a mere scrap, and looked like a dried cod-fish."

So they talked till the dealer took off the coverings, when
Gianni found, in fact, that the oxen had many faults.

"I am sorry to say, my friend," quoth Gianni, "that I
cannot buy them.   I have done you more than one good
turn before now, as you well know, but business is business,
and I am buying for my master, so good-day."

Then the owner was in a great rage, and grated his teeth,
and swore revenge, for there were many round about who

laughed at him, and he resolved to do evil to Gianni, who, however, thought no more of it, but went about the fair till he found a pair of excellent oxen which were the best for sale, and drove them home.

But as soon as they were in the stable they fell on the ground (dead). Gianni was in despair, but the master, who had seen the cattle and found them fine and in good condition when they arrived, did not blame him.

So the next day Gianni went to another fair, and bought another yoke of oxen. But when in the evening they were in the stable, they fell dead at once, as the others had done. Still the master had such faith in him, that although he was greatly vexed at the loss, he bade the man go once more to a fair and try his luck. So he went, and indeed returned with a magnificent pair, which were carefully examined; but there was the same result, for they also fell dead as soon as they were stabled.

Then the master resolved to go and buy cattle for himself, and did so. But there was the same result: these fell dead like the others. And the master, in despair and rage, said to Gianni:

"Here I give thee some money, and now begone, for I believe that thou bringest evil to me. I have lost four yoke of oxen, and will lose no more."

So Gianni went forth with his wife and children, in great suffering. And the master took in his place Dorione. This was the very man who had owned the oxen which Gianni would not buy, and he was one who was versed in all the sorcery of cattle, as such people in the mountains always are, and by his witchcraft he had brought all this to pass.

But under his care all the cattle flourished wonderfully, and the master was much pleased with him. But Gianni was in extreme misery, and could see nothing but beggary before him, because it was reported everywhere that he brought bad luck, and he could get no employment.

One day, when matters were at their worst with him and there was not even a piece of bread in his poor home, he met on the road a troop of cavaliers, at the head of whom were two magnificently clad gentlemen, and these were the Emperor and Virgil.

The poor peasant had stepped aside to admire the procession as it passed, when all at once Virgil looked with a piercing glance at Gianni, and cried:

" Man, what aileth thee that thou seemest so wretched ? For I read in thy face that thou sufferest unjustly, well-nigh to death."

Then Gianni told his story, and Virgil answered:

" For all of this there is a remedy. Now, come with me to the house of thy late master, where there is work to be done."

" But they will drive me out headlong," replied Gianni ; " I dare not go. And if I do not return to my family, who are all ill or starving to death, they will think that some disaster has befallen me."

" For that too there is also a remedy," said Virgil, with a smile. " Have no care. Now to thy master !"

" Why didst thou send away this honest man ?" asked Virgil of the *padrone*.

To which the master replied by telling all about the oxen. " Therefore, because he brought ruin into my house did I dismiss him."

" Well," replied Virgil, " this time thou didst get rid of an honest man and keep the knave. Now let us go and see to thy dead oxen."

So they went apace to the spot where the dead oxen had all been thrown, where the whole eight lay unchanged, for decay had not come upon them, they were as sound as ever.

Then Virgil exclaimed, as he waved his wand:

> " If ye are charmed, retake your breath !
> If you're bewitched, then wake from death !
> Speak with a voice, and tell us why,
> And who it was that made ye die !"

Then all the oxen came to life, and sang in chorus with human voices :

> " Dorione slew us for revenge,
> Because Gianni would not buy his oxen,
> Truly they were greatly ornamented,
> Yet withal were wretched, sorry cattle.
> So he swore to be revenged upon him,
> So he was revenged by witching us."

" You have heard the whole truth," said Virgil to the Emperor. " It is for you to condemn the culprit."

" I condemn him to be at once put to death," replied the Emperor. " Hast thou anything to add ?"

"Yes," said Virgil; "I condemn him to immediately become a goat after death."

Then Dorione was burnt alive for an evil wizard, and he leapt from the flame in the form of a black goat and vanished.

Gianni returned in favour to his master, and all went well with him evermore.

The very singular or unusual name of Dorione intimates a classical origin, and it is true that one of the Danaides, the bride of Cerceste, was called thus; but on this hook hangs no analogy. Dordione was the Roman god of blackguardism *pur et simple*, unto whom people made obscene offerings—which, according to sundry reviewers, might suggest the Dorian of a certain novel of the ultra Greek-æsthetic school, which had many admirers in certain circles, both in America and England. But it is very remarkable that wherever it occurs, be it in pagan antiquity or modern times, the name has always had a certain evil smell about it, a something fish-like and ancient, but not venerable. It is true that I have already given a legend of another Dorione, who was a protégé of Virgil; but even this latter example was sadly given to "rapacious appropriation." The Dorians were all a bad lot from a moral point of view, according to history.

It is remarkable that Dorione, who is a mountain shepherd or herdsman, is noted as a sorcerer. Owing to their solitary lives and knowledge of secrets in the medical treatment and management of cattle, this class in many countries (but especially in France and Italy) is regarded as consisting entirely of sorcerers. This is specially the case with smiths, farriers, and all who exercise the veterinary art.

It may also strike the reader as singular that Dorione

in the tale should be moved to such deadly vengeance, simply because Gianni would not buy his cattle, and preferred others. This is a very common and marked characteristic of Italians. If you examine a man's wares, talk about, and especially if you touch them, you will often be expected to buy as a matter of course. I have been seriously cautioned in a fair, by one who was to the manner born, against examining anything unless I bought it, or something. A few years ago, in Florence, a flower-girl asked an Englishman to buy of her ware, which he declined to do, and then changing his mind, bought a bouquet from another girl close by. Whereupon the first *floriste* stabbed and slew the second —to the great astonishment of the tourist!

There is an unconscious fitness and propriety in making the author of the "Georgics" so familiar with cattle that he is able to raise them from the dead. The chorus of oxen, accusing the evil-doer, is an idea or motive which also occurs in the story of Cain, as given in my "Legends of Florence."

The black goat is, and ever was in Italy, specially accursed as a type of evil. Witches are rarely described as riding brooms—their steed is the goat. Evil spirits, or souls of men accursed, haunt bridges in this form. The perverse and mischievous spirit of the animal, as well as his appearance, is sufficient to explain this.

THE GIRL AND THE FLAGEOLET.

> "Thus playing sweetly on the flageolet,
> He charmed them all; and playing yet again,
> Led them away, won by the magic sound."
>
> *De Pueris Hamleensibus*, 1400.

There is in the Toscana Romagna a place known as La Valle della Fame, or Valley of Hunger, in which dwelt a family of peasants, or three brothers and two sisters. The elder brother had married a wife who was good and beautiful, and she had given birth to a daughter, but died when the babe was only one year old. Then, according to the advice of the sisters and brothers, he married again, that he might have someone to take care of his child. The second wife was a pretty young woman, but after she had been wedded a year she gave birth to a daughter, who was very ugly indeed and evil; but the mother seemed to love her all the more for this, and began to hate the elder, who was as good and beautiful as an angel. And as her hatred grew she beat and abused the poor little girl all day long.

One morning the latter went into the woods to hide herself from her stepmother till it should be evening, when she could return home and be safe with her father and aunts. And while sitting all alone beneath a tree, she heard a bird above her singing so sweetly that she felt enchanted. It was a marvellous sound, at times like the music of a flute played by a fairy, then like a human voice carolling in soft tones, and then like a horn echoing far away. The little girl said:

"Oh dear, sweet bird, I wish I could pipe and play like you!"

As she said this the bird fell from the tree, and when she picked it up she found that it was a *zufolo*, or shepherd's flageolet, in the form of a bird. And when she blew on it, it gave forth such sweet sounds — *suone belle da rimanere incantati*—as would charm all who heard them. And as she practised, she found the art to play it seemed to come of itself, and every now and then she could hear a fairy voice in the sound speaking to her.

Now, this was a miracle which had been wrought by

Virgil the magician, who did so many wonderful things in the olden time.

In the evening she returned home and played on the bird-pipe, and all were charmed except the stepmother, who alone heard in the music a voice which said :

> " Though sweet thy smile, and smooth thy brow,
> Evil and cold at heart art thou ;
> I never yet did harm to thee,
> Yet thou hast beat me cruelly,
> And given me curses fierce and wild
> Because I'm fairer than thy child.
> Unless thou lettest me alone
> Henceforth, all ill shall be thine own,
> With all the suffering I have known."

But to the girl the pipe sang :

> " Sing to thy father, gently say
> That thou the morrow goest away,
> And tell him thou hast borne too long
> Great cruelty and cruel wrong ;
> For truly he was much to blame
> That he so long allowed the same ;
> But now the evil spell is broken,
> The time has come, the word is spoken !"

Then her father would fain have kept her, but the spell was on her, and she went out into the wide world playing on her pipe. And when she was in the woods, the birds and wild beasts came and listened to her and did as she bade ; and when she was in towns, the people gathered round and were charmed to hear her play, and gave her money and often jewels, and no one dared to say an evil word to her, for a spell was on her, and a charm which kept away evil.

So years passed by, and she was blooming into maiden-hood, when one day a young lord, passing with his mother, who was a woman as noble of soul and good as her son, paused to hear the girl play on her pipe and sing, for they thought the marvellous song of the *zufolo* was her voice.

Then the lady asked the girl if she would enter a monastery, where she would be educated and brought up to live in a noble family in return for her music. The girl replied that she had already a great deal of money and many jewels, but that she would be very glad to be better educated and advanced in life. So she entered the convent, where she was very happy, and the end thereof was that she became betrothed to the young signore, and great preparations were made for the wedding.

Now, the stepmother had but one idea in life, which was that her own daughter should make some great match, and for this purpose she was glad when the second went away, as she hoped, to become a mere vagabond, playing the flute for a living. But when she heard that the girl was very prosperous in a convent in Florence, and had not only been educated like a princess in the best society, but would ere long marry a nobleman, she became mad with rage ; and going to a witch, she paid her a great sum to prepare a powder which, if strewed in the path of the bride, would cause her prompt and agonizing pain, and after a time death in the most dreadful suffering. And this was to be laid in the way of the wedding procession. But on that morning the pipe sang :

> " Where'er on earth the wind doth blow,
> All leaves and dust before it go.
> Evil or good, they fly away
> Before its breath, as if in play ;
> And so shall it for thee this day,
> Ashes to ashes and dust to dust,
> And death to the witch, for so it must
> Ever happen as 'twas decreed,
> For death is the pay for an evil deed !"

Now, the bridegroom and all friends had begged the bride to play the flute as she walked in the wedding procession, and she did so, and it seemed to her that it had never played so sweetly. The stepmother was looking on anxiously in the crowd, and when the bride was just coming to the powder in the way, the wicked woman cried :

" Play louder—*louder !*"

The bride, to oblige everyone, blew hard, and a wind came from the pipe which blew all the powder into the stepmother's eyes and open mouth, and in an instant she gave a cry of agony, and then rolled on the ground, screaming ·

"*Il polvore !* I have swallowed the powder !"

And the flute played :

> " By thy mother I was slain ;
> A fairy gave me life again.
> I was killed for jealousy,
> And all as false as false could be.
> Now thou art dead and I am free."

And from that time the pipe played no more. But the young lady married the signore, and all went well with them.

And this was done by Virgil, who was ever benevolent.

The pipe, flute, or whistle, which fascinates all who hear it, is to be found in the traditions of all races, from the story of Orpheus onward; it even forms the plot of what is one of the prettiest tales of the Algonkin Indians,* and one which is probably original with them. What is also common to many is the conception of the one unjustly put to death turned into a musical instrument, which by a song betrays the murderer. But what is peculiar to this story is the power of the pipe to blow away enchantment and dissipate the witch-dust laid in the path. This is a very ingenious addition to the conception of the music and voice.

It is to be observed that sometimes rustic performers on the pipe, who have chiefly learned their music in the woods from birds and Nature, sometimes attain to a very fascinating and singular execution, quite unlike that which is heard from the most cultivated and artistic musicians. The celebrated Dr. Justinus Kerner, whom I have heard play, could produce on the Jew's-harp such results as would be deemed incredible. It struck me as an extraordinary expression of will and character beyond all teaching or imitation.

There are also many learned writers on music who are not aware that the human throat or voice is capable of producing sounds which are not, so to speak, *vocal*, but like those of the musical-box and several wind-instruments. This accomplishment is common among the blacks of the Southern States, and the perform-

* *Vide* "Algonkin Tales of New England," by Charles G. Leland.

ances, as I can bear witness, are most extraordinary and amazing. I once mistook the playing of two coloured boys in Nashville for the sound of a somewhat distant hand-organ. Even the twang of the banjo is thus rendered with startling accuracy. It is also true that reed-pipes can be made which, by combining the voice and blowing (as with the *mirliton*), give results which are very little known, but which probably suggested this and other tales in which the flute or pipe speaks. There are not many people who know the bull-roarer save as a boy's toy—that is to say, a mere flat bit of wood whirled round at the end of a cord—but by modification and combination, this or several of them produce sounds like those of an organ; and when heard by night at a distance, the effect is such as to fairly awe those who are ignorant of its cause. Finally, there is the application by a tube of air to the Æolian harp, etc., so as to produce tunes, which is very remarkable, and as little known as the rest—albeit, a traveller, who found something of the kind among the heathen, avowed his belief that something might be made of it. If people would only find out what resources they all have within themselves, or in very cheap and easily-made instruments, there might be far more music or art in the world than there now is. On which subject the reader may consult a book, written by me, and entitled "The Cheapest Musical Instruments," etc., now being published by Whittaker and Co., 2, White Hart Street, London.

LA BEGHINA DI AREZZO, OR VIRGIL AND THE SORCERESS.

> Beauty, when blent with wickedness,
> Ne'er yet did faile to bring distresse,
> A lovely thing that is an evil
> Is the own daughter of the devil ;
> And what was wicked from the first
> Unto the ende will be accurst,
> And sow, I trow, full sinfull seede,
> As ye may in this story reade !

Once upon a time there was in Arezzo a young woman of rare beauty, though of base condition. This girl showed from her earliest years a very strong character, great and varied talents or gifts, and the outward appearance, at least, of great piety and morality, so that she was always in church or absorbed in thought, which passed for pious meditation, while she never missed early Mass on a single morning.

It came to pass that a young gentleman who was rich, handsome, clever, and of good family, fell in love with her and offered marriage, but this she refused, to the amazement of all, especially her parents. But the girl declared that her disposition to religion made marriage objectionable to her ; and indeed at this time she so devoted herself to devotion that she hardly found time to eat. Yet as she did not become a nun, the Aretini, or people of Arezzo, called her the Beghina (Beguine), or Sister of Charity. Yet in doing all this she had ideas of her own, or more fish in her net than the world was aware of, for the peasants for her services and prayers, regarding her as a saint who could work miracles, because she indeed effected many strange things which seemed to them to be Divine, brought her many gifts, including money, all of which she declared would be devoted in future to the Madonna, regarding all which she had a great work in view.

At last her reputation for sanctity spread over all the country, and it was greatly increased when it was reported that so poor a girl had refused to marry a rich young gentleman, so that she was visited by the nobility, among whom she acquired great influence. And as she declared that it was her ambition to build a small church, and with it a home for herself, they, hoping that this would bring many pilgrims and greatly benefit the town, at last offered her thirty thousand crowns wherewith to carry out her pious purposes, which she with thanks and tears gratefully accepted.

The first thing which she did, however, was to build for herself a house, for which there was (secretly) constructed a long subterranean passage which led out to the river. Then she left her parents, saying that for the present she must lead a life of devotion in absolute seclusion. Then it was observed that from time to time young gentlemen were missing, and more than once their bodies were found floating in the river below the house of La Beghina, yet so great was her reputation for sanctity that no one connected their loss with her name.

So years passed by. But there was one who put no faith in her piety, and this was the signore whom she had refused, and with whom love for her had been succeeded by a bitter love of revenge, and by constant observation and inquiry he found out several things which greatly confirmed his suspicions. The first of these was the discovery of the bodies in the river; and being resolved to find out all the secrets of her house, he visited the mason who had built it, saying that he wished to erect a mansion for himself, and as he greatly admired that of La Beghina, would like to have one exactly like it. To which the old man replied that he was willing, but as every person who built a house kept certain details a secret to secure the safety of persons or property in certain emergencies, he must be excused if he withheld certain particulars. But the young signore replied that he had set his heart on having just such a house in every respect; that he himself wished to conceal all secrets, and, finally, that he would pay a round sum extra to have his desire fulfilled. This was an argument which the mason could not resist, and so explained to his patron every detail of the building, which made more than one mystery clear to him. And having learned the secret of the underground passage which led to the river, he began to watch it by night with great care; and found that the exit by the river was by a stone door, which was so artfully concealed in a rock by bushes that it was hardly perceptible.

One night, when it was very dark, the Signore Primo,

9

for such was his name, being on the watch, heard a noise
and saw the door open. Then there appeared the Beghina,
bearing or dragging a long package or bundle—*un involto*—
which she let fall into the flood. And at this sight the
signore could not restrain a cry of rage, understanding it
all, whereat La Beghina fled in terror into the passage,
leaving the door unfastened behind her. But the young
man, unheeding her, cast himself headlong into the river
after the bundle, which he succeeded in bringing to land,
and on opening it found the body of a young gentleman of
his acquaintance, who was not, however, quite dead, as he
had been merely heavily drugged, and who with care was
restored to life. And truly he had a strange tale to tell,
how he had been inveigled mysteriously and blindfolded,
and introduced to some unknown house where there was a
handsome woman, who, after he had made love with her,
drugged and robbed him, after which he became unconscious.

The Signore Primo conveyed his friend to his own home,
and after caring for his comfort and earnestly recommending
him to keep the whole matter a secret, went back to the
stone door, and finding it open, and having already learned
how the house was built, he entered, and concealed himself
where he could watch the mistress.

Early in the morning there came an elderly lady, who
with many tears and in great emotion told the Beghina that
she had a son gone to the war, and was in great fear lest he
should be slain, and that she had prayed to the Virgin that
he might return safe and sound; and that if the Beghina
by her piety would bring this to pass, she would at once
give her fifty gold crowns, and a very much larger sum in
case her son should come to her again soon and well. To
which La Beghina replied that she could go home with a
happy heart, for in a few days she should have her son with
her. So the lady departed.

Then the Beghina went into a secret room [but the
Signore Primo continued to follow and observe her] and
taking a pack of cards and a chain, she threw them against
the wall and beat on the ground, saying:

> " Diavoli tutti che siete nell' inferno !
> Scatenatevi, e damme portatevi,
> Un comando
> Vi voglio dare

Fino alla città
Dov'é la guerra dovete andare,
E salvare
Il figlio della signora ;
Che pochanzi damme e venuta
E portatelo subito a casa sua,
In carne anima ed ossa,
Se questa grazia mi farete
L'anima di quel giovane l'avrete !"

' All ye devils who are in hell,
Loosen your chains, and come at once to me !
I give you a command—
Go to the city where the war is waged,
And save the life of the son
Of the lady who came to me of late,
And bear him quickly to her in her home !
Bear him in flesh, soul and bones !
If ye do me this favour,
Ye shall have the soul of that youth !"

And when this was sung many devils appeared and saluted her as a queen.

The Signore Primo was indeed amazed and terrified, for now he realized that the Beghina was worse than he had supposed, or a witch of the most malignant kind. But he left the place, and going to the lady, told her all he had witnessed. Then she in great terror fainted, and when restored to life declared that, if anyone could save the soul of her son, he should have all her fortune.

Then the Signore Primo told her that if anyone could defeat the evil witch it was a great magician who by lucky chance was in Arezzo, and that she should seek him forthwith. This great magician was no other than Virgil. And as soon as the lady appeared, Virgil said :

" I know why thou art come."

Then he led her to the form of an angel clad in a rose-coloured garb, and, kneeling before it, said :

" O tu angelo del paradiso !
Ma benche puro e innocente sei stato
In questa terra confinata
Per salvare tua madre de suoi peccati,
Ma anche nel altro mondo
Ne fa sempre di peggio,
E per questo sarai liberato te
E confinata nel tuo posto,
La compagna e complice
Di tua madre la Beghina
La Beghina di Arezzo.

> Vai tu angelo beato !
> Da l'angelo custode !
> E dilli che invochi
> Lo spirito che di la ha piu comando,
> E potenza di volere salvare
> L'anima di quel giovane,
> Che la Beghina le ha venduta
> E cosi tu tu sarai in pace !"

> " Oh, thou angel of Paradise !
> Yet who, though pure and ever innocent,
> Hast been enchanted on this earth
> (Confined in the form which thou wearest),
> To save thy mother for her sins ;
> Yet even in another world
> She will ever be worse.
> Therefore thou shalt now be freed,
> And thy mother and her accomplice
> Be enchanted in thy place.
> The Beghina of Arezzo,
> Go, thou blessed angel,
> To the angel who guards thee !
> Bid him invoke the spirit who has most power
> To save the soul of that youth
> Whom the Beghina has sold ;
> Thus shalt thou be in peace."

At that instant there was heard a clap of thunder, the sound of a roaring storm, and there fell down before them two human beings like two corpses, yet not dead, and these were La Beghina and her companion witch.

Then there entered a grand sun-ray, which flashed in light upon the angel whom Virgil had summoned. And it said :

" The youth is saved, and whoever doeth good shall find good even in another world. Farewell ; I too am saved !"

Then the Beghina and her companion began to spit fire and flame, and they were condemned to wander for ever, without resting, from one town to another, ever possessed with a mad desire to do evil, but without the ability, for Virgil had taken the power from them.

This story seemed to me in the original, after more than one reading, so confused and high-flown, that I was on the point of rejecting it, when a friend who had also perused it persuaded me that, under all its dialectic mis-spellings, barbarous divisions of words, and manifest omissions (as, for instance, what became of the Sieur Buridan of the Italian Tour de Nesle, who was so nearly drowned), there was a legend which was manifestly the mangled version of a far better original. Therefore I have translated it very faithfully, and would specify that there was from me no suggestion or hint of any kind, but that it is entirely of the people.

Firstly, it may be observed that the long-continued, deliberately-contrived hypocrisy of the Beghina, as well as the Red Indian-like vindictiveness of the hero, is perfectly Italian or natural. The construction of secret passages and hiding-places in buildings is almost common even to-day. The idea of a holy spirit who undergoes a penance, *confinata*, or enchanted and imprisoned in a statue to redeem her mother, is also finely conceived, as is the final statement that the Beghina and her mysterious accomplice, who is so abruptly introduced, are condemned to wander for ever, tormented with a desire to do evil which they are unable to satisfy.

The Beghina is an incarnation of hypocrisy, deceit, lust and treachery. The four symbols for these were the serpent, wren, chameleon, and goose—the latter because a certain Athenian named Lampon was wont to swear "by the goose!" and then break his oath. Possibly the origin of the saying "He is sound upon the goose" is derived from this.

But I sometimes think that to decide between tradition or borrowing and independent creation is beyond the folklore of the present day.

THE SPIRIT OF THE SNOW OF COLLE ALTO.

> "And hence, O virgin mother mild,
> Though plenteous flowers around thee blow,
> Not only from the dreary strife
> Of winter, but the storms of life,
> Thee have thy votaries aptly styled
> Our Lady of the Snow."
>
> WORDSWORTH: *Tour on the Continent.*

Once in the olden time, in Colle Alto, the snow fell in one night many yards in depth, and the people were astonished and frightened when they awoke in the morning at beholding it spreading far and wide. Many tried to shovel it away, but were discouraged, because, as they removed it, as much came in its place, so that at last they all remained at home, for no one could pass through the snow, and they were afraid of being buried in it.

But the poor, who had but scant provision in their homes, suffered from hunger. And among these was a good man to whom his five children pitifully cried:

"*Babbo-il pane !*"—Papa, give us bread !

And he replied :

"My children weep, and I must risk my life to save them." And looking out, he cried unthinkingly :

> "And yet the snow is very beautiful !
> O Spirit of the Snow—no mortal knows
> How beautiful thou art. Be kind to us !"

As he said this there appeared before the window, and then among them, a lady of marvellous beauty and dazzling brightness, all clad in white, who said :

"What wilt thou have, since thou hast invoked me ?"

"Lady," replied the astonished peasant, "I know not who thou art, nor did I call thee !"

"Yes ; in thy speech thou didst pronounce my name in invocation, and to those who do that, and deserve it, I give my aid. Follow me !"

---

* In the original "La Dea della Neve." In Italy the word "goddess" is more familiarly and frequently used than it is by peasants in England, but rather with application to great and good spirits of any kind than to deities.

The poor man was surprised and bewildered, but he followed, while trembling, the lady.

And she spoke in a voice which was heard in every house far and near in Colle Alto :

" Let him who will come forth without fear, for this good man hath opened unto you the way. But it is only the poor who can do this, because, while they have suffered and starved in their homes, not one of the rich who dwell here have made any effort to relieve the suffering, therefore none of them shall come forth till the snow is gone."

Then all the poor folk found that they could walk upon the snow,* which was a pleasure, but the gentlefolk could not stir a step out of doors till it melted. And it vexed them sorely to stand at their windows and see women and children running merrily over the snow, so that some of them cursed their wealth, and wished that they were of the poor and free.

For fifteen days not a flake of snow disappeared, and then all at once it went away, and the poor, on opening their windows in the morning, found the sun shining, and a warm breeze blowing, which was scented as with roses, and the streets and roofs all as clean as if new. Then all the poor gathered every man a stone, and meeting in one place, they there built a little church (*chiesina*), and called it the Chapel of the Goddess of the Snow, and adored her as if she had been the Madonna or a saint.

Then for some time, as usually happens, there was great enthusiasm—*vie un gran fanatismo*—and then again all was gradually forgotten. So with the Goddess of the Snow : as years went by people talked about her less and less, and she was even ridiculed by those who were of evil hearts and souls, such as abuse and ill-treat their benefactors—as was shown by a certain waggoner, who found himself one day many miles afar from any house, when snow began to fall. And with it he began to curse, so as to shock even a sinner ; whereupon it drifted round him so deeply that he with his waggon could get no further. And so he kept on blaspheming. His poor starved horses looked at him with meaning, as if calling his attention, and then cast their glances to the wall or a shrine, whereon was depicted an image of the Goddess of the Snow, as if begging him to

* This was probably due to the very rapid formation of a frozen crust. *Vide* Nansen's work.

notice or to appeal to it. And the wretch beholding it, swore
worse than ever, saying that she was an accursed (witch).

He had not time to pronounce the word ere he sank
down (into the snow), so that only his head remained uncovered. And his horses also were in the same place, but
a warm wind began to blow. And so the man remained
fast, freezing and starving, for three days, but it did not
make him repent, and he swore more than ever.

Then, on the third day, Virgil, the great magician, passed
by, and was amazed at seeing the horses quietly feeding on
grass in the warm sunshine, while a pleasant breeze was
blowing, and close by them a man buried to his neck in the
snow. And being questioned, the waggoner replied that he
was thus buried for blaspheming the Goddess of the Snow.

Virgil asked him if he repented it.

" I will repent," replied the waggoner, " when I see it
proved by a miracle—but in miracles I put no faith."

" Well," said Virgil, " pray to the goddess to pardon you.
Pray with me thus :

> " ' Dea della neve che sei candida,
> E pura la sera a lume di Luna,
> Un bel lenzuola candida sembra
> Distesa sulla terra e sui tetti :
> Col sol sei splendida e rilucente :
> E vero ti sprezzai, ma non fu io
> Fu il diavolo che mia ha tentato.
> E spero da oggi non mi tentera più,
> Perche amo essere in grazia tua e come,
> Stella tu sei bella, sei bianca,
> Sei candida e pura e sei l'unica
> Che fra le Dee non faccia altro
> Che bene, e mai male, bella dea !
> O dea della Neve tu che sei
> L'unico mio pensiero, unica speme,
> Unica mia speranza—da ora avanti,
> Tutti e tutti miei pensieri
> Saranna a te rivolti—neppur da casa
> Mi partero prima di fare a te
> Una preghiera che possa spiegar
> Il mio pensier al dar farsi
> Partir o restar a te domandero,
> A te domandero che devo far.
> Tutto questo a te rivago
> E sempre rivolgero se tu mi perdonerai
> E questa grazia mi farai
> Che son pentito assai
> Di farmi sortir di qui

Che tanto sofro—farmi sortir—
Sano e salvo che io posso tornar
In braccio alla mia famiglia !
Che da tre sere mi chiamami desidera !' "

"O Goddess of the Snow, who art so white
And pure that in the evening, in the light
Of the full moon, thou seem'st to be
A fair bright sheet spread over earth and roofs
(That all may sleep beneath it and in peace),
But who art splendid with a ruddy glow
In the rising sunlight—it is very true
That I did scorn thee, yet it was not I.
For 'twas the devil in truth who tempted me,
And who, I hope, will never tempt me more,
Because I fain would be in thy good grace !
O Star, thou art most beautiful and white,
Candid and pure, because thou truly art
Among the goddesses the only one
Who only doest good, and by no chance
Art sullied with aught evil—O most fair !
O Goddess of the Snow, who art indeed
My only thought, my only hope in life,
My only trust from now till ever on !
My all and every thought shall turn to thee
Nor will I ever from my house depart
Till I have offered thee a fervent prayer,
In which I'll lay before thee all my soul,
And ask of thee what 'tis that I must do,
And if I must remain or mend my way !
All this do I repeat to thee again,
And ever will repeat if thou wilt but
Pardon my sin and grant to me the grace,
Having repented from my very heart,
To draw me from this place of suffering,
That safe and sound I may return again
Unto the embraces of my family,
Who for three nights have called to me in vain !"

He had hardly ended this invocation before a voice replied :

"Alzati e cammina e porta con te
Anche i tuoi animali ma non bestemmiare
Mai più, perche questaltra voltra
Sprafonderesti nell' abisso dove
Gnenti (niente) più bastarrebbe per levarti
Dall' inferno." . . .

"Rise and depart, and take away with thee
Thy beasts in peace, but never more blaspheme,
Because another time thou'lt sink so deep
To the abyss that nothing will avail
To draw thee out, for thou wilt fall to hell !"

Then the waggoner took his horses and rode home at double-quick speed. He related to all what had happened, and the chapel was again restored with the image of the goddess. But even among the experienced (*conoscenti*) none could tell him [for a long time] who was the one who had taught him what to do. But it was at last made known to them that it was the great magician and the great poet Virgil, because the Goddess of the Snow and Virgil are good spirits.*

So this waggoner, from being evil became so good that one could not find his equal.

Our Lady of the Snow, or Maria vom Schnee, is one of the more familiar avatars of the Madonna all over Middle and Northern Italy and Germany, including Austria and Switzerland. One of the commonest halfpenny or *soldo* pamphlets sold at corners in Florence is devoted to her. A very famous Madonna of the Snow is that of Laveno, to whom there is a special festival. Wordsworth has devoted a poem to her.

In the legend which I have given the general resemblance of the whole to the Madonna tales, as in the building a chapel, the threat of hell, and the punishment for profanity, suggest that it is borrowed from a Catholic source. This I doubt, for several reasons. It is of the witch witchy, and heathen, as shown by calling the lady a goddess, and especially by the long *scongiurazione* or evocations in which the sorcerer takes such delight that for him they form the solid portion of the whole, possibly because they are, if not actually prohibited, at least secret things, cryptic or of esoteric lore. Now, be it noted that wherever, as regards other legends, as in that of the Madonna del Fuoco, given in my " Etrusco-Roman Legends," the witch claims that her tradition has been borrowed by the priests,

* Anime.

she is probably in the right. But what gives colour to the opinion that this Madonna is of heathen origin is the fact that in the Old German mythology, as Friedrich declares, there is a deity known as Lady Holde, Holle, or Hilda (who may be again found in the Christian Maria), who is a kind and friendly being. She was the Goddess of the Snow, hence it is commonly said when it snows that Lady Holde is making her bed and shaking out the feathers. As there is no German supernatural character, especially in the fairy mythology, which does not exist in Northern Italy, it would be very remarkable indeed if such a widely known and popular spirit as the Lady of the Snow had not been known there long before the Christian Madonna. I would add that this is purely and literally a legend of the people, not asked for by me, and not the result of any inquiry or suggestion.

The Madonna della Neve is especially honoured at Laveno, where there is an annual procession in her honour. I am indebted to the kindness of the Rev. Arthur Mangles, who knew that I was interested in the subject, for the following, translated by him from some small local book there published :

THE LEGEND OF LA MADONNA DELLA NEVE.

In the fourth century there lived in Rome two devout people, husband and wife, who, having no children, prayed to the Virgin that she would indicate to them the best way in which to leave their money.

On the night of the fifth of August, A.D. 352, the Virgin appeared to them and told them to build a church upon the summit of the Esquiline Hill, in Rome, exactly upon the area then covered with snow.

The Pope had the same vision of the Virgin, with the same communication as that of the husband and wife.

Therefore he sent to the place indicated a messenger, accompanied by many priests, who found the snow.

The husband and wife forthwith built a handsome church upon the spot.

The church, which is now on the same hill, and on the foundation of the early edifice, is that of Santa Maria Maggiore.

Snow in August is rather a thin miracle whereon to found a legend, or a church, but it may pass. The one which I have translated seems to me to have a greater air of antiquity, with its retribution and beautiful Latin-like invocation to the Spirit of the Snow.

THE MAGICIAN VIRGIL; A LEGEND FROM THE SABINE.

The following tale was obtained by Miss Roma Lister from the vicinity of Rome, and from an old woman who is learned in sorcery and incantations. It begins with the note that, on February 8, 1897, it was taken down as given, literally word for word, and I translate it accordingly verbatim.

There were a husband, a wizard, and his wife (who was a witch), who had a beautiful daughter, and a house with a fine garden which was full of broccoli — oh, the finest broccoli in the world!

And opposite to this, or overlooking the garden, dwelt two women, and one of these was *incinta*, or with child, and she said to the other woman:

"*Comare*,* how I would like to have two broccoli from the magician's garden. They're so nice!"

"Yes, *comare*, but how to get them? It would be dangerous!"

* *Comare*, godmother, gossip, a familiar form of address. In French *commère;* Scotch, *cummer*.

"*La cosa si farà*—it can be done, at midnight when the sorcerer is asleep, by stealing a little."

And so they did, for at midnight both went with a sack, climbed over the iron gate, and, having filled their bag, went away.*

In the morning the magician Virgilio went to his garden and found that many broccoli were gone. In a rage he ran to his wife, and said : "What's to be done ?"

She replied : "This night we'll set the cat on guard upon the gate."

Which was done. That evening, *fra il lusco e il brusco,*† the one said :

"Ah, gossip, this night it can't be done."

"And why not, my dear ?"

"Why ! Because they've set a guard."

"Guard ! An old cat, you mean. Are you afraid of her ?"

"Yes, because she mews when she sees something."

"I say, I'll tell you what to do. Take a bit of meat, and when she opens her mouth to mew, pitch it in. That'll keep her jaws quiet while we pick the broccoli."

And so it was done, and they got away with another bagful of broccoli.

In the morning the *mago* Virgil found that he had been robbed again. He complained again to his wife, who said :

"Well, to-night we will put the dog on."

Said and done. But the dame at the window was on the watch. And seeing all, she said :

"No broccoli to-night, gossip. This time they've put the dog to look out."

"Oh, bother the dog ! When he opens *his* jaws to bark, I'll pitch in a good bit of hard cheese. That'll keep him quiet."

Said and done again. The next morning the magician found a still greater disappearance of broccoli from his garden.

"The thing is becoming serious," he said. "To-night I will watch myself."

With that he went to his gate and remained there, looking closely at all those who passed by. So he said to the first :

"What is your trade ?"

---

* "Andiede bene"—Cut their lucky.

† "I find this is a peasant's expression for the 'gloaming.' *Verso sera* was the explanation" (Roma Lister). Literally "between the dim and the dark." "Entre chien et loup"—the owl's light.

" I'm a carpenter."

" Pass on," replied the magician. "You're not the man I want."

There came another.

" What's your calling ?"

" I'm a tailor."

" Pass on—*non fate per me* " (you won't do).

There came a baker. He was not wanted. But the next was a digger of ditches and of graves—a *fossaruolo*—and the wizard cried :

" Bravo ! You're my man ! Come with me ; I want you to dig a pit in my garden."

So the poor man went, for he was as much frightened at the terrible face and stature of the wizard as he was in hope of being paid. And being directed, he dug a hole nearly as deep as the magician was tall.

" Now," said the master, "get some light sticks and cover over the pit while I stand in it, and then strew some twigs and leaves over it, with a few leaves to hide the top of my head."

It was done, and there he stood covered. The ditcher, or sexton, hurried away, glad that he had dug this strange grave for another, and not for himself.

Evening came, and the gossip looked out.

" Good ! There is not even a dog on guard. Come, let us hurry ! This time we will take all that remains of the broccoli."

Said and done. And when they had gathered the last plant, the gossip cried :

" See what beautiful mushrooms ! Let us pick them."

She had seen the two ears of the sorcerer, which peeped out uncovered. So she took hold of one and pulled.

" It will not come out !" she cried. "Do thou pull at one, while I draw at this."

Each pulled, when the magician raised his awful face and glared at them. *E sorte fuori la terribile testa del mago !*

" Now you shall die for robbing me !" he exclaimed.

They were in a fine fright. At last Virgil said :

" I will spare thy life, if thou wilt give me all thou bearest —all within thee."

She consented, and they departed. After a time she became a mother, and the magician came and demanded the child. And as she had promised it, she consented to give it to him, but begged that it might be left to her for a time.

"I will give it to thee for seven years," he replied.

Saying this, he left her in peace for a long time.

So the child, which was a boy, was born, and as he grew older was sent every day to school.

One morning the magician met him, and said:

"Tell thy mother to remember her promise."

Then he gave the child some sweets, and left him.

When at home the boy said:

"Mamma, a gentleman met me to-day at the door of the school, and said to me that I should tell you to remember your promise. Then he gave me some comfits."

The poor mother was in a great fright.

"Tell him, when you next meet him," she answered, "that you forgot to give his message to me."

The next day the boy met the magician, and said to him that he had forgotten all about it, and told his mother nothing.

"Very well, tell her this evening, and be sure to remember."

The mother heard this, and bade him tell the sorcerer the same thing again.

When he met the magician Virgil again and told the same story, the latter smiled, and said:

"It seems that thou hast a bad memory. This time I will give thee something by which to remember me. Give me thy hand."

The boy gave his hand; the magician bit into one finger, and as the child screamed, he said:

"This time thou wilt remember."

The boy ran yelling home.

"See what has happened to me, *brutta mammacia*—you naughty mamma—because I did what you bade, and told the gentleman that I forgot."

The poor woman, hearing herself called *brutta mammacia*,* was overcome with grief and shame, and said, "*Vai bene*—I will tell him myself." So the next day she took the child and gave him to the magician, who led him to his home.

But when his wife, the witch, beheld the boy, she cried:

"Kill that child at once, for I read it in his face that he will be the ruin of our daughter Marietta!"

* Literally "ugly mammy."

But the magician declared that nothing would induce him to harm the boy, so the little fellow remained, and was treated by the master like a son. In due time he became a tall and handsome young man, and he was called Antonuccio. But the witch always said:

" We should kill and eat him, for he will be the ruin of our Marietta."

At last the magician, weary of her complaints, said:

" *Bene!* I will set him a task, and if he cannot accomplish it, that same night shall he be slain."

Now, Antonuccio, as he slept in the next room, had overheard all this.

The next morning the magician took the youth to a stable which was very large and horribly filthy, such as no one had ever seen, and said:

" Now, Antonuccio, you must clean this stable out and out—*bene e bene*—repave it on the ground, and whitewash all above it; and moreover, when I speak, an echo shall answer me."*

The poor youth went to work, but soon found that he could do next to nothing. So he sat down in despair.

At noon came Marietta, to bring him his lunch, and found him in tears.

" What's the matter, Antonuccio?"

" If you knew that I am to be killed this evening——"

" What for?"

" Your father has said that unless I clean out the stable, and pave and whitewash it to the echo——"

" Is that all? *Sta allegro*—be of good cheer—I'll attend to that."

Marietta went home, and stealing in on tip-toe while the sorcerer slept, softly carried away his magic wand, and with a few words cleaned out the stable to the echo, and Antonuccio was delighted.

In the evening the magician came, and finding the stable clean as a new pin, was much pleased, and kissed him and took him home. The witch-wife was furious at learning that the stable had been cleaned, and declared that Marietta had done it, and ended by screaming for his life. At last the wizard said:

---

* This conveys the idea of complete cleanliness, as well-scoured bare walls and floors are most easily vibrated by currents of air, and consequently most echoing.

" To-morrow I will set him another task, and should he fail in that, he shall surely die."

The next morning he led the youth into a dense forest of mighty trees, and said :

" Thou seest this wood ? In one day it must be all cut down and cleared away to a clean field, in which must be growing all kinds of plants which are to be found in the world."

And Antonuccio began to hew with an axe, and worked well, but soon gave up the task in despair.

At noon came Marietta with her basket.

" What, crying again ! What is the trouble to-day ?"

" Only to clear away all this forest, make a clean field, and plant it with all the herbs in the world."

" Oh, well, eat your lunch, and I will see about it. It is lucky that it is not something difficult !"

She ran home, got a magic wand, and went to work. Down the trees came crashing—away they flew ! 'Twas a fine sight, upon my word ! And then up sprouted all kinds of herbs and flowers, till there was the finest garden in the world.

In the evening came the magician, and was well pleased at finding how well Antonuccio had done the work. But when his wife heard all, she raged more than ever, declaring that it had all been done by Marietta, who was destined to be ruined by the boy.

" Well, well !" exclaimed the wizard. " If you will give me no peace, I must put an end to this trouble. I will give the boy nothing to do to-morrow—he may remain idle—and in the evening I will chop off his head with this axe."

Antonuccio heard this speech as he had done the others, and this time was in despair. In the morning Marietta found him weeping.

" What is the matter, Antonuccio ?"

" I am to do no work to-day, but this evening I am to have my head chopped off."

" Is that all ? Be of good cheer—*sta allegro*—I will see what can be done."

She put the pot on the fire to boil, and began to make the macaroni. When she had cooked a great deal, they fed all the furniture, pots and pans, chairs and tables, to please them, and induce them to be silent—all except the hearth-brush, whom by oversight they forgot.

10

"And now," said Marietta, "we must be off and away; it is time for us to go!"

So away they ran. After a while the wizard and his wife returned and knocked at the door. No answer. They rapped and called, but got no reply. At last the hearth-brush cried:

"Who's there?"

"Marietta, open the door—it is I."

"I'm not Marietta. She has run away with Antonuccio. First they fed everybody with ever so much macaroni, but gave me none."

Then the witch cried to the wizard:

"Hurry—hasten—catch them if you can!"

The good man did as he was bid, and began to travel—travel far and fast.

All at once, while the lovers were on their way, Antonuccio turned his head and saw afar their pursuer on a mountain-road, and cried:

"Marietta, I see your father coming."

"Then, my dear, I will become a fair church and thou shalt be the fine sexton (*sacristano*). And he will ask thee if thou hast seen a girl and youth pass, and thou shalt reply that he must first repeat the Paternoster and not the Ave Maria. And if he asks again, tell him to say the Ave Maria and not the Paternoster. And then, out of patience, he will depart."

So it came to pass, and the wizard was deceived. When he had returned, his wife asked him what he had seen.

"Nothing but a church and a sacristan."

"Stupid that you are! The church was Marietta—fly, fly and catch them!"

So he set forth again, and again he was seen from afar by Antonuccio.

"Marietta, I see your father coming."

"Good. Now I will become a beautiful garden, and thou the gardener. And when my father comes and asks if thou hast seen a couple pass, reply that thou weedest lettuces, not broccoli. And when he asks again, answer that thou weedest broccoli, not lettuces."

So it all came to pass, and the wizard, out of patience, returned home.

"Well, and what did you see?" inquired his wife.

"Only a garden and a gardener."

"*Ahi—stupido!* Those were the two. Start! This time I will go with you!"

After a while Antonuccio saw the two following, and gaining on them rapidly.

"Marietta, here come your father and mother. Now we are in a nice mess."*

"Don't be afraid. Now I will become a fountain fair and broad, like a small lake, and thou a pretty pigeon, to whom they will call; but for mercy's sake don't let yourself be taken, for then all will be over with us."

The wizard and his wife came to the fountain and saw the dove, and tried to inveigle and catch it with grain. But it would not be caught, neither could the witch quench her thirst with the water. So, finding that both were beyond her power, she cried in a rage:

> "When Antonuccio kisses his mother,
> He'll forget Marietta and every other."

So, when the parents were gone, the pair set forth again, till they came to a place not far from where the mother of Antonuccio lived.

"I will go and see my mother," he said.

"Do not go, for she will kiss thee, and thou wilt forget me," replied Marietta.

"But I will take good care that she does not kiss me," answered Antonuccio. "Only wait a day."

He went and saw his mother, and both were in great joy at meeting again, but he implored her not to kiss him. And being weary, he went to sleep, and his mother, unheeding his request, kissed him while he slept. And when he awoke, Marietta was completely forgotten.

So the curse of the witch came to pass. And he lived with his mother, and in time fell in love with another girl. Then they appointed a day for their wedding.

Meanwhile, Marietta lived where she had been left, and made a fairy friend who knew all that was going on far and near. One day she told Marietta that Antonuccio was to be married.

Marietta begged her to go and steal some dough (from the house of the bride). The friend did so, and Marietta made of the dough two cakes in the form of puppets, or children, and one she called Antonuccio and the other Marietta.

* "Ora siamo belli fritti."

Then, on the day of the feast, the first day of the wedding, she begged her friend to go and put the two puppets on the bridal table.

She did so, and when all were assembled, the puppet Marietta began to speak :

> " Dost thou remember, Antonuccio,
> How, when my father brought thee to his house,
> My mother wished to take away thy life ?
> And how he bade thee sweep the stable clean ?"

And the other replied :

> " Passing away, passing away,
> Well do I remember the day." *

Then Marietta sang :

> " Dost thou remember, Antonuccio,
> How 'twas I aided thee to clear the field ?"

He replied :

> " Passing away, passing away,
> Well do I remember the day."

She sang again :

> " Dost thou remember how thou hadst no work
> Upon the day when they would murder thee,
> And how we fled together to escape ?"

He replied :

> " Passing away, passing away,
> Well do I remember the day."

Meanwhile the true Antonuccio, who was present, began to remember what had taken place.

Then the puppet Marietta sang again :

> " Dost thou remember how I was the church,
> And thou of it becam'st the sacristan ?"

He answered :

> " Passing away, passing away,
> Well do I remember the day."

> " Dost thou remember how I was a garden,
> And how thou didst become its gardener ?"

---

* " Passegiando, passegiando,
  Me ne vengo, ricordando,"
or " walking away."

> " Passing away, passing away,
> Well do I now remember the day."

> " Dost thou remember how I was a fountain,
> And thou a pigeon flying over it ?"

> " Passing away, passing away,
> Well do I now remember the day."

> " Dost thou remember, Antonuccio,
> How 'twas my mother laid a curse on me,
> And how she said before she went away—
> ' When Antonuccio kisses his mother
> He'll forget Marietta and every other ?' "

> " Passing away, passing away,
> Well do I now remember the day."

Then Antonuccio himself remembered it all, and rising from the table, ran from the house to where Marietta dwelt —and married her.

This story, adds Miss Lister, is somewhat abbreviated, since in the original the puppet Marietta, for the edification of all assembled, repeats the whole story.

It will be at once observed that there is in all this no special reference to Virgil as a character, as he appears in other legends, the reason being that the old woman who narrated it simply understood by the word Virgilio *any* magician of any kind. So in another tale a youth exclaims, "Art thou what is called *a* Virgil ?" This is curious as indicating that the word has become generic in Italian folk-lore. But Virgil is even here, as elsewhere on the whole, a man of kind heart. He has had his garden robbed and his daughter stolen, but he displays at all times a kindly feeling to Antonuccio. It is his wife, the witch, who shows all the spite.

Nor is this, like the rest, a witch-story which belongs entirely to esoteric, unholy, or secret lore, specially embodying instruction and an incantation. It is a mere nursery legend, the commonest of Italian

fairy-tales, to be found in all collections in whole or in
part. It is spread all over Europe, and has found its
way through Canadian-French to the Red Indians of
North America—apropos of which I would remind a
certain very clever reviewer and learned folk-lorist
that because many French tales are found among the
Algonkin tribes, it does not follow, as he really intimates, that the said Redskins have no other traditions.

But even in this version there are classic traces.
The cleaning out of the Augean stables by Hercules is
one, and the spell of oblivion another.

I do not know what the origin may be of the head
of the sorcerer rising from the surface of the earth
with ears like mushrooms, implying that they were
very large ; but I find in an edition of the " Meditations
of Saint Augustin," Venice, A.D. 1588, illustrated with
rude, quaint pictures, one in which the holy father is
kneeling before a crucifix, while there rises from the
ground before him a great and terrible head with one
very long ear. By it lies the usual skull, one-fifth its
size. Were two women substituted for the saint, it
would be a perfect illustration of the strange scene
described in the story. It is, to say the least, a singular
coincidence.

This story is therefore of some value as indicating
that the general term of sorcerer, magician or wizard,
is used as a synonym for Virgil, or *vice versâ*. As
Lucan writes in his " Pharsalia " : " Nec sua Virgilio
permisit nomina soli."*

It is worth noting that there is in the Museum of
Florence an Etruscan mirror on which Mercury and
Minerva are represented as looking at a human head
apparently coming from the ground. It may be that

* M. Annæi Lucani, " De Bello Civili, vel Pharsaliæ," Liber X., 225.

of Orpheus lying upon it; in any case, it is strangely
suggestive of these tales. I am indebted for a tracing
of this mirror to the Rev. J. Wood Brown, author of
the "Life of Michael Scott, the Magician and Philosopher," wherein the latter hath a dual affinity to
Virgil, and it is very remarkable, as I have elsewhere
noted, that the splitting a hill into three is near Rome
ascribed to the Roman poet.

A curious book could be written on heads, decapi-
tated, which have spoken. There is, I believe, a
legend to the effect that the caput of John the Baptist
thus conversed, and it may be that the New Testament
only gives a fragment of the original history. The
belief that Herodias was a sorceress, and a counterpart of Diana as queen of the witches, was generally
established so early as the second century, but is far
older, the original Herodias having been a form of
Lilith.*

It is specially to be noted in connection with this
tale that one of the older legends given in "Virgilius
the Sorcerer of Rome" expressly declares that

"Virgilius made an iron head which could not only speak,
but also foretell the future; and, as some say, it was by
misinterpreting the oracle that Virgilius met his death in
this wise. Being about to undertake a journey, he asked
the head if it would come to a good end. The reply was:
'Yes, if he took care of *his head*.' Taking this to mean the
oracle itself, Virgilius took every measure to secure it, and
with light heart went his way, but while journeying, exposed
to sunshine, he was seized with a fever in the head, of which
he died."

This is again like the death of Michael Scott.

* The reader will find this Herodias-Lilith fully described in a little
work entitled "Aradia; or, The Gospel of the Witches," by Charles
Godfrey Leland. London: D. Nutt.

VIRGIL, THE WICKED PRINCESS, AND THE IRON MAN.

> " An iron man who did on her attend,
> His name was Talus, made of yron mould,
> Immoveable, resistless—without end."
> SPENSER : *Faerie Queene,* v. c. i.

There once lived a Princess who was beautiful beyond words, but wicked beyond belief; her whole soul was given to murder and licentiousness; yet she was so crafty as to escape all suspicion, and this pleased her best of all, for deceit was to her as dear as life itself. And this she managed, as many another did in those days, by inveigling through her agents handsome young men into her palace by night, where they were invited to a banquet and then to a bed, and all went gaily till the next morning at breakfast, when the Princess gave her victim in wine or food a terrible and rapid poison, after which the corpse was carried away secretly by her servants to be thrown into the river, or hidden in some secret vault ; and thus it was the lady sinned in secret while she kept up a white name before the world.

Now it came to pass that a young man, who was a great friend of Virgil, was taken in the snare by this Princess, and put to death and no more heard of, when the great poet by his magic art learned the whole truth. Then for revenge or punishment he made a man of iron with golden locks, very beautiful to behold as a man, with sympathetic, pleasing air, one who conversed fluently and in a winning voice; and yet he was all of iron, and the spirit who was conjured into him was one without pity or mercy.

Then Virgil bade the Iron Man walk to and fro past the palace of the Princess, and she, seeing him, was more pleased than she had ever been before, and at once sent out a messenger, who invited him to enter by a secret gate, which he did, and was warmly received, and treated with a great display of love. And in the morning at breakfast, as the Princess hesitated to give him the deadly drink, for she had at last fallen madly in love, he said :

" Well, where is the poison ? Don't keep me waiting ! Quick, that I may drink !"

And when she heard that she was indeed terrified, thinking, " This man knows all my secret." But as she hesitated, he took the deadly cup and drained it to the last drop. " And now," she thought, " I am saved."

But the Iron Man said with scorn :

" Do you call *that* stuff poison ? Why, it would hardly kill a mouse. Give me stronger, I say—stronger ! I live on poison, and the stronger it is the better I like it."

Hearing this, the Princess felt from head to foot as if her blood were all turned to ice, for now she knew that she was lost, and her punishment at hand.

" And now," said the Iron Man, " since all the poisoning and treachery and putting away of young gentlemen is at an end, you must come with me ;" and with this he took her under his left arm and went forth.

At her screams all her retainers came armed, and after them twenty soldiers, but all were of no avail against such an enemy, whom they could neither pierce with steel nor restrain by strength ; and escaping with her, he mounted a black steed, which a Moor was holding outside, and with his victim flew over the land till they came to a dark and savage place in the mountains. And here he bore her into a vast cavern, where many men were seated round a table, and as she looked she saw that they were all the lovers whom she had put to death. Then they all cried :

" *Ecco la nostra moglie !* Behold our wife ! Behold our Drusiana !"

And another said :

" Let us give her to drink, and let us drink to her !"

And they gave her a full goblet, which she could not help swallowing, and the wine was like fire, the fire of hell itself in all her veins. The men assembled round burst into laughter at seeing her suffering, and one shouted :

> " Drink, Princess, drink !
> Thou feelest the same fire,
> Only in greater measure,
> Hotter, wilder and fiercer,
> Which thou didst feel before,
> When thy blood boiled with passion,
> And with love of secret murder ;
> Then thou didst feel it a little,
> Now thou shalt feel it greatly ;
> Once it ran drop by drop,
> Now in full goblets and frequent."

Then another gave her a glass of wine which she could

not help swallowing, and it was cold, and her blood again
grew cold as ice, and she shivered in an agony of freezing.
And so it went on, everyone giving her first the scalding hot
wine and then the cold, while all sang in chorus :

> "We give thee again in thy heart
> What thou didst give to us :
> The heat of love which burned in us,
> Burned in us and in thee,
> And the cold of desire when satisfied.
> Thou hadst no mercy on us :
> We have as little for thee."

The connection of Virgil with the classic Talus, or
Iron Man, and so many other ancient legends, as shown
in these which I have gathered, renders the more striking
the assertion that "after the sixteenth century the
Vergilian legends disappear, and become known only to
scholars," as worded by E. F. M. Beneche in his translation of Comparetti's work.   The truth is, that as the
age of credulity and mere marvels passed away among
the higher classes, the learned ceased to collect or take
an interest in heaping up "wonders upon wonders."
But the people went on telling and making tales about
Virgil, just as they had always done.   And the full
proof that there was not a soul who for centuries took
the least interest in folklore or popular tradition in
Central and Northern Italy is to be found in the fact
that, while such material *abounds* in the English, French,
and especially German literature of later ages, there is
hardly a trace of it in a single Roman or Tuscan writer
till of late years.   Even at the present day there is
small search or seeking in Northern Italy for the rich
treasures of old Roman tradition which still exist among
the people.

GIOVANNI DI BOLOGNA AND THE GOD MERCURY.

"Mercurium omnium Deorum antiquorum vigilantissimum ac maxime negotiis implicatum, scribit Hesiodus in Theogonia."—NATALIS COMITIS : *Mythologia*, lib. v., 1616.

In the old times in Florence the Tuscans worshipped the idols of Jupiter, and Bacchus, and Venus, and Mercury in their temples. And sometimes those gōds when conjured* came down to earth.

In those times there was in Florence† a sculptor of Bologna named Giovanni, the same who made the Diavolino in the Mercato Vecchio. He was tormented by the desire to make a statue of such beauty that there should not be its like in all the world ; and he, moreover, desired that this statue should be as if living, one not stiff and fixed, but one like Mercury, all activity, and he was so full of this thought that he had no rest even by night, for a certain gentleman had said to him :

" All in vain dost thou intoxicate thyself by studying statues, saying, ' This one is beautiful, that still more so ; this sculptor—*è bravo*—has talent, that even cleverer ;' but, after all, the best of their work is motionless, and produces on me the effect of a corpse. I should call him a clever sculptor who could make a statue inspired with motion like a living man—*che caminasse o magari saltasse*—who runs and hops, but not a piece of marble merely carved."

And this moved Giovanni to make a statue which should not have its equal in the world. And thinking of Mercury, the liveliest and quickest of all the gods, who is ever flying like a falcon, he said :

> " If I could behold him,
> Though 'twere but for once.
> I should have the model
> Of a wondrous statue
> Inspired unto life !"

One evening Giovanni found himself in the Temple of Mercury, that which is to-day called the Baptistery of Saint

* " Scongiurati "—evoked.
† The sentence is twice repeated in the original.

John [and there he found Virgilio], to whom he said that he
so greatly longed to see Mercury living and in flight.

Virgilio replied :

"Go at midnight to the hill of Vallombrosa when the
moon is full, and call the fairy Bellaria, who will aid thee."

Giovanni went to the hill and called to Bellaria, but she
made no reply.   So he returned to Virgilio, who said :

"It is not enough to simply call to her, she must be
scongiurata—called by an incantation."

Then Giovanni, having learned this, thus conjured her :

> "Stella lucente,
> Ed aria splendente,
> Col tuo splendor,
> Bell' Aria infiamma
> Mercurio, e fa lo scendere
> In terra che io posso
> Levarne il modello !
> Tu che siei bella,
> Bella quanto buona,
> Fa mi questa grazia ;
> Perche io sono molto,
> Molto infelice,
> Se non faro una statua
> Come il desiderio mio,
> Vedi Bellaria.
> Finquaseù in questo monte,
> Son venuto per potermi
> A te raccomandare ;
> Tù prego non indugiare
> A far mi questa grazia,
> Perche sono infelice."

> "Shining star !
> Resplendent glowing air,[*]
> With thy burning splendour,
> Bell' Aria, inflame,
> Inspire great Mercury,
> Make him descend to earth
> That he may copied be.
> Thou who art beautiful,
> As beautiful as good,
> Grant me, I pray, this grace,
> For I am lost in grief
> Because I cannot make
> A statue as I wish.
> Behold, Bellaria !
> I've come unto this hill
> To beg this thing of thee !

---

[*] "Ed aria resplendente," a play on the name Bell' Aria.

> I pray thee grant my prayer,
> For I am suffering."

Then Bellaria thus evoked Mercury :

> " Mercurio mio, bel Mercurio,
> Per quell' acqua corrente,
> E cel (cielo) splendente,
> E tu risplendi, risplendi amor
> Di bellezza, e come il vento,
> Come il fulmine lesto sici,
> Io sono stata
> Scongiurata,
> Scongiurata pel mio splendor,
> Per infiammarti
> Del mio calor
> Che tu scenda in terra
> Che vié Giovanni
> Gian di Bologna,
> Primo scultore, vuol prendere da te
> Il modello,
> Ti prego di scendere
> Come un baleno
> Perche fino che non sarai sesato,
> Ne pure a me tornerebbe
> La mia pace perche
> Mi hanno scongiurata per te ;
> Se questa grazia mi farai
> Non per me, ma per Giovanni,
> Tre segni mi darai—
> Lampo, tuono e fulmine
> Se questa grazi mi farai,
> I tre seguali mi darai !"

> " Mercury, beauteous God !
> By the rushing water !
> By the glowing heaven !
> As thou shinest, reflecting again
> Their beauty, and as the wind
> Or the lightning thou art fleet.
> Even so am I
> Conjured and compelled
> Even by mine own splendour
> To inspire, inflame
> Thee by mine own heat !
> That thou descend to earth,
> That Giovanni, born
> In Bologna, may
> As sculptor copy thee !
> I pray thee to descend,
> Even like lightning's flash,
> Since till thou art measured,

> I shall not be in peace,
> Being myself invoked.
> If thou wilt grant this grace,
> Yet not for me but *Gian*,
> Accord to me three signs :
> The flash, the crash and bolt ;
> Even as lightning comes,
> I pray thee grant me this !"

And in an instant there came all together in one the flash and roar and thunderbolt, and Giovanni di Bologna beheld Mercury flying in the heaven, and said :

> "E troppo leggiadro, troppo bello !
> Non posso dipingere una Stella
> Ne il vento, ne un balén,
> E finito la mia speranza.   Amen !"

> "Thou art too little and light, by far !
> I cannot paint a shining star,
> Nor the wild wind or lightning—then
> All hope is lost, ah me !   Amen !"

Then the beautiful Bellaria said :

" If thou canst not depict Mercury flying through the air, it may be that thou canst make him passing over the waves, for then his speed is not so great." [So she invoked Mercury again, and he was seen flitting over the ocean.*]

But when Giovanni di Bologna beheld Mercury leaping from wave to wave like a dolphin, he cried :

> " Bel Mercurio, sempre *vale*!
> Io non sono che un mortale,
> Io non posso tanto fare,
> Ne le tue grazzie combinare."

> " Farewell, fair Mercury, all is o'er,
> I'm but a mortal and no more,
> I cannot give again thy face,
> And least of all thy wondrous grace."

Bellaria said to him :

" Thou hast asked too much ; it is not possible for thee to make fire and water to the life.   Yet be at ease, for what may not be done in water or in air may come to pass with ease upon the earth."

Bellaria again invoked Mercury, who descended like the wind in a leap, even as a man leaps down and alights on earth.

* This I have supplied to fill a blank.

Then Giovanni cried :

" Grazia à Dio !
Io ho l' ideà !"

" Thanks to God divine !
The *idea* is mine !"

And so Giovanni made the beautiful statue of Mercury in bronze ; and so long as the Tuscans worshipped their idols it was wont to dance, but after they ceased this worship, it danced no more. [At present, the beautiful statue of Mercury in bronze is in the Bargello.]

It is said that Bellaria is the sister of Mercury, and that both fly in the air. When the *Fate* or fairies, or good witches die, Bellaria descends, and then bears their souls to heaven.

Mercury is the god of all people who are in haste, who have occasion to go rapidly—as, for instance, those who wish to send a letter quickly and receive a speedy reply. To do this, you must have an image of Mercury cast in bronze, and it must be made to shine like silver, with a bright colour like a looking-glass ;* and this should be worshipped before going to bed, and on rising in the morning adore it again. And to invoke Mercury, this is the manner : You must have a basin full of water, taken from a stream when agitated (*i.e.*, running water), and in the evening, as in the morning, take that basin and make a cross on the earth where you kneel down, and then say :

" Acqua corrente
E vento furente,
Avanti la statua di Mercurio
Mi inghinnocchio, perche Mercurio,
E il mio idole, Mercurio !
E il mio dio ;
Acqua corrente
E vento furente,
Infuriate Mercurio
A farmi questa grazia !"

" Running water, raging wind !
Before the form of Mercury I kneel,
For Mercury is my idol and my god !
Running water, raging wind,
Inspire great Mercury
To do what I desire !"

---

* Evidently with quicksilver or mercury—*similia similibus.*

Then you shall pause and sing again :

> " Mercurio, Mercurio !
> Tu che siei il mio Dio !
> Fammi questa grazia
> Che io ti chiedo,
> Se questa grazia a me concedi
> Tre cose fammi vedere ;
> Tuono, lampo e vento infuriato !"

> " Mercury, Mercury divine !
> Who ever art a god of mine !
> Grant me that which I do need,
> And if't be given me indeed,
> Cause me then three things to see—
> The lightning's flash,
> The thunder crash,
> And the wind roaring furiously !"

And where the water from the running stream has been poured it must be carefully covered over, so that no one can tread thereon, or else from that time the favour of Mercury will cease.

It would seem as if this story were originally intended to imply that the sculptor, unable to give a higher conception of vivacity or motion, represented the mobile god as in the moment of descending on earth, still preserving the attitude of flight. This conception was probably too subtle for the narrator, who describes the image as having been a kind of marionette, or dancing Jack. " Whate'er it be, it is a curious tale."

The connection of Mercury with moving water is also remarkable. He bears serpents on his *caduceus* or wand ; and among other ancient myth-fancies, a rushing river, from its shape or windings and its apparent life, was a symbol of a serpent.

It is hardly worth while to note that Giovanni di Bologna was really a Frenchman—Jean de Boulogne. The bronze Mercury by him described in this story, and now in the Bargello Museum, is supposed to have suggested the allusion to the god as

> "just alighted
> On a heaven-kissing hill,"

and the probability is indeed of the strongest. Many judges good and true are of the opinion that, as regards motive or conception, this is the best statue ever made by any save a Greek, as there is assuredly none in which the lightness of motion is so perfectly expressed in matter. I believe, however, that Giovanni di Bologna was indebted for this figure to some earlier type or motive. There is something not unlike it among the old Etruscan small bronze *figurini*.

THE DOUBLE-FACED STATUE, OR HOW VIRGILIO CONJURED JANUS.

> " Now by two-headed Janus!
> Nature hath formed strange fellows in her time !"
> SHAKESPEARE.

" There were in Rome many temples of Janus, some unto him as *bifrons*, or double-faced. Caylus has published pictures of Greek vases on which are seen two heads thus united, the one of an elderly man, the other of a young woman."—*Dizionario Mitologico.*

There was once in Florence, in the Tower della Zeccha, a statue of great antiquity, and it had only one body, or bust, but two heads; and one of these was of a man and the other of a woman, a thing marvellous to behold.

And Virgil, seeing this when it was first found in digging amid old ruins, had it placed upright and said :

" Behold two beings who form but a single person! I will conjure the image; it shall be a charm to do good; it shall teach a lesson to all."

Thus he conjured ·

> " Statua da due faccie
> Due, e un corpo solo,
> Due faccie ed avete
> Un sol cervello.   Siete

11

Due esseri l' uno per altro,
Dovete essere marito e moglie,
Dovete peccare con un sol pensiero.

" Avete bene quattro occhi
Ma una sol vista,
Come tutti i mariti,
E moglie dorebbere essere,
E dovete fare la buona fortuna
Di tutti gli inamorati."

" Statue gifted with two faces,
Two and yet a single body !
Two and but one brain—then art thou
Two intended for each other—
Two who should be wife and husband,
Acting by the same reflection.

" Unto you four eyes are given,
And but a single sight—ye are then
What indeed all wives and husbands
Ought to be if they'd be happy ;
Therefore shalt thou bring good fortune
Unto all devoted lovers !"

Then Virgil touched the statue with his rod, and it replied :

" Tutti quelli che mi pregherano.
Di cuore sincera, amanti o sposi,
Tutti quelli saranno felice !"

" All of those who'll come here to adore me,
Be they lovers, be they married couples,
I will ever make them truly happy."

The conception of a head with two faces, one male and the other female, is still very common in Italy. In the cloister of Santa Maria Novella in Florence the portraits of a husband and wife are thus united on a marble monumental tablet. And in Baveno, among the many *graffiti* or sketches and scrawls made by children on the walls on or near the church, there is one which is evidently traditional, representing Janus. This double-headed deity was continued in the Baphomet of the Knights Templars.

In the older legends are two tales declaring that Virgil made and enchanted two statues. This appears to be a variation of the story of Janus.

VIRGIL AND HIS COURTIERS.

"Virgilius also made a belfry."—*The Wonderful History of Virgilius the Sorcerer of Rome.*

> "To be a crow and seem a swan,
> To look all truth, possessing none,
> To appear a saint by every act,
> And be a devil meanwhile at heart,
> To prove that black is white, in sooth,
> And cover up the false with truth ;
> And be a living lie, in short—
> Such are the lives men lead at court."
> *Old Italian saying cited by* FRANCESCO PANICO *in his* "*Poetiche Dicerie*" (1643) ; article, Courtiers.

"Above all lying is the lie as practised by evil *courtiers*, it being false-hood *par excellence.* For they are the arch-architects, the cleverest of artists at forming lies, pre-eminent in cooking, seasoning, serving them with the honey of flattery or the vinegar of reproof."—FRANCESCO PANICO (1643).

On a time Virgilio remained for many weeks alone at home, and never went to court. And during this retirement he made seven bells of gold, and on every one there was engraved a name or word.

On the first there was "Bugiardo" (or lying), on the second "Chiacchiera" (or tattling gossip), on the third "Malignità" (or evil spite), on the fourth "Chalugna" (or calumny), on the fifth "Maldicenza" (or vituperation), on the sixth "Invidia" (or envy), and on the seventh "Bassezza" (or vileness).

And these he hung up in a draught of air, so that as they swung in the breeze they rang and tinkled, first one alone, and then all.

One day the Emperor sent a messenger to Virgilio, asking him why he never came to court as of old. And Virgilio wrote in reply :

"MY DEAR EMPEROR,

"It is no longer necessary that I should come to court to learn all that is said there. For where I am at home I hear all day long the voices of Falsehood, Tattling, Evil Spite, Calumny, Vituperation, Envy, and Vileness."

And then he showed the bells to the messenger. The

11—2

Emperor, when he had read the letter and heard all, laughed heartily, and said :

" So Virgilio keeps a court of his own !   Yes, and a finer one than mine, for all his courtiers are clad in gold."

VIRGIL AND THE THREE SHEPHERDS.

A LEGEND OF THE MONTE SYBILLA, NEAR ROME.

> " And, warrior, I could tell to thee
> The words which split Eildon Hill in three,
> And bridled the Tweed with a curb of stone ;
> But to speak them were a deadly sin,
> And for having but thought them my heart within
> A treble penance must be done."—SCOTT.

Miss Roma Lister, when residing in Florence, having written to her old nurse Maria, in Rome, asking her if she knew, or could find, any tales of Virgil, received after a while the following letter, written out by her son, who has evidently been well educated, to judge by his style and admirable handwriting :

"ROME, *January* 28, 1897.

" MIA BUONA SIGNORINA,

" I have been seeking for some old person, a native of the Castelli Romani, who knew something relative to the magician Virgil, and I found in a street of the new quarters of Rome an old acquaintance, a man who is more than eighty years of age ; and on asking him for what I wanted, he, after some reflection, recalled the following story :

" ' I was a small boy when my parents told me that in the Montagna della Sibilla there was once an old man who was indeed so very old that the most ancient people had ever known him as appearing of the same age, and he was called the magician Virgilio.

" ' One day three shepherds were in a cabin at the foot of the mountain, when the magician entered, and they were at first afraid of him, knowing his reputation. But he calmed them by saying that he never did harm to anyone, and that he had come down from the mountain to beg a favour from them.

"' "There is," he continued, "half-way up the mountain, a grotto, in which there is a great serpent which keeps me from entering. Therefore I beg you do me the kindness to capture it."

"'The shepherds replied that they would do so, thinking that he wanted them to kill the snake, but he explained to them that he wished to have it taken in a very large bottle (*grandissimo boccione*),* by means of certain herbs which he had provided.

"'And the next day he came with the bottle and certain herbs which were strange to them, and certainly not grown in the country. And he said:

"' "Go to the grotto, and lay the bottle down with its mouth towards the cavern, and when the serpent shall smell the herbs he will enter the bottle. Then do ye close it quickly and bring it to me. And all of this must be done without a word being spoken, else ye will meet with disaster."

"'So the three shepherds went their way, and after a time came to the grotto, which they entered, and did as the magician had ordered. Then, after a quarter of an hour, the serpent, smelling the herbs, came forth and entered the bottle. No sooner was he in it than one of the shepherds adroitly closed it, and cried unthinkingly:

"' "Now you're caught !"

"'When all at once they felt the whole mountain shake, and heard an awful roar, and crashing timber round on every side, so that they fell on the ground half dead with fear. When they came to their senses each one found himself on the summit of a mountain, and the three peaks were far apart. It took them several days to return to their cabin, and all of them died a few days after.

"'From that time the magician Virgil was no more seen in the land.'

"This is all which I could learn; should I hear more I will write at once to you."

---

* Bottles for wine are sometimes made to contain several gallons.

This is beyond question an imperfectly-told tale. What the sorcerer intended and effected was to divide a mountain into three peaks, as did Michael Scott, of whom legends are still left in Italy, as the reader may find by consulting the interesting work by the Rev. J. Wood Brown.*   In the Italian tale the three shepherds who were together find themselves suddenly apart on the tops of three peaks, which clearly indicates the real aim of the narrative.

An old Indian woman, widow of an Indian governor, told me, as a thing unknown, that the three hills of Boston had been thus split by Glusgábe or Glooscap, the great Algonkin god.   As this deity introduced culture to North America, it will be at once perceived that there was something truly *weirdly*, or strangely prophetic, in this act.   As Glooscap was the first to lay out Boston—*à la Trinité*—he certainly ought to be regarded as the patron saint of that cultured city, and have at least a library, a lyceum, or a hotel named after him in the American Athens.   The coincidence is very singular—Rome and Boston !

Eildon Hill, by which, as I have heard, Andrew Lang was born, is one of the picturesque places which attract legends and masters in folk-lore.   Of it I have a strange souvenir.   While in its vicinity I for three nights saw in a dream the Fairy Queen, and the "vision" was remarkably vivid, or so much so as to leave a strong or haunting impression on my waking hours.   It was like a glimpse into elf-land.   Of course it was simply the result of my recalling and thinking deeply on the legend of "True Thomas," but the dream was very pleasant and sympathetic.

---

* "An Enquiry into the Life and Legend of Michael Scott," by the Rev. J. Wood Brown, M.A.   Edinburgh, David Douglas, 1897.

THE GOLDEN PINE-CONE.

"Quid sibi vult, illa *Pinus*, quàm semper statis diebus in deum matris intromittis sanctuarium?"—ARNOBIUS, i. 5.

There was once a young man named Constanzo, who was blessed, as they say, in form and fortune, he being both fair in face and rich. Now, whether it was that what he had seen and learned of ladies at court had displeased him, is not recorded or remembered, but one thing is certain, that he had made up his mind to marry a poor girl, and so began to look about among humble folk at the maids, which indeed pleased many of them beyond belief, though it was taken ill by their parents, who had but small faith in such attentions.

But the one whom it displeased most of all was the mother of Constanzo, who, when he said that he would marry a poor girl, declared in a rage that he should do nothing of the kind, because she would allow no such person to come in the house. To which he replied that as he was of age, and the master, he would do as he pleased. Then there were ill words, for the mother had a bad temper and worse will, and had gone the worst way to work, because of all things her son could least endure being governed. And she was the more enraged because her son had hitherto always been docile and quiet, but she now found that she had driven him up to a height which he had not before dreamed of occupying and where he would now remain. But she vowed vengeance in her heart, saying: "Marry or not—this shall cost thee dear. *Te lo farò pagare!*"

Many months passed, and no more was said, when one day the young gentleman went to the chase with his friends, and impelled by some strange influence, took a road and went afar into a part of the country which was unknown to him. At noon they dismounted to rest, when, being very thirsty, Constanzo expressed a desire for water.

And just as he said it there came by a *contadina*, carrying two jars of water, cold and dripping, fresh from a fountain. And the young signor having drunk, observed that the girl was of enchanting or dazzling beauty, with a charming expression of innocence, which went to his heart.

"What is thy name?" he asked.

"Constanza," the girl replied.

"And I am Constanzo," he cried; "and as our names so our hearts shall be—one made for the other!"

"But you are a rich lord, and I am a poor girl," she slowly answered, "so it can never be."

But as both had loved at sight, and sincerely, it was soon arranged, and the end was that the pair were married, and Constanza became a signora and went to live in the castle with her lord. His mother, who was more his enemy than ever, and ten times that of his wife, made no sign of anger, but professed love and devotion, expressing delight every day and oftener that her son had chosen so fair a wife, and one so worthy of him.

It came to pass that Constanza was about to become a mother, and at this time her husband was called to the wars, and that so far away that many days must pass before he could send a letter to his home. But his mother showed herself so kind, though she had death and revenge at her heart, that Constanzo was greatly relieved, and departed almost light of heart, for he was a brave man, as well as good, and such people borrow no trouble ere it is due.

But the old signora looked after him with bitterness, saying, "Thou shalt pay me, and the hour is not far off." And when she saw his wife she murmured:

> "Now revenge shall take its shape;
> Truly thou canst not escape;
> Be it death or be it dole,
> I will sting thee to the soul."

Then when the hour came that the countess was to be confined, the old woman told her that she herself alone would serve and attend to all—*e che avrebbe fatto tutto da se*. But going forth, she found a pine-tree and took from it a cone, which she in secret set to boil in water, singing to it:

> "Bolli, bolli!
> Senza posa.
> Che nel letto
> Vi é la sposa,
> Un fanciullo
> Alla luce mi dara,
> E una pina diventera!"

" Bolli, bolli !
Mio decotto
Bolli, bolli !
Senza posa !
Il profumo
Che tu spandi,
Si spanda
In corpo alla
Alla sposa e il figlio,
Il figlio che farà
Pina d' oro diventerà !"

" Boil and boil,
Rest defying !
In the bed
The wife is lying ;
Soon her babe
The light will see,
But a pine-cone
It shall be !

" Boil and boil,
And well digest !
Boil and boil,
And never rest !
May the perfume
Which you spread
Thrill the body
To the head,
And the child
Which we shall see,
A golden pine-cone
Let it be !"

And soon the countess gave birth to a beautiful daughter with golden hair, but the old woman promptly took the little one and bathed it in the water in which she had boiled the pine-cone, whereupon it became a golden pine-cone, and the poor mother was made to believe that this was her first-born ; and the same was written to the father, who replied to his wife that, whatever might happen, he would ever remain as he had been.

The mother-in-law took the pine-cone and placed it on a mantelpiece, as such curious or odd things are generally disposed of. And when her son returned she contrived in so many ways and with craft to calumniate his wife that the poor lady was ere long imprisoned in a tower.

But a strange thing now happened, for every night the pine-cone, unseen by all, left like a living thing its place on the chimney-piece and wandered over the castle, returning at five o'clock to its place, but ever going just below the lady's window, where it sang :

> " O cara madre mia !
>   Luce degli occhi miei !
>   Cessa quel pianto,
>   E non farmi più soffrir !"

> " O mother, darling mother,
>   Light of my eyes, I pray
>   That thou wilt cease thy weeping,
>   So mine may pass away."

Yet, after he had shut his wife up in the tower, Constanzo had not an instant's peace of mind. Therefore, to be assured, he one day went to consult the great magician Virgil. And having told all that had happened, the wise man said :

" Thou hast imprisoned thy wife, she who is pure and true, in a tower, and all on the lying words and slanders of that vile witch your mother. And thou hast suffered bitterly, and well deserved it, as all do who are weak enough to believe evil reports of a single witness ; for who is there who may not lie, especially among women, when they are jealous and full of revenge ? Now do thou set free thy wife (and bid her come to me and I will teach her what to do)."

So the count obeyed.

Then the mother took the pine-cone and threw it up three times into the air, singing :

> " Pina, mia bella pina !
>   Dei pini tu sei regina !
>   Dei pini sei prottetrice,
>   D' un pino pianta la radice !
>   E torna una fanciulla bella
>   Come un occhio
>   Di sole in braccio
>   A tuo padre
>   Ed a tua madre !

> " Pine, the fairest ever seen,
>   Of all cones thou art the queen !
>   Guarding them in sun or shade,
>   And 'tis granted that, when planted,
>   Thou shalt be a charming maid,
>   Ever sweet and ever true
>   To thy sire and mother too."

And this was done, and the cone forthwith grew up a fair maid, who was the joy of her parents' life. But the people in a rage seized on the old witch, who was covered with a coat of pitch and burned alive in the public square.

This legend was gathered in and sent to me from Siena. As a narrative it is a fairy-tale of the most commonplace description, its incidents being found in many others. But so far as the pine-cone is concerned it is of great originality, and retains remarkable relics of old Latin lore. The pine-tree was a favourite of Cybele, and it was consecrated to Silvanus, who is still known and has a cult in the mountains of the Romagna Toscana. This rural deity often bore a pine-cone in his hand. Propertius also assigns the pine to Pan. The cone was pre-eminently a phallic emblem, therefore specially holy ; in this sense it was placed on the staff borne by the specially initiated to Bacchus. It was incredibly popular as an amulet, on account of its supposed magical virtues, therefore no one object is more frequently produced in ancient art. A modern writer, observing this, and not being able to account for it, very feebly attributes it to the fact that the object is so common that it is naturally used for a model. " Artists," he says, " in fact prefer to use what comes ready to hand, and to copy such plants as are ever under their eye." So writes the great dilettante Caylus, forgetting that a thousand objects quite as suitable to decoration as the pine-cone, and quite as common, were not used at all.

The pine typified a new birth, according to Friedrich ; this was because it was evergreen, and therefore sacred as immortal to Cybele. Thus Ovid (" Metamorphoses," x. 103) writes, " *Pinus grata deum matri.*" The French Layard, in the new " Annales de l'Institut

Archæologique," vol. xix., has emphatically indicated the connection of the pine-cone with the cult of Venus, and as a reproductive symbol. It is in this sense clearly set forth in the Italian or Sienese legend, where the pine-cone planted in the earth grows up as the girl with golden locks. This is very probably indeed the relic of an old Roman mythical tale or poem.

The golden pine-cone appears in other tales. Wolf ("Zeitschrift für deutsche Mythologie," vol. i., p. 297) says that in Franconia there were once three travelling *Handwerksburschen*, or craftsmen, who met with a beautiful lady, who when asked for alms gave to each a pine-cone from a tree. Two of them threw the gifts away, but the third found his changed to solid gold. In order to make an amulet which is kept in the house, pine-cones are often gilded in Italy. I have seen them here in Florence, and very pretty ornaments they make.

VIRGIL'S MAGIC LOOM.

"I heard a loom at work, and thus it spoke,
As though its clatter like a metre woke,
And echoed in my mind like an old song,
Rising while growing dimmer e'en like smoke.

"And thus it spoke, 'God is a loom like me,
His chiefest weaving is Humanity,
And man and woman are the warp and woof,
Which make a mingling light of mystery.'"
The Loom : C. G. L.

Gega was a girl of fifteen years of age, and without parents or friends, with nothing in the world but eyes to weep and arms to work. Yet she had this luck, that an old woman who was a fellow-lodger in the place where she lived,* moved by compassion, took the girl to live with her,

* "Pigionale come si dei ebbe volgarmente" (original text).

though all she had was a very small room, in which was a poor bed and a little loom, so crazy-looking and old that it seemed impossible to work with it.

Nunzia,* for such was the old woman's name, took Gega indeed as a daughter, and taught her to weave, which was a good trade in those days, and in that place where few practised it. So it came to pass that they made money, which was laid by. [This was no great wonder, for the old loom had a strange enchantment in it, by which marvellous work could be produced.]

The old woman very often bade Gega take great care of the loom, and the girl could not understand why Nunzia thought so much of it, since it seemed to her to be like any other. [For it never appeared strange to her that when she wove the cloth seemed to almost come of itself—a great deal for a little thread—and that its quality or kind improved as she applied herself to work, for in her ignorance she believed that this was the way with all weaving.]

At last the old Mamma Nunzia died, and Gega, left alone, began to make acquaintances and friends with other girls who came to visit her. Among these was one named Ermelinda, who was at heart as treacherous and rapacious as she was shrewd, yet one withal who, what with her beauty and deceitful airs, knew how to flatter and persuade to perfection, so that she could make a simple girl like Gega believe that the moon was a pewter plate, or a black fly white.

Now, the first time that she and several others, who were all weavers, saw Gega at work, they were greatly amazed, for the cloth seemed to come of itself from a wretched old loom which appeared to be incapable of making anything, and it was so fine and even, and had such a gloss that it looked like silk.

"How wonderful! One would say it was silk!" cried a girl.

"Oh, I can make silk when I try," answered Gega; and applying her will to it, she presently spun from cotton-thread a yard of what was certainly real silk stuff.

And seeing this, all present declared that Gega must be a witch.

"Nonsense," she replied; "you could all do it if you tried as I do. As for being a witch, it is Ermelinda and

* Annunziata.

not I who should be so, for she first said it was like silk, and made it so."

Then Ermelinda saw that there was magic in the loom, of which Gega knew nothing, so she resolved to do all in her power to obtain it. And this she effected firstly by flattery, and giving the innocent girl extravagant ideas of her beauty, assuring her that she had an attractiveness which could not fail to win her a noble husband, and that, having laid by a large sum of money, she should live on it in style till married, and that in any case she could go back to her weaving. But that on which she laid most stress was that Gega should leave her old lodging and get rid of her dirty old furniture, and especially of that horrible, crazy old loom, persuading her that, if she ever should have occasion to weave again, she, with her talent, could do far better with a new loom, and probably gain thrice as much, all of which the simple girl believed, and so let her false friend dispose of everything, in doing which Ermelinda did not fail to keep the loom herself, declaring that nobody would buy it.

"Now," said the latter, "I am content. Thou art very beautiful; all that thou needest is to be elegantly dressed, and have fine things about thee, to soon catch a fine husband."

Gega assented to this, but was loth to part with her old loom, which she had promised Nuñzia should never be neglected; but Ermelinda promised so faithfully to keep it carefully for her, that she was persuaded to let her have it. Then the young girl took a fine apartment, well furnished, and bought herself beautiful clothes, and, guided by her false friend, began to go to entertainments and make fashionable friends, and live as if she were rich.

Then Ermelinda, having obtained the old loom, went to work with it, in full hope that she too could spin silk out of cotton, but found out to her amazement and rage that she could do nothing of the kind—nay, she could not so much as weave common cloth from it; all that she got after hours of fruitless effort was a headache, and the conviction that she had thrown away all her time and trouble, which made her hate Gega all the more.

Meanwhile the latter for a time enjoyed life as she had never done before; but though she looked anxiously to the right and the left for a husband, found none, the well-to-do young men being quite as anxious to wed wealth as she was, and all of them soon discovered on inquiry that she had little or nothing, despite her style of living, and her money rapidly melted away, till at last she found that to live she must work—there was no help for it. With what remained she bought a fine loom and thread, and sat down to weave ; but though she succeeded in making common stuff like others, it was not silk, nor anything like it, nor was there anyone who would buy what she made. In despair she remembered what Mamma Nunzia had solemnly said to her, that she must never part from the old loom, so she went to Ermelinda to reclaim it. But her false friend, although she could do nothing with the loom herself, was not willing that Gega, whom she hated with all her heart, should in any way profit, and declared that her mother had broken up and burned the rubbishy old thing, and to this story she adhered, and when Gega insisted on proof of it, drove her in a rage out of the house.

While Mamma Nunzia was living she, being a very wise woman, had taught Gega with care the properties and nature of plants, roots, herbs, and flowers, saying that some day it might be of value to her, as it is to everyone. So whenever they had a holiday they had gone into the fields and woods, where the girl became so expert that she could have taught many a doctor very strange secrets; and withal, the Mamma also made her learn the charms and incantations which increase the power of the plants. So now, having come to her last coin, and finding there was some profit in it, she began to gather herbs for medicine, which she sold to chemists and others in the towns. And finding a deserted old tower in a wild and rocky place, she was allowed to make it her home ; and indeed, after all she had gone through, and her disappointment both as to friends and lovers, she found herself far happier when alone than when in a town, where she was ashamed to meet people who had known her when she lived in style.

One evening as she was returning home she heard a groaning in the woods as of someone in great suffering, and, guided by the sound, found a poor old woman seated on a stone, who told her that she had hurt her leg by slipping from a rock. And Gega, who was as strong as she was kind and compassionate, carried the poor soul in her arms to the tower, where she bound an application of healing herbs to the wound, and bade her remain and welcome.

"I have nothing to give you for it all," said the old woman on the following day.

"Nor did I do it in the hope of aught," replied Gega.

"And yet," said the sufferer, "I might be of use to you. If, for example, you have lost anything, I can tell you how to recover it or where it is."

"Ah!" cried Gega, "if thou canst do that, thou wilt be a friend indeed, for I have lost my fortune—it was a loom which was left to me by Mamma Nunzia. I did not regard her advice never to part with it, and I have bitterly repented my folly. I trusted it to a friend, who betrayed me, for she burned it."

"No, my dear, she did nothing of the kind," replied the old woman; "she has it yet, and I will make it return to thee."

Then she repeated this invocation:

"Telaio! Telaio! Telaio!
Che per opera e virtú
Del gran mago Virgilio
Fosti fabricato,
E di tante virtù adornato
Ti prego per opera e virtu
Del gran mago Virgilio
Tu possa di una tela
Di oro di argento
Essere ordito.
E come il vento,
Dalla casa di Ermelinda,
Tu possa sortire,
Sortire e tornare
Nella vecchia sofitta
Della figlia mia
Per opera e virtú
Dal gran mago Virgilio!"

"Loom! Loom! O loom!
Who by the labour and skill
Of the great magician Virgil
Wert made so long ago,
And gifted with such power!
I pray thee by that skill
And labour given by
Virgil, the great magician,
As thou canst spin a web
Of silver or of gold,
Fly like the wind away
From Ermelinda's house

Into the small old room
Where once my daughter dwelt,
All by the skill and power
Of great Virgilius !"

When in an instant they were borne away on a mighty
wind and found themselves in the old room, and there also
they found the loom, from which Gega could now weave at
will cloth of gold or silver as well as silk.

Then the old woman looked steadily at Gega, and the girl
saw the features of the former change to those of Nunzia,
and as she embraced her, the old woman said :

"Yes, I am Mamma Nunzia, and I came from afar to
restore to thee thy loom ; but guard it well now, for if lost
thou canst never recover it again. But if thou shouldst
ever need aught, then invoke the grand magician Virgil,
because he has always been my god."[*]

Having said this, she departed, and Gega knew now that
Nunzia was a white witch or a fairy. So, becoming rich,
she was a lady, and ever after took good care of her loom
and distrusted flattering friends.

This legend exists as a fairy-tale in many forms, and
may be found in many countries ; perhaps its beginning
was in that of the princess who could spin straw into
gold. To have some object which produces food or
money *ad libitum* when called on, to be cheated out of it,
and finally be revenged on the cheater, is known to all.

Virgil is in one of these tales naïvely called a saint,
and in this he is seriously addressed as a god, by which
we, of course, understand a classical heathen deity, or
any spirit powerful enough to answer prayer with
personal favours. But Virgil as the maker of a magic
loom which yields gold and silk, and as a *god* at the
same time, indicates a very possible derivation from a
very grand ancient myth. The reader is probably
familiar with the address of the Time Spirit in Goethe's
" Faust ":

* " Perche e stato sempre il mio dio."

" In Being's flood, in action's storm,
  I work and weave, above, beneath—
  Work and weave in endless motion
  Birth and Death—an infinite ocean,
      A-seizing and giving
      The fire of the Living.
  'Tis thus at the roaring loom of Time I ply,
  And weave for God the garment thou see'st Him by."

Thomas Carlyle informs us, in " Sartor Resartus,"
that of the thousands who have spouted this really very
intelligible formula of pantheism, none have understood
it—implying thereby that to him it was no mystery.
But Carlyle apparently did not know, else he would
surely have told the reader, that the idea was derived
from the Sanskrit myth that Maya (delusion or appearance), "the feminine half of the divine primitive
creator (Urwesen), was represented as weaving the
palpable universe from herself, for which reason she
was typified as a spider."*   Hence Maia of the Greeks;
and it is a curious coincidence that Maia in the
Neapolitan legends is the mother of Virgil, all of which
is confused, and may be accidental, but there may also
be in it the remains of some curious and very ancient
tradition.   The spider was, however, certainly the
emblem of domestic, stay-at-home, steady industry, as
Friedrich illustrates, therefore of prosperity, hence it is
believed to bring luck to those on whom it crawls, as
set forth in the novel of " The Red Spider."   And it is
evident that the moral of this tale of Virgil's loom is to
the effect that the heroine gained her good fortune by
hard work at home, and came to grief by gadding abroad
and playing the belle.

That Maia, or Illusion or Glamour, should, according to our tradition, be the mother of the greatest
thaumaturgist, wonder-worker, poet, and sorcerer of

* Vollmer, "Wörterbuch der gesammten Mythologie," p. 1162.

yore is curious. That the original Maya of India should be the living loom from which the universe is spun, and that in another tale the *same* magician, her son, is a god who makes a magic loom which spins gold, silver, and silk, may be all mere chance coincidence, but, if so, it is strange enough to rank as a miracle *per se*.

The name Gega, with *g* the second soft, is very nearly *Gaia*, the Goddess of the Earth, who was one with Maia, as a type of the Universe.

As I regard this as a tradition of some importance, I would state that it owes nothing whatever to any inquiry, hint, or suggestion from me; that it was gathered from witch authority by Maddalena, near Prato; and, finally, that it is very faithfully translated, with the exception of the passages indicated by brackets, which were inserted by me to make the text clearer—a very necessary thing in most of these tales, where much is often palpably omitted. I have seldom had a story so badly written as this was; it appears to have been taken down without correction from some illiterate old woman, who hardly understood what she was narrating.

It is to be observed that in a number of these tales the proper names are strangely antique and significant. They are not such as are in use among the people, they would not even be known to most who are tolerably well read. I have only found several after special search in mythologies, etc.; and yet they are, I sincerely believe, in all cases appropriate to the tradition as in this case.

VIRGIL AND THE PRIEST.

" Beware, beware of the Black Friar,
Who sitteth by Norman stone."—BYRON.

" Seven times shall he be accursed who returns evil for good, and seven
times seven he who lives for himself alone, but seventy times seven the
one who wrongs the orphan, the weak, the helpless, the widow or the
young !"—*The Ladder of Sin.*

There is in Arezzo a lonely old lane or silent street where
few people care to go after dark, nor do they love it much
even by daylight, the reason being that it is haunted, for
many have seen walking up and down in it after midnight
the form of a ghostly friar, who is ever muttering to himself.
So he wanders, speaking to none, but now and then he
seems to be in great distress, and screams as if in agony,
when light dim flames fly from his mouth and nostrils, and
then he suddenly vanishes.

It is said that long, long ago there lived in or near Arezzo
a poor young orphan girl who had no relations, and had
been taken in charity as a servant in a farmer's family,
where she was not unkindly treated, but where everything
was in harsh contrast to the life which she had led at home,
for her parents, though poor, were gentle folk, and had
brought her up tenderly.

So it happened that when at Easter she was ordered to
kill for the usual feast a pet lamb, because all the rest were
too busy to attend to it, she could not bring herself to do it,
and wept bitterly when the lamb looked at her, which the
master and mistress could not understand, and thought her
very silly. And being deeply grieved at all this, she could
eat nothing, and so went along weeping, wishing that her
life were at an end. And while walking she met a priest,
who was indeed a black sheep of the flock, or rather a wolf,
for he was a hardened villain at heart, and ready for any
knavery; and he, seeing that the girl, whose name was
Ortenzia, was in distress, drew from her all her sad story,
and was very much interested at learning that she had some
small store of money and a few jewels and clothes, which
her mother had charged her not to part with, but to keep till
she should be married or for dire need.

Then the priest, pretending great sympathy and pity, said that the farm was no place for her, and that he himself was in great need of a maid-servant, and if she would come and live with him she should be to him as a daughter, and treated like a lady, with much more honeyed talk of the kind, till at last she assented to his request, at which he greatly rejoiced, and bade her be careful to bring with her all her property; whereupon he lost no time in inducing her to sign a paper transferring it all to him, which she in her ignorance very willingly did.

The poor child found very soon indeed that she had only changed the frying-pan for the fire, for the same night the priest made proposals to her, which she rejected in anger, when he attempted force, which she resisted, being strong and resolute, and declared that she would leave his house at once. But when she asked for her money and small property he jeered at her, saying that she had *given* it to him, and all the law in the land could not take it away. And more than this, he declared she was possessed by a devil, and would certainly be damned for resisting him, and that he would excommunicate and curse her. Hearing all this, the girl became mad in fact, and rushed forth. For a long time she went roaming about the roads, in woods, and living on what people gave her in pity; but no one knew what it was that had turned her brain, and the priest, of course, said all that was ill and false of her.

One day, as the poor lunatic sat in a lonely place singing and making bouquets of wild-flowers, the priest passed, and he, seeing her still young and beautiful, was again inspired by passion, and threw his arms about her. She, seized with horror, again resisted, when all at once a voice was heard, and there stood before them a tall and dignified man, who said to the priest :

"Leave untouched that poor girl, who is all purity and goodness, thou who art all that is vile and foul!"

Then the priest, in great terror and white as death, replied :

"Pardon me, Signore Virgilio!"

"What thou hast deserved, thou must endure," replied Virgil, "and long and bitter must thy penance be; but first of all restore to this poor creature all that of which thou hast robbed her, and make a public avowal of her innocence and of all thy crimes."

And this he did; when Virgil said :

"Now from this hour thy spirit shall haunt the street where thou hast lived, and thou shalt never leave it, but wander up and down, thinking of all the evil thou hast wrought. And when thou wouldst curse or rage, it shall come forth from thy mouth in flames, and therewith thou shalt have some short relief."

As for the girl, she was restored to health, and Virgil made for her a happy life, and she married well, and after a long and prosperous life passed away, having founded a great family in the land.

But the goblin friar still haunts the street in Arezzo, for he has not yet fully and truly repented, and a life as evil as his leaves its stain long after death.

IL GIGLIO DI FIRENZE, OR THE STORY OF VIRGIL AND THE LILIES.

"The lily is the symbol of beauty and love. By the Greeks it was called Χαρμα Αφροδιτης, the joy of Venus, and according to Alciatus, Venus Urania was represented with a lily in her hand."—J. B. FRIEDRICH : *Die Symbolik der Natur.*

This story is of the lily, or the *stemma*, or crest of Florence. One day Virgilio went forth to walk when he met with a Florentine, who saluted him, saying :

"Thou truly shouldst be a Florentine, since thou art by name a *vero giglio*"—a true lily (*Ver'-giglio*).

Then the poet replied :

"Truly I am entitled to the name, since our first ancestors were as the lilies of the field, who toiled not, neither did they spin, hence it came that they left me nothing."

"But thou wilt leave a lordly heritage," replied the nobleman, smiling ; "the glory of a great name which shall honour all thy fellow-citizens, and which will ever remain in the shield as the flower of Florence."*

This is a pretty tale, though it turns on a pun, and has nothing more than that in it. Much has been

* "Anche dopo morte rimarrai la stemma di Firenze, ovunque si trovera il Giglio."

written to prove that the lilies in the shields of France and Florence and on the ends of sceptres are not lilies, but there can be no reasonable doubt of its Latin symbolical origin. Among the Romans the lily was the emblem of public hope, of patriotic expectation, hence we see Roman coins with lilies bearing the mottoes: *Spes Publica, Spes Augusta, Spes Populi Romani,* and Virgil himself, in referring to Marcellus, the presumed heir to the throne of Augustus, makes Anchises cry : " Bring handfuls of lilies !"

This did not occur to me till after translating the foregoing little tradition, and it is appropriate enough to suggest that it may have had some connection with the tale. The idea of its being attached to power, probably in reference to the community governed, was ancient and widely spread. Not only was the garment of the Olympian Jupiter adorned with lilies,* but the old German Thor held in one hand the lightning and in the other a lily sceptre† indicating peace and purity, or the welfare of the people. The lily was also the type of purity from its whiteness, the origin of which came from Susanna the Chaste, who during the Babylonian captivity remained the only virgin. Susan is in Hebrew *Shusam,* which means a lily. " This was transferred to the Virgin Mary." Hence the legend that Saint Ægidius, when the immaculateness of the Virgin was questioned, wrote in sand the query as to whether she was a maid before, during, and after the Conception, whereupon a lily at once grew forth out of the sand, as is set forth in a poem by the German Smetz—of which lily-legends of many kinds there are enough to make a book as large as this of mine.

* Pausanias, v. 11.
† " Christliche Kunstsymbolik," p. 28 ; Frankfort, 1839, *apud* Friedrich

The cult of the lily in a poetical sense was carried to a great extent at one time. The Dominican P. Tommaso Caraffa, in his " Poetiche Dicerie," or avowed efforts at fine writing, devotes a page of affected and certainly florid Italian to the " Giglio," and there are Latin poems or passages on it by Bisselius, P. Laurent le Brun, P. Alb. Ines, given by Gandutius (" Descriptiones Poeticæ "), Leo Sanctius and A. Chanutius. There is also a passage in Martial eulogizing the flower in comparing to it the white tunic given to him by Parthenio :

> " Lilia tu vincis, nec adhuc dilapsa ligustra,
> Et Tiburtino monte quod albet ebur.
> Spartanus tibi cedit color, Paphiæque columna
> Cedit Erithræis eruta gemma vadis."

I saw once upon a time in Venice a magnificent snow-white carpet covered with lilies—a present from the Sultan to the well-known English diplomat and scholar, Layard—to which it seems to me that those lines of the Latin poet would be far more applicable than they could have been to what was in reality about the same as an ordinary clean shirt or blouse—for such was in fact the Roman tunic. It must, however, be candidly admitted that he does good service to humanity who in any way renders romantic, poetic, or popular, clean linen or personal purity of any kind.

VIRGIL AND THE BEAUTIFUL LADY OF THE LILY.

" Ecce tibi viridi se *Lilia* candice tollunt,
  Atque humiles alto despactant vertice flores
  Virginea ridente coma."
  P. LAURENCE LE BRUN, *El.* 50, l. 7.

Once the Emperor went hunting, when he heard a marvellously sweet voice as of a lady singing, and all his dogs, as if called, ran into the forest.

The Emperor followed and was amazed at seeing a lady, beautiful beyond any he had ever beheld, holding in one hand a lily and wearing a broad girdle as of steel and gold, which shone like diamonds. The dogs fawned round her when the Emperor addressed her, but as he spoke she sank into the ground, and left no trace.

The Emperor came the second day also, alone, and beheld her again, when she disappeared as before.

The third day he told the whole to Virgil, and took the sage with him. And when the lady appeared Virgil touched her with his wand, and she stood still as a statue.

Then Virgil said :

"Oh, my lord, consider well this Lady of the Lily, and especially her girdle ; for in the time when that lady shall lose that girdle Florence will gain more in one year than it now increases in ten."

And with this the lady vanished as before, and they returned home.

VIRGIL AND THE DAUGHTER OF THE EMPEROR OF ROME.

" As the lily dies away
  In the garden, in the plain,
  Then as beautiful and gay
  In the summer comes again ;
  So may life, when love is o'er,
  In a child appear once more."

The following strange legend, which was taken down by Maddalena from some authority to me unknown, near Arezzo, is so imperfectly told in the original, and is, moreover, so evidently repieced and botched by an ignorant narrator, that I at first rejected it altogether; but finding on consideration that it had some curious relations with other tales, I determined to give it for what it may be worth.

Once the Emperor of Rome was in his palace very melancholy, nor could he rally (*ralegrarla*), do what he might. Then he went forth into the groves to hear the birds sing, for this generally cheered him, but now it was of no avail.

Then he sent a courier to Florence, and bade him call Virgil with all haste.

Virgil followed the messenger at full speed.

"What wilt thou of me?" asked the sorcerer of the Emperor.

"I wish to be relieved from the melancholy which oppresses me. I want joy."

"Do like me, and thou wilt always have a peaceful mind:

> "'I work no evil to any man;
> I ever do what good I can.
> He who acts thus has ever the power
> To turn to peace the darkest hour!'"

"Nor do I recall that I ever did anything to regret," replied the Emperor.

"Well, then, come with me, for I think that a little journey will be the best means of distracting your mind and relieving you from melancholy."

"Very well," replied the Emperor. "Lead where you will; anything for a change."

"We will take a look at all the small districts of Tuscany," answered Virgil.

> "Going from the Florentino,
> Through Valdarno to Casentino;
> Where'er we see the olives bloom,
> And smell the lily's rich perfume,
> And mountains rise and rivulets flow,
> Thither, my lord, we two will go."

To which the Emperor replied:

"Where'er you will, all things to see,
High or low—'tis all one to me,
If I can only happy be."

So they travelled on through many places, but the
Emperor was ever dull and sad; but when in Cortona he
said that he felt a little better, and went forth with Virgil to
look about the town.

[And it was unto this place and to a certain end that
Virgil led his lord.]

Passing along a street, they saw at a window a girl of
extraordinary beauty, who was knitting. . . .*

The girl instead of being angered, laughed, showing two
rows of beautiful teeth, and said :

" Thou mayst become gold, and the skein a twist of
gold."

The girl was utterly surprised and confused at this, and
knew not whether to accept or refuse (the gift offered).

The Emperor said to Virgil :

" Just see how beautiful she is. I would like to win her
love, and make her mine."

" Always the same song," replied Virgil. " You never
so much as say, ' I wish she were my daughter.' "

" She can never be my daughter," answered the Emperor ;
" but as she is as poor as she is beautiful, she may very
easily become my love. Honour is of no value to a poor
person."

" Nay," replied Virgil, " when the poor know its value,
it is worth as much to them as gold to you who are
wealthy.† And it is from your neglecting this that you have
so long suffered, you knew not why [but an evil deed will
burn, though you see no light and know not what it is].
For thus didst thou once betray a poor maid, and then cast
her away without a further thought, not even bestowing
aught upon her. And thou hadst a daughter, and her
mother now lies ill and is well nigh to death. And it is this
which afflicted thee [for every deed sends its light or
shadow at some time unto the doer]. And now, if thou dost
not repair this wrong, thou wilt never more know peace, and
shalt ever sit in the chair of penitence."

* Here there is a manifest omission. It would appear that the Emperor
made love to the girl, and that the first speech which follows was by him
and not by her.

† Here the remark and answer are run together in absurd confusion,
but I believe that I have correctly restored the original.

" And where is my daughter and her mother ?" asked the Emperor.

" That girl is the daughter, and if you would see her mother, follow me," replied Virgil.

When they entered the room where the dying woman lay, the Emperor recognised in her one whom he had loved.

" Truly," he said, " she was the most beautiful to me of all."

And he embraced and kissed her ; she was of marvellous beauty ; she asked him if he recognised their daughter.

" I recognise and acknowledge her," he replied. " Wilt thou live ?"

" No," she replied ; " for I have lived to the end, and return to life. [I am a fairy (*fata*) who came to earth to teach thee that fortune and power are given to the great not to oppress the weak and poor, but to benefit."]

Saying this she died, and there remained a great bouquet of flowers.

The Emperor took his daughter to the palace, where she passed for his niece, and with her the flowers in which he ever beheld his old fairy love, and thus he lived happy and contented.

To supply a very important omission in this legend, I would add that the bouquet was certainly of lilies, as occurs in other legends, and the real meaning of the whole is a very significant illustration of the history and meaning of the flower. Old writers and mythic symbolism, as Friedrich and many more have shown, believed that Nature taught, not vaguely and metaphorically, but directly, many moral lessons, and that of the lily was purity and truth. By comparing this with the other stories relating to this flower which I have given, it will hardly be denied that my conjectural emendations formed part of the original, which the narrator had not remembered or understood.

There is something beautifully poetical in the fancy that spirits, *fata*, assume human form, that they by their influence on great men, princes or kaisars, may

change their lives, and teach them lessons by means
of love or flowers. This makes of the tale an allegory.
It was in this light that Dante saw all the poems of
Virgil, as appears by passages in the " Convito," in
which curious book (p. 36, ed. 1490) there is a passage
declaring that the world is round and hath a North and
South Pole, in the former of which there is a city named
Maria, and on the other one called Lucia, and that
Rome is 2,600 miles from the one, " more or less," and
7,500 miles from the other.

> "And thus do men, each in his different way,
> From fancies unto wilder fancies stray."

Or as the same great poet expresses it in the same
curious book : " Man is like unto a weary pilgrim upon
a road which he hath never before travelled, who every
time that he sees from afar a house, deems that it is
the lodging which he seeks, and finding his mistake,
believes it is the next, and so he erreth on from place
to place until he finds the tavern which he seeks. And
'tis the same, be it with boys seeking apples or birds, or
their elders taking fancies to garments, or a horse, or
a woman, or wealth, ever wanting something else or
more and so ever on."

The lily in Italian tales is the flower of happy, saintly
deaths ; it fills the beds of the departing, it sprouts
from the graves of the holy and the good. In one
legend it is the white flower of the departing soul
which changes into a white bird. But in this story
it has a doubly significant meaning, as the crest of
Florence and as conveying a significant meaning to its
ruler.

The " Convito " of Dante is not nearly so well known
as the " Commedia," but it deserves study. The only

copy which I have ever read is the editio princeps of 1490, which I bought of an itinerant street-vendor for 4 soldi, or twopence.

VIRGIL AND POLLIONE, OR THE SPIRIT OF THE PROVERB.

"A Proverb is a relic or remain of ancient philosophy, preserved among many ruins by its brevity and fitness."—Aristotle ap. Synesius.

"I Proverbi e la sapienza dell uomo
El Proverbio no fale."
Proverbi Veneti, da Pasqualigo.

"He who leaves money leaves what may be lost,
But he who leaves a *Proverb* keen and true
Leaves that wherein his soul will never die."
C. G. Leland.

"Tremendo leone, destriero animoso
Che in lungo riposo giaceste al suo piè.
Mostrate agli audaci cui grato e l' errore
Che 'l vostro vigore scemato non è."
Gabriel Rossetti (1832).

There was once a young man of genius, and honest; he was a true gentleman (*vero galantuomo*), with a good heart.

At that time there was also in Rome a great magician who was called the Poet, but his real name was Virgilio. And the honest youth, whose name was Pollione, was a student with Virgilio, and also his servant.

Everybody may have heard who Virgilio was, and how he was a sorcerer above all others. He had a custom of giving to his friends sayings and proverbs, or sentences[*] wherein there was always wisdom or a moral. His friends did not know it, but with every one of these sayings there went a spirit, and if they gave heed to the saying[†] the spirit took care that from it some good resulted to them.

One day when Virgil gave sayings to his friends, he said to Pollione:

"When a man speaks to you, hear to the end all that he has to say before answering."

[*] "Sentenze," as defined by D'Ambra, "Apothegms."
[†] Avviso, "Quando l' amico guardara (o), ricordava bene l' avviso, cosi lo spirito lo guardava, e cosi quella persona diveniva buona."

After a while Pollione left Rome, and went to Florence. While wandering, he found himself not far from Lucca, in a solitary forest. And while resting he observed a stone, almost hidden under the grass, on which stone were letters, and, clearing it away, he read the word "Lift." So he raised the stone, and found under it a small ancient vase, in which was a gold ring. Then he took the ring, and went his way.

And after weary wandering he found a small house, empty, into which he entered. It was one of the cabins in which peasants store chestnuts or grain or their implements for work. Therein was a partition of boards, and the youth lay down behind it and went to sleep.

After a little time there entered two friars, who never suspected there was anybody behind the screen, so they began to talk freely. And Pollione, awaking, listened to them.

One friar said to the other:

"It is now a year since old Father Girolamo died, who on his deathbed left to us both, to wear by turns, the gold ring which is hid somewhere in this wood in a vase under a stone on which is the word 'Lift.' Pity that he died before he could tell us just where it is. So we have sought and sought in vain, and so we must seek on, seek ever."

When Pollione heard that, in the honesty of his heart, he was about to show himself and cry out, "Here is your ring!" when all at once he recalled the proverb of Virgilio to always hear all that a man has to say before answering. So he kept quiet, while the other friar said:

"Thou knowest that with that ring one can turn any man or woman into any kind of an animal. What wouldst thou do with it if it were thine?"

"I," replied the other, "would at once change our Abbot into an ass, and beat him half to death ten times a day, because he put me *in penitenza* and in prison because I got drunk."

"And I," answered the second friar, "would change the proud, beautiful daughter of the count who lives in the castle yonder into a female dog, and keep her in that form till she should consent to be my mistress. Truly, I would give her a good lesson, and make her repent having scorned me."

When Pollione heard such talk as this he reflected:

"I think I would do well to keep the ring myself."
Then he took a piece of paper and wrote on it:

> "L' anello non avrai,
> Ma asinello tu sarai,
> Tu asinello diventerai
> E non l'Abate,
> Cosi dicono le Fate."

> "The ring of gold is not for thee,
> For thou thyself an ass shalt be;
> Not the Abbot, but thou in truth,
> This the Fairies say in sooth."

This poem he placed on the stone which had covered the ring. And when the two friars found and read it, and discovered that the ring was gone, they verily believed that the fairies had overheard them and taken away the ring, and so, full of sorrow, returned to their convent.

Then Pollione, ever travelling on, one day met in Verona a clever, bold-looking young man, who was playing marvellous juggler's tricks in a public place. And, looking closely at one another, each recognised in his observer the wizard who knew hidden things.

"Let us go together," said Pollione. "We shall do better by mutual aid."

So they went into partnership.

One evening they found themselves in a castle, where the signore treated them very kindly; and this lord had a beautiful daughter, who looked at Pollione with long glances, nor were his at her one whit shorter.

But the father seemed to be dying with some great sorrow; and at last he said to Pollione:

"Thou art a gentleman, and a man who is learned in books and wise. It may be that thou canst give me good advice and save me. If thou canst, there is nothing of mine which I will not give thee. And this is the story:

"A year ago I was sent on State affairs to Constantinople, where the Sultan promised me that within a certain time he would send me a lion as a gift for our Grand Duke.

"And after I had returned to Italy I told the Duke of this, at which he was greatly pleased. But when the time had come to an end the lion did not arrive. Then several of the courtiers who were my envious enemies made the Duke believe that the tale of the lion was all a lie, and a mere boast of mine.

" Then the Duke said to me that if the lion did not arrive within six months I should lose my head, and the allotted time is nearly past."

"I believe that I can save you," replied Pollione. "I will do it, if only to please your daughter."

" Do it, and she shall be thine," answered the father.

And the daughter smiled.

So the signore wrote to the Grand Duke that on a certain day the lion would be his, and invited him with all the court to his castle to see it.

Then there was at the time appointed a grand pavilion, in which was the Grand Duke, with all the courtiers and music.

The sorcerer Jannes, who was the companion of Pollione, had formed a deep attachment to the signore, as the latter had to him. Then the magician asked the lord to point out carefully to him all those who were his enemies.

And then from a tent there came forth a great lion. It was the magician, who had been touched by the ring.

The music sounded, and the people cried, "*Evviva il lione !*" Hurrah for the lion !

But when the lion, running round the course, came to the courtiers, he roared and became like a raging devil. He leaped over the barrier, and, attacking the courtiers, tore them limb from limb, and did terrible things. Nor could the Duke say anything, for it was his own fault.

Then the lion bounded away and was seen no more.

So the signore was saved, and Pollione wedded his daughter, and became very wealthy and a great lord.

And it is a true thing that there are wizards' sayings or proverbs which cause good luck—*buona fortuna ;* and if such a proverb remains always in the memory the spirit of the proverb will aid him who knows it. And to secure his aid one should repeat this spell :

> " Spirito del proverbio !
> Ti prego di stampare
> Questo proverbio corretamente
> Per sempre nella mia mente,
> Ti prego di aiutarlo,
> Sempre cosi la detta sara
> Cagione della felicità."

> " Spirit of the proverb,
> I pray thee to impress

> This proverb exactly
> And for ever in my mind,
> So that it may ever be
> A blessing and a joy to me."

And this done, the proverb or poem will become a living spirit, which will aid you to become learned and wise.[*]

As the *Jatakas* of Buddha, which perhaps give the origin of the fable, were all intended to set forth the great doctrine of the immortality of the soul in transmigrations, so most stories like the preceding have for an aim or object the teaching of a spell. That which is here explained is very singular, yet the idea is one which would naturally occur to a student of magic. It is that in a deep meaning or moral there is a *charm*, and every charm implies a spirit. Hence a spirit may go with a proverb, which in its form is like a spell. It is simply a perception of the similarity of a saying or proverb to a charm. As the Pythagoreans and Neo-Platonists believed there were spirits in numbers and ideas, so a believer might even more rationally conceive of a soul in a wise saying.

VIRGIL AND MATTEO, OR ANOTHER PROVERB OF VIRGILIO.

" Proverbi, noti spontaneamente, e quasi inconsciamente sulle labbre del popolo, oltre contenere una profonda sapienza . . . manifestano la prontezza, il brio."—DA AUGUSTO ALFANI : *Proverbi e Modi Proverbiali* (1882).

The following story is translated from the Romognola, or mountain dialect, also called Bolognesa, which is a rude, strange patois, believed to be very

[*] " Il proverbio o poema divena
Uno spirito vivente,
Che ti aiutera
A divenire savio e sapiente."

ancient. It was written by a native of Rocca Cas-
ciano, near Forli. The beginning of it in the original
is as follows :

"*Un Eter proverbi di Virgilio.*—Ho iera una volta un
om co des a Verzeglie che un su usen lera un ledre e vieva
rube quaicosa, e é bon om ed nom Matei, e pregheva
Verzeglie ed ulei de un det, ho proverbi, incontre a e le der."

There was once a man who said to Virgil that one of his
neighbours was a thief, who had stolen something from him,
and the man, whose name was Matteo, begged Virgil to
give him a saying or a proverb against the thief.

Virgil replied : " Truly thou hast been robbed ; but be of
good cheer, and thou mayst regain thine own again if thou
wilt remember this saying :

> " Se un dievele ti disprezza,
> Tu guent un dievele e mezza,
> E quan e lup la e tu agnel,
> L' e temp et tolá su pel."

> " If a devil should injure thee,
> Doubly a devil thou shouldst be ;
> And if a wolf thy lamb should win,
> 'Tis time for thee to take his skin."

Matteo had learned that the thief, whose name was
Bandelone, was in the habit of sitting by a pool or pond,
and whenever any traveller came by he would cry that he
had let fall a bag of gold into the water, and, being very
lame and ill, could not dive for it. So he would promise a
great reward to him who would recover it.

Then the traveller, deluded by the tale, would strip himself and dive into the pool, which was very deep, with steep
banks. And while he was under water the crafty thief
would seize on his clothes, arms, and money, mount his
horse, and ride away.

Matteo reflected on this. Then he got a small bag and
filled it with nails, so that it seemed to be heavy, as if with
money. So he went to the pool, where Bandelone was
waiting like a spider for flies, and seeing Matteo, whom he
did not recognise, because the latter was disguised, he
began to cry :

" Oh, kind sir, have pity on a poor man who has lost his
whole fortune !" And so he went on to tell how he had

dropped his bag full of gold in the water, and was too weak to dive for it, with all the rest of the tale.

Then Matteo consented to dive for the purse; but first of all put his horse, with all his arms and clothes, on the opposite bank, where they would be in safety.

Bandelone was angry enough at this, and cried:

"Why do you do that? Do you think I am a thief?"

"No, friend," answered Matteo. "But if a thief should come to take my things thou wouldst be too weak to defend them, and he might do thee harm. It is all for thy good that I take such care."

Bandelone wished all this kind care to the devil, but he had to submit. Then Matteo dived twice or thrice, and then came out of the water as if overjoyed, crying, as he held his bag of nails* on high:

"Ech! Ho alo trovè e sac d' oro! Com le grand!"
—Behold, I have found the bag of gold! How large it is!

Bandelone was indeed surprised at this; but, believing that Matteo had by chance really found a treasure, he cried:

"Yes, that is mine! Give it to me!"

"*Zentiment!* Fair and softly, friend," replied Matteo. "Give me half, or I will keep it all."

Bandelone would by no means consent to this. At last Matteo said:

"Well, as I do not know what is in the bag, I will take a risk. Give me your horse and sword and cloak for the bag. That is my last word, and if you utter another I will ride away with the bag and keep all."

So Bandelone gave him his horse and cloak and a fine sword. And Matteo, when mounted, pitched him the bag, and rode away singing merrily:

> "If a devil should injure thee,
> Doubly a devil thou must be;
> And if a wolf thy lamb should win,
> 'Tis time for thee to take his skin."

---

* The Bag of Nails was once a tavern sign in England. It was con-ectured to be a corruption of *Bacchanals*—a very unlikely derivation.

VIRGILIO AND THE FATHER OF TWELVE CHILDREN.

A LEGEND FROM COLLE DI VAL D'ELSA, TUSCANY.

" In the earliest form of the legend, Virgil appears not only as doing no harm, but also as a great benefactor."—COMPARETTI: *Virgil in the Middle Ages.*

Once when Virgil was in Colle di Val d'Elsa, he found that the utmost poverty and wretchedness prevailed among the people. Everywhere were men and women wailing and weeping because they could not get food for their children.

Virgil began by giving alms right and left, but was obliged to cease, finding that all his means would be but a trifle towards relieving such suffering. Therefore he resolved to go to the Emperor and beg him to use his authority in the matter. But while in the first furlong of his journey he met a man wailing bitterly, and on asking the cause, the one who wept replied:

"*Caro Signore*, I weep in despair not for myself, but for my twelve children, who, starving, lie on the bare ground. And this day we are to be turned out of the house because I owe for the rent. And I have gone hither and thither to seek work and found none, and now thou knowest all."

Then Virgil, who was kind of heart, replied:

" Be not afraid of the future. Holy Providence which takes care of the birds of the air will also provide for you."

" My dear lord," replied the poor man, " I trust it is true what you tell me, but I have waited a long time now for Holy Providence without seeing it."

"Hope yet a little longer," answered Virgil. " Just now I will go with you to your house and see how I can aid you."

"Thank you, my lord," replied the poor man, whose doubts in a Holy Providence began to weaken. So they went together, and truly found twelve children with their mother, well-nigh dying from cold, hunger, and exposure.

Then Virgil, having relieved them, thought deeply what could be done to help all this wretchedness, and invoked a certain spirit in whom he trusted—*un spirito di sua fiducia*—asking how he could aid the suffering *Colligiani*."

And the spirit replied:

" Sorti da quella casa,
　E passa disotto a una torre,
　E nel passare
　Si senti a chiamare
　A nome, alze il capo,
　Ma non videte nessuno,
　Soltanto senti una voce,
　Una voce che le disse
　' Sali su questa torre !' "

" Leave this house, in going,
　Thou'lt pass beneath a tower,　·
　And hear a voice which calls thee,
　Yet looking, thou'lt see nothing,
　Yet still will hear it crying,
　' Virgil, ascend the tower !' "

Virgil did this, and heard the Voice call him, when he ascended the tower and there beheld a small red goblin, who was visible to him alone, because Virgil had invoked him.　And the Spirit said to him :

" Behold this little dog.　Return with it to the house whence thou hast come, and go forth with the poor man, and take the dog with you.　And where the dog stops there dig !"

And they did so.　And they went away, and at last the dog stopped at a place, and the poor man began to dig. And lo! ere long the earth became red, and he came to iron ore.　And from this discovery resulted the iron factory of Colle, and by it that of glass; wherever the dog led they found minerals.　So from that time there was no more suffering because there was work for all.

This legend is a full confirmation of what I have elsewhere remarked, that these " witch-stories " have almost invariably a deeper meaning or moral than is to be found in the " popular tales " generally prevalent among peasants and children.　Thus, while we find in this the magician Virgil, his invocation to a familiar spirit, the apparition of the Red Goblin of the Tower and the mystical dog of the Kobold, or goblins of the mines, there is with it a noble reflection that the best way to relieve suffering is to provide work.　In an ordinary fairy-tale the magician would have simply conjured up a treasure and have given it to the poor.

Apropos of the word *goblin*, which is generally supposed to be from the German *Kobold*, I would observe that the Greek κοβάλι or *cobali* are defined in a curious old French work as *lutins*, "household spirits, or domestic fairies."

VIRGILIO AS A PHYSICIAN, OR VIRGIL AND THE MOUSE.

"Now to signify destruction and death they paint a *mouse*. For it gnaweth all things, and works ruin." — HORI APOLLI : *Hieroglyphica ; Rome*, 1606.

There once lived in Florence a young gentleman—*un gran signore*—who wedded a beautiful young lady to whom he was passionately attached, as she indeed was for a time to him. But "fickle and fair is nothing rare," and it came to pass that before long she gave her love again to an intimate friend of her husband. And the latter did not indeed perceive the cause, but he was much grieved at the indifference to him which his wife began to show.

Then the wife began to tell her lover how her husband had scolded her for her neglect, and how much afraid she was lest their intrigue would be discovered, and that she was so uneasy that she was ready to poison her spouse "if she could only get rid of him !"

The lover replied that there were many ways to get rid of a man without really killing him, for that a violent death would lead to suspicion, inquiry, scandal, and perhaps legal punishment. And then he hinted that a better method would be to consult a witch.

The lady lost no time in running to one, to whom she told her whole story, and what she wanted, and as she began by paying a large fee, the sorceress promised she should have her wish.

Then the witch prepared with magic skill a flask of water,

and a powder. The water she gave to the wife, and bade
her sprinkle it over her husband's clothes. But she changed
herself into a mouse, and having been carried to the bed-
room which the married couple occupied, she gnawed a hole
in the mattress, and crawling in, dragged after her the bag,
and so remained hidden.

When the husband went to bed, there came over him an
utter weakness and sickness, so that he lay in pain as if
dead, and this grew worse day by day. His parents in vain
called in the first physicians, and every remedy was resorted
to without result.

Then Virgilio, who knew much and suspected all the rest
of this affair, was angry that so vile a woman and her
gallant should inflict such torture on an excellent and
innocent man, and resolved to have a hand in the affair.

Therewith he dressed himself as a *medico*, or doctor, from
some distant land, saying that he had heard of this extraordinary case of illness, and would like to see the sufferer.
To which the parents replied that he was welcome to do so,
since all the professors of medicine in Florence could make
nothing of it.

The doctor looked steadily for some time at the patient,
who appeared to be in such utter prostration and misery
as might have moved the hardest heart. By him sat his
wife, pretending to weep, but counting to herself with
pleasure the time which would pass before her husband
should die—giving now and then a suspicious glance at the
new-comer.

Then Virgilio said to the wife :

" Signora, I beg you to leave the room for a while. I
must be alone with this man !"

Whereupon she, with a great show of tears and passion,
declared she would not leave the room, because her husband
might die at any minute, and she could never forgive herself were she to be absent, and so on. To which Virgilio
angrily replied, that she might depart in peace, with the
assurance that her husband would be cured. So she went
out, cursing him in her heart, if there was a chance that he
could do as he declared.

Then Virgilio took a mirror which he had brought with
him, and placing it before the eyes of the invalid, bade him
look at it as steadily and as long as he could. The young
man did so, and then said, as if in despair ·

" For me there is no remedy, O doctor, for what you show me is worse than my disorder, as I supposed it to be. Truly I see death, and not myself."

" Courage !" replied Virgilio. " You shall be cured."

" Cure me," he answered, "and you shall have all that I possess."

" Nay, I will cure you first," said Virgilio, "and then settle on easier terms."

The patient looked steadily at the mirror. Virgilio rapped thrice with a wand, when there suddenly leaped from the bed a mouse, which uttered three horrible, piercing screams. The doctor bade the invalid continue to look steadily at himself in the mirror, and for his life not to cease doing so. Without turning round, the doctor ordered the mouse to enter the bed and lick up and bring away with her on her tongue all the water which the wife had sprinkled on the clothes. And this done, he bade her bring again out of the bed all the powder which she had placed there. Which being effected, he ordered the mouse to make of it a pellet, and devour it ; but here she resisted, for to do that meant death to her and a cure to the invalid.

But the doctor was inflexible, and she had to obey. Nor had she begun to eat it before he bade the husband rise, which he did, feeling perfectly recovered, though much confused at such a sudden change.

Then Virgilio ordered the mouse to mount the bed, and lo ! she changed to a woman, for she was, of course, the witch who had done all this devil's work. And the sorceress bade them call parents and wife and all. And when they came the witch said :

" Evil my life has been, and evil will be the death which in a few minutes will come to me ; yet am I not so evil as this woman, who would have killed by the worst suffering the husband who loved her. For hell hath many who are bad, but the worst are they who return evil for good. And he who hath ended this thing by his power is the great Virgilio, who is the lord of magic in all this land."

Then she told, step by step, how the wife had turned her heart from her husband, almost as soon as she was married, and wished to kill him, and had paid her to bewitch him. Then Virgilio opened the window and the witch indeed died, or it was the last seen of her, for with a horrible howl she vanished in the night, flying away.

The husband recovered, and would have given Virgilio all his wealth, but he would accept nothing but the young man's friendship. And the guilty wife was imprisoned for life in a castle, far away in the mountains and alone.

Virgil appears as a *physician* so distinctly in this and other tales as to induce the question whether he had not, quite apart from his reputation as poet and magician, some fame as professor of the healing art. And in fact, as I have shown in the legend of Virgil and the Spirit of Mirth, he on one occasion at least is, by Pæonia, identified with Esculapius. The latter is described as having "a countenance bright with joy and serenity," and being very benevolent and genial—wherein he agrees with the poet. The God of Medicine, it is expressly stated, used "sweet incantations," or poetical spells, which is also significant. He was also associated with Apollo and the Muses, as in the temple of Messina. The author of the great "Dizionario Storico Mitologico" (1824) plainly declares that "Esculapius is another form of Apollo, in whom poetry and medicine were combined. In the temple devoted to him in Sycione, Esculapius is associated with Diana. In a Roman bas-relief he appears with the Three Graces; in one of these legends Virgil is associated with four Venuses." Making every allowance, it must be admitted that, comparing all that is known of the God of Medicine with what appears in these legends of the Mantuan bard, there is a remarkable general likeness between the two. Virgil is also, here and there, curiously identified with the serpent and the staff, which were the symbols of Esculapius; and, as I have before noted, Buddha, who had so much in common with Virgil, was in his first incarnation a physician.

THE ONION OF CETTARDO.

"On, Stanley, on !"—MARMION.

"Were I in noble Stanley's place,
When Marmion urged him to the chase,
The word which you would then descry
Might bring a tear to every eye."—ANONYMOUS.

Virgil is introduced, I may say, almost incidentally in the following tale, not by any means as *coryphæus* or hero, as is indeed the case in several other stories, which fact, on due reflection, is of importance, because it indicates unmistakably that he is so well known in popular tradition as to be recognisable even in a minor rôle. It is as when one swears by a saint, or Bacchus —in Florence one hears the latter invoked forty times where a Christian deity is apostrophized once—'tis not to form a portion of the sentence, but to give it force, as Chinese artillerymen, when they fire a ball at an enemy, sometimes grease the mouth of a gun, to increase the loudness of the report and thereby frighten the foe. Which figure of a saint is not that of Saint Malapropos, because, as the reader may note in another tale, Virgil is very seriously described as a santo.

Now to the narrative. *Sancte Virgile, ora pro nobis!*

In very ancient times there were few families in Cettardo, and these were all perfectly equal, there being among them neither rich nor poor. They all worked hard in fields or forests for a living, and were like a company of friends or brothers.

And of evenings, when they were not too weary, they met many together in some house, all in love and harmony, to talk about the crops, and their children, or repeat the *rosario*,* or discuss their clothing, or cattle, or whatever interested them.

* This means here the recitation of five prayers, after which stories are told or traditions imparted and discussed. An immense amount of folk-lore can be gathered on such occasions.

These people were all as one, and had no head or chief.* But one evening a very little girl came out with a thing (*sorti con una cosa*) which astonished all who were present, because the child had received no instruction, and did not know what a school meant. And what she said was this:

"*Babbo*—papa—I wish to tell thee something in presence of all who are here assembled, with all due respect to them, since there are certainly so many here who could with greater propriety set it forth.† Therefore, I trust you will pardon and bear with me, because I am but an infant."

Then all exclaimed in chorus: "Speak, and we will listen to thee!"

And then the infant, in this fashion, spoke:

"Know that this night I have spoken with a spirit, the *bel Folettino col berretta rossa*—the beautiful fairy with the red cap—and it told me that for this our land we have no name or coat of arms. But the time has come to have that which shall represent the country, and therefore we should choose a chief who will open commerce for us, and found a school so that our young people shall escape from ignorance."

"Truly, thou hast spoken well!" cried all present. "*Evviva il capo*—hurrah for a chief!—and that chief shall be thy father, dear child!"

"Moreover," added the good girl, "I will, to show my gratitude, give you the design for the armorial bearings, and in due time tell you all that is needful to be done. All of that will I find out, and also a name for the country."

"Do so, and deserve our gratitude."

"I thank you again," said the girl, "and I will pay attention to the subject, since you show such sympathy."

The next day she went to herd a flock of sheep, as was her custom; and then, lying down on the ground as wild boars are wont to do,‡ said:

> "Spirito, capo di tutti i spiriti !
> Re dei ré dei Maghi !

---

* "Ne avevano un capo e ne gnente"—No head and no nothing—in the original.

† The speech as given by the precocious maiden in the original text is an amusing effort at fine talk or elevated language by an illiterate person, its object being to strengthen the marvel of the child's inspiration.

‡ That is, on her face. To do this in a pig-sty was a special means of invoking dreams or inspirations, as described in Norse sagas. It is fully illustrated in my "Etrusco-Roman Remains."

Portami qui presenti un hoggetto
Che possa servirmi per rappresentare
Un arme."

" Una voce le rispose :

" Chiama e chiama più forte.
E chiama ancora per tre volte
E chiama il tuo prottetore,
Chi é con te a tutte le ore
E mai non ti lascera se sempre
Lui invochera."

" Spirit, who art the chief of all the spirits !
Who art the king of all the sorcerers !
Bring unto me some object which may serve
To represent our land, and be its crest."

" To which a voice replied :

"Call out aloud, then more forcibly,
And yet again three times, and unto him
Who is thy guardian and ever with thee,
And who will never leave thee—call to him !"

"And who art thou who speakest to me ?" asked the girl.
" I am the Spirit of the Red Cap."
" And who is my protector ?"
" The magician Virgil," replied the Voice.
Then she invoked Virgil, who appeared in person, and
asked what she would have.
She replied that she had been charged to find a name and
object to represent the land.
" It is well," answered Virgil. " I have already written
the name on a leaf; now take this thing in thy hand "—
here he gave her an onion—"and cast it into yonder cavern,
from which there is an underground way."
The girl obeyed; the onion spun round and rolled away ;
she followed it afar, till at last it stopped at a leaf on which
was written " Cettardo." And it was in this spot where
the onion stopped that the town in after time was built,
and where the girl found the leaf is now the municipal
palace. And so, one by one, great buildings rose. Thus
came the name and arms of Cettardo.
In due time the maid had a lover, and it was said that
these two were the only ones who could go through the
subterranean passage.
And it hath been, and may be still, proved that any

person attempting this passage will after a few steps be suffocated, and can go no further.

If we compare this legend with other traditions, there can be little doubt that it is at least of Roman origin. The great veneration for the onion among the Egyptians—"Happy people," wrote Juvenal, "to have gods growing in their gardens!"—which passed to the Romans, probably, in later days through the priests of Serapis and Isis,* and the many mysteries connected with it, fully account for its being chosen as the symbol of a city. Its traditions were greatly mingled and confused with those of the garlic and the leek, but it was above all other plants a protector against sorcery; that is, against *all* evil influence. Where onions could not help, nothing availed, or as it was expressed, *bulbus nihil profuerit*. It would appear from the conjectures of Nork (*Andeutung eines Systemes der Mythologie*, p. 125) that the onion was the sign or crest of the pyramid of Cheops, as it is of Cettardo.

It is, however, in the mention of a subterranean passage full of mephitic vapour, which seems to have no connection with the tale whatever, that the clue to the whole tradition may be found. The people wanting a name and a site for a city, receive them from a pythoness or sibyl, the two being identified in many legends. The grotto of the Sybil near Naples is approached by a long subterranean road, over which I have myself passed—being carried on the back of a strong peasant-guide.

Just in the middle of the wet, winding cavern, I said: "You are a good horse."

* Their temples were the last which were abandoned in Rome, as Wilkie Collins has minutely described in a novel.

"I am particularly good at eating macaroni," he replied, and stopped. This was equivalent to begging.

"Horses who talk need the spur," I replied, giving him a gentle reminder with my heel. He laughed, and trotted on. However, he got his "macaroni."

That the pythoness, or female oracle, was first intoxicated with the vapour of carbonic acid gas in a cavern, and that her utterances were recorded on leaves which blew about loosely and were then gathered and put together, is well known, and it is this, apparently, which is meant in this tale by the flying leaf bearing the name of Cettardo. Plutarch, in his "Treatise on Abandoned Oracles," declares that "the terrestrial effluvium was the conductor of the god into the body of the Pythia." As the vapours disappeared, the oracle became dumb, or, as Cicero expresses it:

"They ceased because this terrestrial virtue, which moved the soul of the Pythia by divine inspiration, disappeared in time, as we have seen rivers dried up or turned away into other beds."

The onion was a symbol of fertility and increase of population, therefore it was well adapted to serve as a fetish for a new city. It was also among the Egyptians *par eminence* typical of the resurrection, so that no woman was buried without one.*

It may be observed that in this legend Virgil appears as a guardian spirit or god, certainly not as a mortal.

It would almost seem as if there were an undercurrent of genial satire or mockery in the part where

---

* "Wegen ihrer erregenden Eigenschaft wurde die Zwiebel ein erotisches Symbol; deshalb *salaces* genannt ; daher in die Schamtheile weiblicher Mumien als Sinnbilder der Auferstehung gelegt wurden."— Friedrich, "Symbolik."

the young Pythia graciously assures the simple peasants that, out of sheer gratitude and to oblige them, she will consult with—of all the gods—the Robin Good-fellow, or goblin of the red-cap! who in all tales, Italian as well as English, is ever a tricksy sprite, more given to teasing and kissing servant-girls, and playing with children and cats, than aught more dignified. When we remember that the object of this gracious benevolence is to make her father chief or king, it verily appears as if the whole were a "put-up job" between parent and child.

THE END.

Elliot Stock, 62, Paternoster Row, London.

www.ingramcontent.com/pod-product-compliance
Lightning Source LLC
Chambersburg PA
CBHW030117030726
47498CB00007B/2432